BLUEWATER QUEST

THE 14TH NOVEL IN THE CARIBBEAN MYSTERY AND ADVENTURE SERIES

C.L.R. DOUGHERTY

rev 1

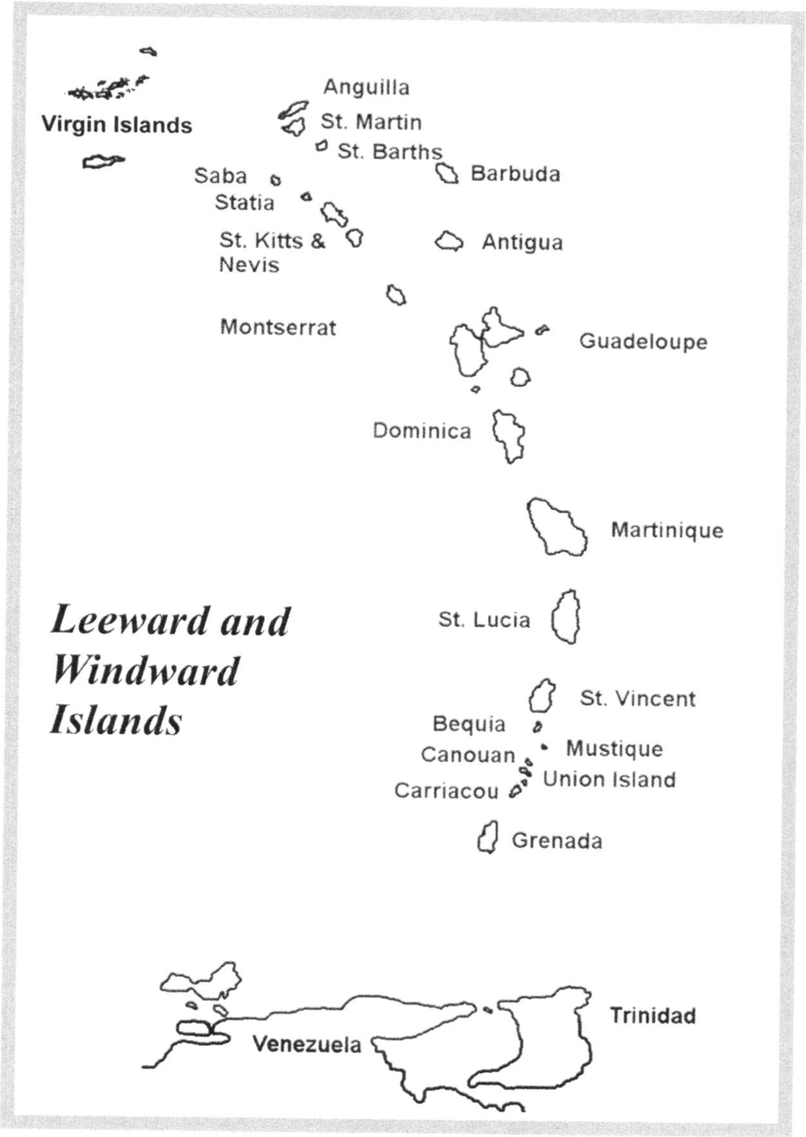

Leeward and Windward Islands

Virgin Islands
Anguilla
St. Martin
St. Barths
Saba
Barbuda
Statia
St. Kitts & Nevis
Antigua
Montserrat
Guadeloupe
Dominica
Martinique
St. Lucia
St. Vincent
Bequia
Mustique
Canouan
Union Island
Carriacou
Grenada
Trinidad
Venezuela

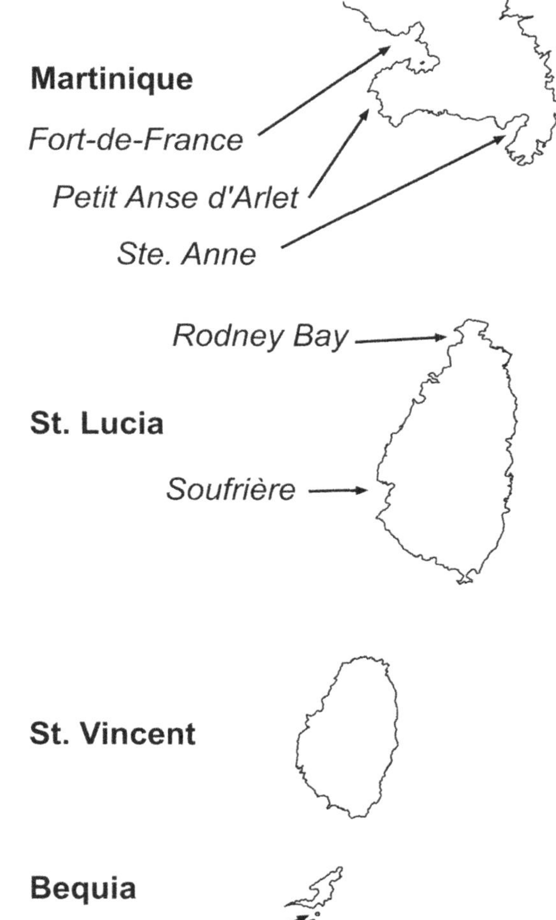

Southern Martinique to Bequia

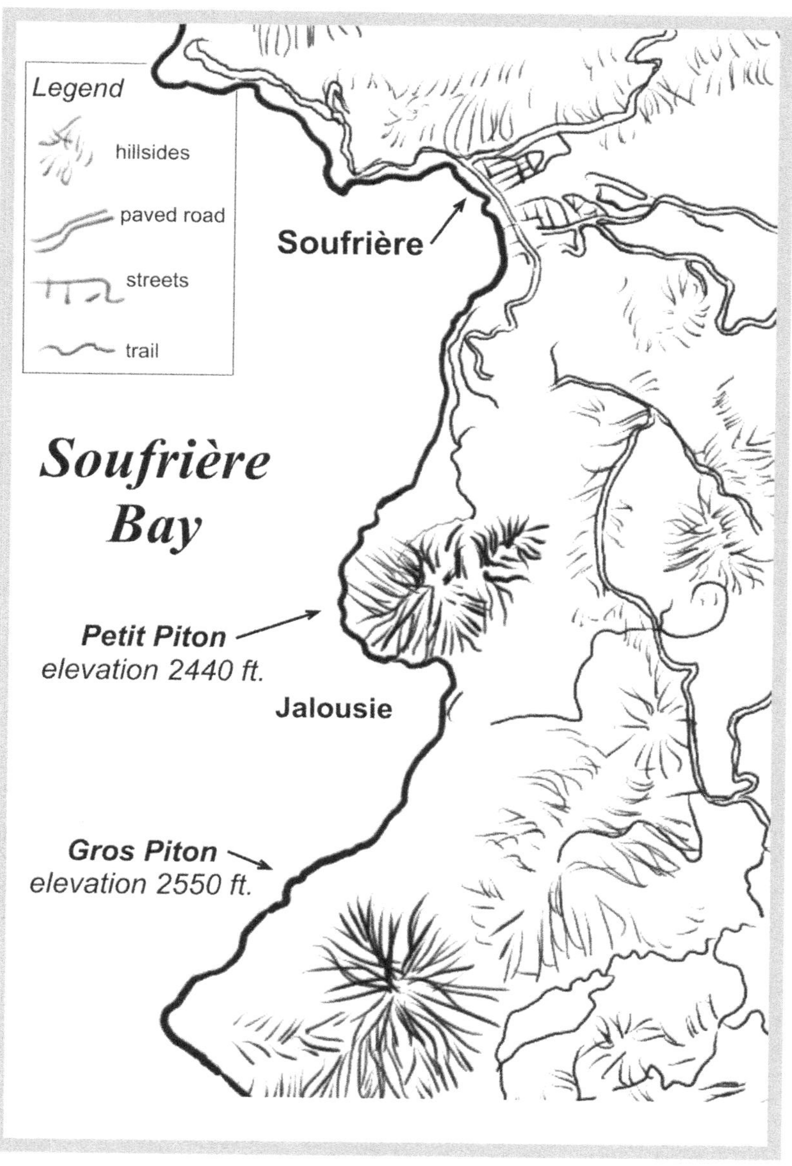
Legend
hillsides
paved road
streets
trail
Soufrière
Soufrière Bay
Petit Piton
elevation 2440 ft.
Jalousie
Gros Piton
elevation 2550 ft.

1

"Bullshit! A *quest*? To prove the Moors discovered America?" Dani Berger's face reflected her disbelief. She took a sip of passion fruit juice and put her glass back on the cockpit table.

Liz Chirac smiled at her partner's reaction. She and Dani were aboard *Vengeance*, at a dock in the marina in St. George's, Grenada. "I told Elaine that's what you would say; I almost got it verbatim."

"Who are these people? They actually believe that load of crap propaganda from the president of Turkey?"

"A couple of university professors," Liz said. "Richard and Michelle Everett."

"Academics," Dani said, shaking her head. "How did they come up with this? They must be rich. And gullible, to spend money on such a bullshit 'quest.' I'll bet they've got some kind of grant."

"I don't know," Liz said, "but Elaine says the money was wired to her escrow account on their behalf the day they booked the charter."

"Really? On their behalf? So they're not footing the bill themselves," Dani said, her frown fading. "This is serious, then? Or do you think this could be some kind of scam? A boondoggle?"

"If it's a boondoggle, Everett's got some heavy financial backing," Liz said. "The deposit came from some foundation in Washington."

"How long's the charter?" Dani asked.

"They're committed for a month, with the option to extend it for two more, depending on how their quest develops."

"Whoa! Quest? There's that word, again. That makes it sound like a treasure hunt, or a crusade, or something."

"Elaine said 'quest' was his word. It does sound kind of quaint, doesn't it?"

"Academics talk like that, I guess, but three months is forever, Liz. We'll lose prime-time business if they cancel after a month; Elaine can't book anybody else all winter if they've got an option that ties us up like that."

"Take it easy, Dani. Elaine got the three months paid up front. The first month's guaranteed, and they've got a thirty-day notice for cancellation after that. So effectively, they're committed for two months once they show up today. We're golden; our winter's revenue is in the bag, already."

"That's a quarter million dollars," Dani said, awestruck. "What kind of foundation is this?"

"I don't know. Elaine told me the name, but it didn't mean anything to me. You can ask them this afternoon."

"When are they getting in?"

"Three o'clock, on the Miami flight. Felix is meeting them and bringing them straight here."

"That's an awful lot of money," Dani said. "Why would anybody think it was worth that much to find out if some Moorish fleet beat Columbus here by 600 years? You know that's foolishness. There's no way they can prove that, even if it did happen. There has to be more to this. Nobody would put up that kind of money for an academic exercise with no payoff."

"You'll have to ask him," Liz said. "I *thought* you might find it interesting."

"It is interesting. I can't imagine what could be behind this; I'll definitely ask him." Dani took another sip of her juice, and they passed several seconds in silence, watching a flock of seagulls fighting over a dead fish out in the harbor.

"What did you and Connie talk about while I was chatting with Elaine?" Liz asked, after one of the seagulls managed to fly away with the prize. "You were on the phone for a long time."

"That showdown she and Paul had with Montalba. I'm still pissed off about that."

"I can tell. But why?"

"She didn't even kill the bastard. She had him dead to rights. I wouldn't have let the scumbag go to prison. He deserves to be dead," Dani said. "Stealing my boat. Bastard."

"Well, there's not much you can do about that now. And we got *Vengeance* back with no damage. You're just frustrated because you missed the action," Liz said. "Try to put it behind you. We've got an open-ended charter for most of the winter. We're lucky to have the business, after all the hurricane damage up north."

"I'm still pissed at Connie."

"Of course you are."

"And Phillip and Sharktooth. And Marie. They deliberately cut me out of the Montalba thing."

"Get over it, Dani. Elaine thinks we'll enjoy the Everetts. She says they're really nice people. Let's focus on their 'quest,' as he called it. It might even be fun. We're bound to learn something out of it, however it turns out."

"You're right, Liz. Sorry for being grouchy about the other. I'd almost put it behind me until Connie called and reminded me of it."

"That's not why she called, is it?"

"No. She didn't bring it up; I did. I wish I hadn't, now."

"What was on her mind, then?"

"She just wanted to let us know they'd be in Ste. Anne in three weeks. If we're up that way, they'd like to get together for a few days."

"That would be nice," Liz said. "Maybe it'll work out for the Everetts to meet them. Who knows?"

"Maybe. That could be a blast. Everybody enjoys Connie and Paul."

"That's more like it," Liz said, smiling. "Try to stay positive for our guests, okay?"

Dani's face lit in an easy smile. "I'm okay, now. Thanks for talking me around, Liz. You saved me from myself one more time."

"That's what friends are for," Liz said. "Part of my job, skipper."

"I hope Elaine's right about the Everetts," Dani said. "I'm up for some pleasant company. Guess we'd better get to work and get *Vengeance* squared away. Three o'clock's not far off."

"THE AMERICAN PROFESSOR and his wife are *en route* to Grenada, your highness," the Saudi colonel reported, when Abdullah al Saud, one of the many princes of the House of Saud, had acknowledged him.

"How much does he know?" the prince asked.

"Only what we agreed upon. He has been manipulated by our agents so that he believes his own research led him to request the documents from our archives. A translation of Abul-Hassan's work was forwarded to him, and he now plans to search the islands for artifacts which would substantiate the voyage of Khashkhash ibn Saeed ibn Aswad."

Khashkhash sailed from Palos, Spain, in 889 CE, to explore what then was known as the sea of darkness and fog, now called the Atlantic Ocean. After many months, Khashkhash's fleet had returned laden with treasure. The voyage had been documented a few years after its conclusion by Abul-Hassan, a well-known historian and geographer. His original work was among the many items in Saudi Arabia's archives. The translation mentioned by the colonel had been prepared for the professor from Abul-Hassan's manuscript.

Ali ibn Abi Bakr, a mullah who had accompanied the fleet, had elected to remain behind with three ships and a sizable party of the faithful. He intended to establish a trading center and explore and map the islands. He also planned to investigate rumors of larger land masses to the northwest and south.

Ali, a scholar and a distant relative of Mohammed, had been carrying an ivory quran case containing documents which he was compiling into a history of Islam. He was the last man known to have possessed an eighth-century document written by Ibn Ishaq, one of the most important biographers of the Prophet.

Entitled *Sirah Rasul Allah (Life of God's Messenger)*, the document was a history of the life of Mohammed. Ibn Ishaq had assembled it from near-contemporaneous accounts of the prophet's companions. His work had disappeared with Ali, though its previous existence was well established.

Some of the documents in Ali's casque were believed to have been written by the prophet himself. All of this information was in the translated material which had been provided in response to the professor's request.

"Does the professor have a copy of the map fragment?"

"Yes, your highness. He will begin by visiting the islands which might be shown by the facsimile of the map fragment, hoping to find one which matches the geographic features depicted on the fragment."

"And does he understand the sensitive nature of our involvement?"

"No, your highness. In fact, he doesn't know of our interest. As far as he knows, his funding comes from a grant established by an anonymous American donor who is interested in determining the accuracy of the claim by the Turkish president, Recep Tayyip Erdoğan, that Columbus was attempting to retrace the route that Khashkhash took to the West Indies."

"Very well done, colonel. Keep me apprised of his progress."

"CAN you even believe this is happening?" Michelle Everett asked.

Her husband grinned at her and shook his head before he took a sip of coffee. "I've never flown first-class before," he said. "These foundation people have a different attitude about travel expense."

"They've booked this yacht for three months, Rick?"

"He said, 'Up to three months.' They're hoping we'll finish sooner."

"Why are they doing this? What's in it for them?"

"Bragging rights, I guess. If they're right, we'll be part of rewriting history. That's for sure."

"Do you believe it?" she asked. "That the Arabs discovered America before Columbus, I mean."

"Stranger things have happened. It's certainly possible. We know the Vikings began to colonize North America in the late tenth century, and fishermen from Europe were probably working the Grand Banks before that. It's not hard to imagine that some of them spotted the coastline, is it?"

"No, but that's different."

"Why do you say that, Shellie?"

"You said the documents mentioned a hundred ships, or something."

"Actually, Abul-Hassan alluded to hundreds of ships, not a hundred."

"How can that be, Rick? Columbus only had three ships."

He shrugged. "Columbus was a beggar. The Moors ruled the Iberian Peninsula for hundreds of years. Khashkhash was a wealthy man. He would have sailed when their rule was at its peak, I think. So it's not crazy that he would have had a big fleet. It's possible that he knew where he was going, too. The Arabs led the world in terms of geography and all the sciences back then. His skill as a navigator probably far exceeded that of Columbus.

"Besides, Abul-Hassan would have been in his late teens when the fleet left. He didn't write about it until later in his life. There could have been some embellishment. And this could be behind all the rumors that Columbus knew perfectly well where he was going. He could have found references in some of the material the Moors left behind after the Christians re-conquered the Iberian Peninsula."

"Why did the foundation pick you for this?" she asked.

"They liked my background and the work I've published on the role of alien artifacts in documenting prehistoric cross-cultural contacts."

"Like the stashes of Roman coins that pop up in unexpected places?"

"Exactly."

"But you always end up finding an explanation that doesn't involve visitors from the Roman Empire."

"They mentioned that. It was an important factor in their decision; it gives me some extra credibility, in case I find something. There will be plenty of opposition to the idea that the Muslims discovered America hundreds of years before Columbus. We'll need as much credibility as we can get."

"No kidding. You'll be a pariah in the west."

"Only if I find out the theory is right. And if the evidence is convincing, I'll be remembered as one of those people who rewrote the history of the world."

"Yes, you will. And as a traitor to Christianity. Don't forget the way people look at Muslims these days."

"What do you want me to do, Shellie? It's a little late for

second thoughts. Why are you bringing this up now? I didn't just spring it on you."

"No, you didn't. I'm sorry. It's been building up over the last few weeks. I'll get over it. Like you said, it's a big opportunity. I shouldn't look a gift horse in the mouth."

"You were part of the package, you know," he said, patting her on the arm. "Your background in art history was a big factor in their decision. We're looking for distinctive artifacts, after all."

"Yes, you said that before. About my background, I mean. But why didn't they want to interview me? Why just you?"

"Who knows? We got the grant. Try not to let it bother you."

"I'm working on that," she said, as the captain announced their preliminary approach to Grenada.

2

Hossein Rahimi sat at attention across the desk from his commanding officer, the assistant to the deputy commander of the Quds Force.

Little known outside Iran, the Quds Force is a special forces unit of Iran's Revolutionary Guards. Its commander reports directly to the Supreme Leader of Iran, the Ayatollah. The Quds Force, among other things, runs clandestine operations all over the world. Rahimi was responsible for one of the Quds Force's eight geographically defined directorates. His territory encompassed the Arabian Peninsula.

"What do you have for me this evening, Rahimi?" the steely eyed man across the desk asked.

"One of our agents in Saudi Arabia reports that Abdullah al Saud has dispatched an American university professor to the Lesser Antilles to search for evidence that a Moorish fleet that left from Palos in 889 reached the Caribbean Islands."

"Why would the Saudis do such a thing?"

"They want to correct the infidels' notion that the New World was discovered by Christopher Columbus."

"You sound skeptical, Rahimi. Do you question their motive?"

"No, not as far as it goes. But we think there may be a less obvious reason, as well as their stated one. The fleet was under the command of Khashkhash ibn Saeed ibn Aswad. It returned after an extended period, laden with treasures of the sort that the Spaniards plundered hundreds of years later." Rahimi paused and took a sip of the tea his host had ordered for him.

"So they believe this Khashkhash was successful," the steely eyed man said. "How do they know what you have told me so far? Where does their information come from?"

"The voyage was documented by Abul-Hassan, the historian and geographer, not long after the voyage. His work is in their archives."

"So they seek to validate his history? Is that it?"

"Yes, but there is more. A mullah remained behind when the fleet returned to Spain. He retained three ships and a hundred men. His name was Ali ibn Abi Bakr. The mullah had in his possession some documents which dated from the time of Mohammed. Our source thinks there may have been writings from the prophet himself. Ali ibn Abi Bakr was supposedly a distant relative of the prophet."

"And this Ali ibn Abi Bakr, what became of him?"

"There is no record that we know of. The presumption is that he died in the New World, but the Saudis may know more. We are checking."

"You think the Saudis are looking for the documents this mullah had?"

"Our source in Abdullah al Saud's organization thinks that is a strong possibility. The prince thinks the documents may have a significant impact on Islam."

"If that is true and those Sunni bastards want them, it cannot bode well for us. Give me a full written report; I need to brief the commander. Perhaps even the Ayatollah. What do you know about this mullah?"

"We are researching him. I will include our findings in the report."

"Very well, Rahimi. Carry on."

"WELCOME ABOARD," Liz said, raising a moisture-beaded glass of chilled white wine.

"Yes, welcome to *Vengeance*," Dani said, raising her own glass. They sat in *Vengeance's* cockpit, tied to a dock in the luxury marina in St. George's, Grenada. Their guests had been aboard long enough to unpack and freshen up from their day's travel.

"Thank you," Richard Everett said. "We're glad to be here."

"Your yacht's a beauty," his wife said, as the four of them touched the rims of their glasses together. After they had each taken a sip of the wine, she asked, "Is *Vengeance* an antique? She has classic lines."

Dani grinned. "Thanks, Doctor Everett. You have a good eye. She's actually a reproduction of a classic design by L. Francis Herreshoff."

"Oh, call me Shellie. And this Herreshoff must have had an artist's eye. The visual harmony is lovely. It's a pleasure just to look at her."

"Thanks, Shellie," Liz said. "Are you by chance an artist?"

"Oh, I wish. But I'm afraid my only gift is the ability to draw pleasure from the work of others."

"She's being modest," Rick said. "Her background is in art history, and in spite of her protests to the contrary, she's quite talented in her own right. She's just too busy to pursue that these days. And by the way, I'm Rick. Forget the professor stuff. We may work in academia, but it's just a job. We don't let it define who we are."

"I couldn't help noticing the paintings in the main cabin,"

Shellie said. "They're so precise they almost look like photos. Who's the artist? I couldn't make out the signature."

"Liz did those," Dani said.

"You're quite good," Shellie said. "If I could paint like that, I'm not sure I'd ever do anything else. You could make a living from your work."

"You're kind to say so," Liz said, "but I'm not sure I could paint for money. Then it would just be work. Now, it's my escape."

"I understand the escape part. It's that way for me, too. But I don't paint as well as you."

"I feel that way when I look at other people's work," Liz said. "Did you notice the impressionist sunset on the forward bulkhead of the saloon?"

"I did!" Shellie said. "It's a real departure from your others. You're quite versatile."

Liz smiled. "Not that versatile. I look at that and it makes me feel so ... I guess unimaginative is the word I'm searching for."

"So you didn't paint that?" Shellie asked.

"No. A friend of ours did."

"It's awesome. Is your friend someone I might have heard of?"

Liz chuckled.

"It's doubtful," Dani said. "But if you had, you'd remember it. He lives in Dominica. If we go up that way, maybe we can introduce you."

"Has he done many paintings?"

"Quite a few," Liz said. "His wife paints, as well. She runs a gallery there."

"And what's his name?" Shellie asked.

"Sharktooth," Liz said.

"Huh? Sharktooth? Is that like a stage name or something?"

"Or something," Liz said. "It's the only name he'll answer to, for whatever reason. Tell us about yourselves. You're both professors?"

"Yes," Rick said. "My field's the pre-Columbian history of

North America, which means I get to dabble in archaeology, as well." He looked at Shellie.

"And my background is art history. I have a special interest in east Asian and Middle Eastern works. My focus is the era from the Holy Roman Empire through the Middle Ages."

"So, there's some overlap in your interests, at least in the sense of the time period," Liz said.

"Right," Shellie said. "That's how we first encountered one another. We were both involved in the study of some artifacts that were recovered from an Inca site in southwest Colombia."

"Someone found a jeweled dagger that was of obvious Arabic origin. The site was at first thought to predate the Spanish period, partly because of the engraving on the dagger," Rick said.

"There was a notion that the Arabs were there before the Spanish?" Dani asked, raising her eyebrows. "In South America?"

"Yes. But Shellie managed to pin down the origin of the dagger to a Moorish artisan in Spain. He did his work in the days before the Spanish took back the Iberian Peninsula. The dates matched up, but the dagger itself was mentioned in some records that were much later, consistent with the idea that Francisco Pizarro, or one of the noblemen in his party, owned it. It was valuable and distinctive enough to appear in some documents that put it in Spain well after the beginnings of the Spanish conquest. Perhaps they left it with some local dignitary as a gift."

"That's quite a story," Liz said. "I can imagine that there was some serious detective work involved in discovering that."

Shellie smiled. "There was, indeed. But the best thing I discovered was Rick."

"That's sweet," Liz said.

"Were the people who found the dagger disappointed?" Dani asked.

"Oh, maybe a little, but the site was important enough to keep them excited even without tying it to the Moors," Rick said. "I'm sure it would have been fun for them if it turned out that the

Spanish didn't leave it there. Just imagine; it could have turned back the clock on the discovery of the new world by several hundred years."

"Is that related to your current project?" Liz asked. "Our charter broker told us you were looking for evidence to support that same kind of theory."

"It sort of is," Rick said. "Our work on the dagger is what attracted the attention of our sponsor and led them to us. How much did your charter broker tell you? Elaine, right? She's your broker?"

"Yes," Liz said. "I just told you everything we know. It sounds like an interesting project. Can you tell us more about it?"

Rick and Shellie traded looks for a few seconds. "Sure," he said. "But we'll need your commitment that it goes no farther without our okay."

"That's not a problem," Dani said. "We trade on protecting our guests' privacy."

"Elaine assured us of that. She recommended you two because of your background, Dani."

"Our background?" Dani frowned.

"Yours, individually," Rick said.

"She said you grew up in the islands. Your family's from Martinique?" Shellie asked.

"My father's family, yes. Why is that important to you?"

"We need someone with more than a casual knowledge of local politics and culture. We'll be depending on you to keep us straight with the authorities."

"How do you mean that?" Dani asked, her frown deepening.

"We don't want to cross any boundaries, legally or culturally. It may come to the point where we're doing some minor excavating, looking for artifacts."

"I'm afraid I don't know much about that," Dani said. "Doesn't it involve a lot of red tape?"

"Sometimes. Our sponsor has people who can handle that; it's the sensitivity to that kind of issue, and the ability to interpret local reactions that we're looking for from you," Shellie said.

"The Caribbean countries don't have well-defined regulations for protecting historic sites. Pillaging has always been a problem here," Rick said. "But people are becoming more conscious of the need to stop that. Your sense of the local attitudes is what we need."

"Oh, okay. I do know the people on the different islands pretty well, if that will help."

"That's exactly what we want."

"So what are you planning?" Liz asked.

"To start with, we have a fragment of a map that is thought to have been drawn by one of the Moors who made this voyage. It was part of a folio we managed to obtain from an archive in a Middle Eastern country that I'm not at liberty to name."

"Does it point to a particular island?" Liz asked.

"It's not that easy," Rick said, grinning. "As I said, it's a fragment. What we have is a photocopy, of course. The documents of the voyage put the fleet somewhere between the islands we call Grenada and Puerto Rico, but based on what we can glean, we don't think they got as far north as Puerto Rico. Our first job is to do a preliminary survey of the islands to try to find a match for the geographic features on the map fragment. We'll be trying to get a feel for how the area would have looked back then, as well."

"I imagine that you've already studied modern maps and charts," Dani said.

"Yes, of course. That's part of why we think the island we're looking for is in the Lesser Antilles. The Virgins and the Greater Antilles don't offer a match, at least not on a preliminary basis."

"How do you want to go about this, then?" Dani asked.

"Well, if it's okay with you, we'll go over that with you in the morning. We've got a little presentation worked out. We thought it might be useful with the local authorities, and we'd like your reaction. It could be that you'll recognize some of the features from the fragment and the text references. Based on the preliminary work we've done, it could even be Grenada."

"Sure, that's fine with me," Dani said. "Liz?"

"Certainly."

"But is there any way we could have an early dinner?" Shellie asked. "I'm beat from the airplane ride. I could use food, a nice walk around the harbor, and an early bedtime."

"Dinner in half an hour?" Liz asked.

"Perfect," Shellie said. "Okay with you, Rick?"

"Yes. Suits me. Liz, if I come below with you, can you help me get on the internet? I have some things I need to check."

"Yes, I can do that." Liz stepped through the companionway and Rick followed her.

Shellie took a sip of wine and gave Dani a warm smile. "Growing up in the islands sounds exciting," she said, putting her glass on the cockpit table.

"I don't know," Dani said. "It was just ... the way I lived, I guess."

"Now, you said your father was from Martinique. Is that where you lived when you were little?"

"Well, sort of," Dani said. "Some of the time, anyway. My parents were divorced, so I had a strange childhood."

"Oh, I went through that, too. I'm sorry if I was prying. I understand if you'd rather not talk about it. My interest was piqued by the notion of growing up down here in paradise."

"No, it's okay," Dani said. "I didn't take it that way. I just don't want to bore you."

"I love hearing about unusual experiences. I'm sure your story's not boring. How did you and Liz end up in business together? She's from Belgium, right?"

"She was on a sabbatical in the islands, and she met this strange guy, who had tried to kill me when I ... Are you sure you want to hear all this? It's a long, involved story."

"It's absolutely tantalizing, with an opener like that. This guy tried to kill you?"

"Yes. It's going to take a while, because a bunch of my friends from childhood played a part."

"We've got weeks. I'd love to hear whatever you're comfortable telling me."

"Don't get her started on that now," Liz said, setting a tray of appetizers on the bridge deck. "It's not good dinner table conversation. Tell them about how you tricked me into cooking for you on *Kayak Spirit* before you conned me into buying *Vengeance* with you."

"You tricked her into cooking for you?" Shellie asked, as Liz ducked back into the galley.

"Was *Kayak Spirit* a boat?" Rick asked.

Dani smiled as she remembered taking Liz sailing that first time. "Yes. She belongs to a friend of mine, and I was living aboard her, doing a little refurbishing, when I met Liz. We were in Antigua, and this boat was for sale at a brokerage there. I had decided I wanted to buy her and go into the charter business, but I would need a partner — somebody who could sail, but more important, somebody who could cook. So, I invited Liz out for a day sail ... "

3

"What do you think of Dani and Liz?" Rick asked, as he and Shellie strolled along the road from the marina toward St. George's.

"Dani's okay, but you spent more time with Liz than I did," Shellie said.

"I was going over my presentation and she was fixing dinner. We didn't talk much. But man, can that woman cook!"

"The broker said she was a gourmet chef," Shellie said.

"She told us the truth. I only got snatches of your conversation, but it sounded like you got quite a bit of Dani's story."

"She was guarded at first, but I got her to relax a little. She was still pretty careful, though, especially talking about her father's business and her teenage years."

"Why were you asking her about her father's business?"

"Oh, it just kind of came up. You wanted to know how extensive her background was in the islands, so I was trying to probe where she had lived down here, and when. And how old she was in each place."

"What did you learn?"

"She had a strange childhood. Her parents divorced when she was an infant. Her mother's part of a wealthy investment banking family in New York, and her father's an international businessman."

"I thought she said his family was from Martinique," Rick said.

"Yes, he was born there. His family's been in the islands since the 1600s, and they were apparently well off. Some of them were, anyhow. Some of his ancestors were in Louisiana, before the purchase. She has distant cousins all over the place, but mostly concentrated in the French islands. Her father lives in Paris now."

"So how did she come to live all over the Caribbean as a kid?"

"It was summers and vacations, mostly. Her mother wasn't particularly interested in her, from what I got. I think there's some strain there. She insisted on Dani going to private schools in the Northeast, but other than that, she didn't pay much attention. Her father took her under his wing, but whatever he was doing to build his business in the islands, he was gone most of the time. So she was passed around among his friends and family when she was nominally in his care."

"What was special about her teenage years? You said she didn't want to talk about them."

"I don't know. I didn't sense anything amiss, there. She just wouldn't say where she spent her time, except that she hung out with a friend of her father's who was almost like a much older brother. He was in the U.S. Army, a military attaché, most of the time. He spent most of his career in the islands and South and Central America."

"That does sound like a strange childhood, but at least she must know her way around this part of the world. That should be a big help."

"Oh, I think so. I think she was much more comfortable in this part of the world than in the States. Still is, for that matter.

Her mother browbeat her into working for the family's bank after she finished college."

"What did she study?"

"Bachelor's in accounting, Master's in finance."

"How'd she find her way into this business, then?"

"Her father's always been a yachtsman. He's got a fleet of big crewed charter yachts in the Mediterranean. She was a deckhand on them off and on from her early teens, when she wasn't kicking around down here. When she got fed up with investment banking, she started crewing on private yachts and ended up down here. She and Liz bumped into one another while Liz was on a sabbatical from working for the E.U. I didn't get to hear the particulars of how they met, but the little I got really blew me away."

"How so?"

"All I got was that Liz met this 'strange guy,' as Dani put it. He had tried to kill Dani, at some point before Liz took up with him. And that was all she said about that. She wandered off into the divorce thing."

"Wow! How could you not grill her on that?"

"Well, like I said, she was guarded. I don't think she's much into small talk. I just let her go where she was comfortable. I mean, all we care about is whether she can be a good fixer for us, with the locals, right? We don't need her complete life story."

"Right, but it sounds like she's really got some tales to tell. Probably Liz, too, if she was seeing the guy who tried to kill Dani."

"No kidding. Anyhow, I don't think the charter broker steered us wrong. I think Dani and Liz are just what we need. And they're pleasant company, too."

"Not to mention Liz's cooking," Rick said.

"Keep that up and you'll make me jealous," Shellie said, smiling up at him as she gave him a gentle elbow to the ribs. "Let's get back to the boat; I'm ready for bed."

Hossein Rahimi was preparing to leave his office for the night; as usual, he had worked until almost midnight. The hours after most people had gone home were his most productive ones. He'd spent the evening studying the material on Ali ibn Abi Bakr that his people had assembled during the afternoon.

The mullah had left his imprint on Islam, even though he had disappeared a thousand years ago. Ali ibn Abi Bakr, according to Rahimi's researchers, was indeed a descendant of the Prophet. Furthermore, he was a proponent of the Sunni interpretation of Mohammed's teachings.

This made Ali a heretic in the eyes of the Shiite clerics who controlled modern Iran. It was clear now, at least to Rahimi, that the Saudis had a broader agenda than claiming the Moors had discovered America. Ali ibn Abi Bakr's writings would support the Saudi's Sunni view of Islam, eroding the credibility of Iran as a major influence in Middle Eastern politics.

Rahimi had prepared a memorandum for his commander's approval granting him the authority to pursue this investigation outside his normal geographic territory. The directorate responsible for the Caribbean included most of the western world, but Rahimi didn't expect to meet any resistance to his request from his counterpart responsible for the west. His request was *pro forma*, an extension of his responsibility for surveillance of the Arab nations.

The agents currently assigned to Rahimi's counterpart for the West were preoccupied with the minions of the Great Satan. They were also pursuing opportunities afforded by the increasing unrest in Venezuela. They didn't have time to devote to chasing an academic who was hunting ghosts, even if the academic had the backing of the Saudis.

Rahimi had sent the memo earlier. Several hours ago, he had begun deploying his own agents in anticipation of his commander's approval. He had a deep-cover team *en route* to the Caribbean. Because of airline connections and his lack of specific information as to the Saudis' plans, the team would start from the French island of Martinique. They would arrive there early in the morning.

"WERE you telling her your life's story, or what?" Liz asked, rinsing a plate and handing it to Dani to dry. Their guests were out for a stroll in the cool of the evening. "I felt like I was interrupting a performance when I brought dinner up into the cockpit."

"Yes. She's really easy to talk to. She drew me out before I even realized it."

"They're both good company," Liz said. "I'm enjoying them; they're nice people."

"They seem to be," Dani said. "You've spent more time with him, but I almost *like* her."

Liz laughed. "You almost like her? You're a mess, Dani. What do you mean, you *almost* like her?"

"Why would she be interested in me, Liz?" Dani frowned. "What's her angle?"

Liz pulled the plug from the sink drain and wiped her hands on the dish towel Dani still held. She took it from Dani and folded it over the towel bar in front of the sink. "Because you're an interesting person, Dani. You've had some unusual experiences."

Dani shook her head and stared into space while Liz filled two glasses with the wine left from their dinner. "Come on up to the cockpit and tell me about it," Liz said. "Did she make you uncomfortable?"

Dani took a glass of wine and followed Liz up the companionway ladder. "A little bit, at first," she said, as she sat down across from Liz.

"But she helped you to get over your reticence?"

"I guess. She backed off right away when I tried to change the subject. She'd asked about growing up in the islands, and I told her it wasn't what it sounded like, that it was a long story, and it was complicated because my parents were divorced."

"Uh-huh," Liz said.

"Her parents were divorced, too. She kind of understood. So she asked how you and I ended up in business together."

"And pretty soon, you were telling her everything?"

"Yes, I guess so. She was just so ... I don't know ... "

"A good listener?"

"I guess so."

"Did she tell you much about herself?"

"Um ... when I asked, she did. She's just really nice. I haven't met many women like that, except you and Connie. You think I screwed up?"

Liz almost laughed, until she saw the look on Dani's face. "No, you didn't screw up. You had a conversation. That's a good thing to do with our guests. It's good business. How did you leave off with her when I served dinner?"

"She wants to hear more. I mostly told her about how we met — Mike Reilly, and all that, but not the details. Then that led to Phillip, and Sharktooth. You know. She wanted to hear about how I got to know all of them when I was little."

"Good, Dani. I've told you before that you have an interesting story and that you should be more open with our guests. Now do you believe me?"

"Maybe. Anyway, I like her. Do you think I can trust her?"

"I think so, Dani. But what's the downside? I like her, too. Both of them, for that matter. Give it a try; making friends is a good thing to do."

"Okay, I will. I'm looking forward to hearing how they're planning to run this quest, or whatever you want to call it."

"Rick was flipping through some slides on his laptop while I was working on dinner; I didn't want to spy on him, but I think he's got quite a presentation to show us in the morning," Liz said.

"Good. Maybe this charter will be fun after all. Let's turn in; I don't think we need to wait up for them, do you?"

"No. Everybody's tired." Liz stood and stepped through the companionway with Dani right behind her.

4

"How do you two stay so slim?" Shellie asked, as she finished her breakfast. "I'd gain weight like crazy if I ate like this all the time."

"Well, there are two things going for us," Liz said. "Sailing *Vengeance* is physically demanding, and we only eat this way when we have guests aboard."

"What do you eat the rest of the time?"

"Fruit and cheese, salads, grilled fish when we catch one."

"What was the filling in that pastry you served with the eggs?" Rick asked.

"Salt fish," Liz said. "It's a staple down here, along with pickled meat — pork, or beef. A lot of people in the islands don't have refrigerators."

"What about fresh meat?" Shellie asked.

"Chicken, or goat," Dani said. "Fresh pork, sometimes. Most of the islands don't have the acreage to support beef cattle, I guess. I would imagine that hasn't changed much since the period you're studying."

"I think you're right. I suspect the early explorers had to be flexible in their diets," Rick said. "I don't know about chicken and goats — whether the Caribs would have had them, or any kind of domestic animals."

"Was there mention of that in the records of this Moorish voyage?" Liz asked. "Their diet?"

"Not much," Rick said. "That fleet would have been made up of seasoned travelers: sailors, soldiers, itinerant merchants. The man in command was Khashkhash ibn Saeed ibn Aswad; he was a wealthy merchant. As best we can tell, he spent more of his life at sea than ashore."

"I don't think of the Arabs as seagoing people," Dani said, "even though I know they were. But I picture them as poking around the Mediterranean, not crossing the Atlantic into the unknown."

"That's true to an extent," Rick said. "But Khashkhash would have been driven by the same motives as Columbus."

"He was looking for a route to Asia?" Liz asked. "I thought the Arabs were already trading in Asia."

"They were. So were the Europeans, but the land routes were treacherous. Moving goods by ship was more efficient then, just as it is now. If you think about it, the relative advantage was probably bigger back then."

"I hadn't really thought about that," Dani said, "but you're right. One ship could carry a lot more stuff than a string of camels, or whatever they were using."

"Exactly," Rick said. "And the Arabs knew their way around; they were ahead of the Europeans in terms of geography and navigation. Finding your way across the desert isn't a lot different from sailing out of sight of land, if you think about it."

"I can see that," Dani said.

"So can I." Liz lifted the carafe of coffee and filled everyone's cups. "What's your agenda for the day? How can we help?"

"Well, I had mentioned giving you our presentation, but we're in a little bit of a time crunch. I got an email last night just before we turned in, and I have an appointment with the curator of the Grenada National Museum in about an hour."

"At the museum?" Liz asked.

"Yes. How long will it take us to get there?"

"Ten or fifteen minutes, if you take a taxi. It's not too far."

Checking his watch, Rick said, "We'd better delay giving you the presentation, then. It's likely to take us a while, because we'll want time for you to really dig into some parts of it. Is that okay?"

"Our time is yours," Dani said. "But I thought you wanted our reaction before you went live with the presentation. Could we do a crash version? Would that help?"

Rick grinned. "Thanks, but it'll work out. I've been trying to line up the meeting with the curator for a while, and he's only blocked out a half hour. We talked about it before we left the States. This will just be a quick, 'get acquainted' session. He's going to set up a meeting with several other people he thinks will want to see the full pitch, maybe tomorrow or the next day."

"We should be back in time to get through the presentation with you before lunch," Shellie said. "That way, we can explore all the details while we eat. Will that work?"

"Sure," Liz said. "I'll put together a nice cold seafood salad while you're gone. That way, we can all sit down and go through your material, and when you're ready, we can eat without interrupting our discussion."

"Sounds good to me," Rick said. "We'd better go below and get ready, I guess. Do we need to reserve a taxi?"

"I'll take care of that for you," Dani said.

As Colonel Rahimi had anticipated, his commanding officer had authorized him to proceed with his proposed mission to monitor the Saudis' Caribbean project. Rahimi sat in his office in

Tehran, drinking strong tea as he reviewed the new material his research team had assembled over the last 24 hours. He had tasked his cyberespionage team with learning as much as possible about the American professor and the people who were supporting him.

Thanks to his agent in Riyadh, Rahimi had a name for the American professor, as well as more information about his plans. The Saudis had funded Dr. Richard Everett's venture through a foundation in Washington which concealed their participation. Rahimi's agent in the Saudi prince's organization reported that the professor didn't know of the Saudi's interest in his work.

As best Everett knew, his grant was funded by an anonymous donor with an interest in the possibility of pre-Columbian contacts between Spain or Portugal and the Americas. Western academics, Everett among them, had long speculated that Columbus was the beneficiary of knowledge from earlier explorers, so Everett was pleased to have his research funded.

The foundation's director and Everett had discussed recent claims by the president of Turkey that Muslims had discovered America some 600 years before Columbus made his voyage. The director had mentioned that the Saudi royal family had procured numerous materials from the period when the Moors occupied the Iberian Peninsula. As a result, the professor had made a request through Saudi diplomatic representatives in the U.S., seeking access to documents related to early voyages across the Atlantic from what is now Spain. The Saudis had pretended some reluctance, but they had allowed themselves to be persuaded by the professor's sincere entreaty.

Rahimi's cyberespionage group had hacked into the foundation's computers and uncovered Everett's credentials and his travel plans, as well as evidence of the Saudis' manipulation. Everett and his wife had flown to Grenada from the U.S., arriving yesterday. The foundation had wired $250,000 U.S. to a charter yacht broker in Fort Lauderdale, Florida, ten days earlier. Surreptitious access to the broker's computer revealed the name of the yacht which had been chartered for Everett's use.

Rahimi studied the website for the yacht *Vengeance*. Surprised to see that it was operated by two young women, he made note of their names as he stared at their pictures. Both were beautiful; he wondered if that would cause friction between Everett and his wife. His interest wasn't prurient; he was looking for any possible source of leverage for his surveillance team to use.

Rahimi wondered about the selection of the yacht. He never assumed that such things were the result of chance. He would rule out all other possibilities before accepting that fate had put the professor on that particular yacht. He closed the report and started typing.

First, he sent a short email to his research team, ordering background information on the Everetts as well as on the two women who ran the boat. As an afterthought, he asked for information on the vessel's ownership and registration.

After he sent that email, he composed another one ordering his field operatives to fly to Grenada from Martinique. He provided as much information as he had on the yacht and instructed them to look for it. If they failed to find it, or if the Everetts weren't aboard, their first priority was to locate the professor and his wife. They should maintain surveillance on the Everetts and the yacht. He wanted to know what the Everetts' business in Grenada was.

Next, he turned his attention to the field operatives' travel arrangements. They should be arriving in Martinique about now. Clicking through airline schedules, he saw that there were a number of inter-island flights on regional carriers. Connections permitting, his team should be on the ground in Grenada in the early afternoon.

~

"How was the meeting?" Liz asked, as she poured coffee for everyone. They sat in the shade of the big awning that was stretched over *Vengeance's* cockpit.

"It went well enough," Rick said. "Dr. Johnson is one of the most knowledgeable people around on the subject of early European influence in the islands. I've read a lot of his work over the years."

"He didn't think a follow-up meeting was necessary, though," Shellie said.

"No?" Dani asked.

"Not yet, anyway," Rick said. "He couldn't pull together anybody he thought could contribute to our project. He did steer me to some references, though. I have some new leads to research."

"Here?" Dani asked.

"On the web, at least to start with. He ran across some material years ago that he thought might help, but he doesn't have the references. It was stuff that he didn't see as relevant to his work at the time."

"I was surprised by that," Shellie said. "I can't believe he didn't chase down those leads."

"Well, like he said, I guess he thought it would be a distraction. One of the hazards of the publish or perish environment is tunnel vision."

"Okay, no fair," Dani said. "What are you two talking about?"

Rick grinned. "Sorry. We've been arguing about it since we left him. Shellie and I see it differently. She's less biased than I am." He looked at Shellie. "Why don't you tell them?"

She took a sip of coffee and nodded, putting her mug down before she spoke. "After Columbus reported what he'd found, the Spanish focused on the Greater Antilles and North and South America. That's where the riches were. They weren't too interested in the little islands, so the French and the English fought over them, along with the Dutch. But mostly the French and the

English. They saw an opportunity for agricultural colonies. The Dutch were more interested in trading, I guess. With me so far?" Shellie paused for another sip of coffee.

Dani and Liz nodded.

"Okay. Dr. Johnson was interested mostly in Grenada. The French got here first. French missionaries, in fact. Johnson was reading some of their early accounts, which were more like diaries and personal correspondence than anything else. Anyway, the French priest Johnson studied the most was swapping letters with a friend in Martinique. That's where he stumbled across the information he thought might help us. The two priests were debating why it was that the Indians had a number of Spanish words and phrases in their language."

"Don't forget the key word, Shellie," Rick said, when she paused for another swallow of coffee.

"Right," she said. "The priest in Martinique was the one who mentioned that the borrowed vocabulary was archaic. Ancient was the way he described it."

"Keep in mind that he was writing in the early 1600s," Rick said. "So when he said ancient, we're talking really old."

Dani frowned. "But that's a hundred years after Columbus, when these priests were writing to each other, right?"

"You're right," Shellie said. "But you have to realize that the Romance languages went through some fairly rapid evolution after the fall of the Holy Roman Empire. Before the Moorish conquest, the people on the Iberian Peninsula spoke various dialects of what's called Vulgar Latin. That was a corrupt, simplified version of Classical Latin, and it evolved into French, Spanish, Portuguese, and Italian."

"Okay," Liz said. "When the French priests said the Spanish phrases were archaic, were they talking about Vulgar Latin?"

"Almost. But the branch of Vulgar Latin which had evolved into Spanish by the early 1600s was heavily influenced by the Moors. They invaded Spain in the early 700s, almost a thousand years before the French missionaries were here in the islands. The Moors interjected Arabic and an Arabic dialect of their own, called Mozarabic, into the Vulgar Latin spoken by the people they conquered. There are thousands of words in modern Spanish that come directly from Arabic."

"Does that mean the missionaries thought the Moors came to the islands before Columbus?" Dani asked.

"It's hard to know what they thought. They may have written their thoughts, or they may not have," Rick said. "Johnson didn't know how much of their correspondence survived until now. He wasn't even sure where he picked up that thread. He thought the reference he recalls might have been a secondary source. And we don't know for sure what they meant by 'ancient Spanish,' either. That's my homework assignment from Dr. Johnson." he smiled.

"That sounds like a whole different project," Liz said. "You could spend a lifetime trying to track that down, couldn't you?"

Rick grinned. "A lifetime, or as long as the funding holds out. It's easy to get sidetracked in this business."

"I can see that," Liz said.

"What's next?" Dani asked.

"Let's get started on our presentation," Shellie said. "We need to think about what we want to accomplish in Grenada, but the presentation's a good start. It'll get you up to speed enough so that you can give us your thoughts on how we should start scouting the islands."

"Good," said Dani.

"Let's go below. I'll set up my laptop on the dining table," Rick said.

5

"Leila, Bert. Have a nice walk?" the man asked, as the couple stopped at his table in the marina's open-air restaurant. He had watched their approach while the attractive blonde sitting with him scanned the dining area.

"Lovely," the trim, dark-haired Leila said. Her companion, Bert, held a chair for her. She sat down and took a sip of the fruit punch that had been delivered in her absence. Leila Kelley, known within Quds Force as Laleh Kazemi, smiled at the man who had spoken to her.

"There's a boat here that caught our attention, Ed," Bert said, as he sat down across from Leila.

Ed, the man who had greeted them, raised his eyebrows and looked around, satisfied that no one was in earshot. It was late enough so that the lunch crowd had cleared out. Ed, named Eshan Gorbhani when he was born, was traveling on a U.S. passport in the name of Edward Gordon. He was in charge of the Quds Force field team assigned to watch Dr. Richard Everett.

"This place is empty; we can talk. Just watch out for the waitress," Ed said. "You found them?"

"Yes," Bert said. His birth name was Hirbod Pahlavi, although his U.S. passport identified him as Herbert Parsons. "The boat's name's on the stern in gold leaf. *Vengeance*. She's a beauty, too."

"Were the people aboard?" the blonde woman asked, continuing to sweep her eyes over their surroundings. Ashraf Esfahani, or Ashley Stevens, as she was calling herself, was their lookout.

Leila nodded. "Yes. All four of them. They were lounging in the cockpit when we walked by on our way to the end of the pier. When we came back, they were going below deck."

Ashley saw the waitress come out of the kitchen with their food. She dropped her napkin and bent to the side to retrieve it. The group fell silent at this prearranged signal. They had worked together for almost a year; they had a well-honed set of nonverbal cues. Posing as two American couples traveling together was a cover that served them well, even when they were working the Arab countries, their normal territory.

Their colloquial American English was flawless. Children of refugees from the fall of the Shah, they had all grown up in the States. Recruited separately, they had been trained in Iran. Only after they had proven themselves on individual assignments had they been formed into a team.

Hossein Rahimi had been one of their instructors. Their initial assignments had been back in the U.S., but Rahimi had kept an eye on them. He'd recognized that they could be far more valuable in the Arab nations, where their western ways would serve as camouflage. Even if the security forces in the Arab countries suspected they were spies, they would misjudge their affiliation. No one would believe that the two American couples were reporting to Tehran.

"We got lucky, finding them so quickly," Ed said. "Now we need to get aboard that yacht and see what Everett has in the way of information. We'll have to watch for them to go ashore, but we can't carry out surveillance from here. We need a boat, here in the marina."

"Security's too tight," Ashley said, "if you're thinking about setting up on one of the unoccupied boats."

"There's a bareboat charter fleet based right here in the marina," Leila said. "Must be 25 or 30 yachts. We saw them on our walk. We could rent one. Bert and I have certificates; we've done some sailing."

"Great," Ed said. "Go for it, once we've finished eating. Ashley and I will head back to the guesthouse and retrieve our stuff. You guys didn't unpack yet, did you?"

"No," Bert said. "Just dumped our bags in the room."

"YOU TELL A FASCINATING STORY," Dani said, as Shellie and Rick finished their presentation.

"Thanks," Rick said, closing his laptop. "It's kind of you to say so. You're the first outsiders who have seen our pitch. But I'm a little worried that we may be overselling the Moorish discovery idea."

"Why's that?" Liz asked. "I mean, you want it to be convincing, don't you?"

Shellie traded looks with Rick, a slight frown wrinkling her brow. "We want it to be plausible, but not overly persuasive," she said.

"You're losing me," Dani said. "You said you planned to use this to encourage local authorities to support your efforts. Doesn't that call for salesmanship?"

"Salesmanship is the kiss of death in the academic world," Rick said. "We want to position ourselves as having open minds about what we might find."

"Or not find," Shellie said. "We're striving for a kind of scientific impartiality. Objectivity, in other words."

"We don't want to come across as treasure hunters, either,"

Rick said. "We're out to help determine what actually happened, not to sell a particular version of history."

"But you want to get people excited, don't you?" Dani asked.

"Well, yes," Rick said. "But excited by the intellectual challenge — new ideas. We both worry that we shouldn't create any particular expectation as to the outcome. We're looking for facts that would support *an* alternative history, not any *specific* alternative history."

"If you think about it, this is a pretty inflammatory notion," Shellie said. "The idea that Muslims found the New World and Columbus was just exploiting their discovery won't be well received in a lot of places."

"Because of the current wave of Islamophobia in the States, you mean?" Liz asked.

"Well, that's certainly part of it," Rick said, "but it's deeper than just that."

"There's the whole idea that western values shaped the fundamental structure of society in North and South America," Shellie said. "Our worldview is built on the assumption that the people who came here in the wake of Columbus had some inherent right to displace the social structures of the indigenous people."

"Throwing Islam into the mix just complicates it further," Rick said. "We need to be careful to avoid appearing to push the idea that European Christians didn't 'discover' America, however you interpret 'discover.'"

"So it's critical that we come across as objective," Shellie said.

"I get that," Dani said, "but I think the attitudes of the people in the islands may be different from what you find on the mainland."

"How so?" Rick asked, his eyebrows rising.

"The islands were colonies until not long ago," Dani said. "There are still some remnants of colonialism, depending on who you ask. Don't forget, in most of the islands, the majority of the population isn't descended from European immigrants, either."

"You mean the heritage of African slavery?" Shellie asked.

"Not just that. Almost everybody here descended from slaves or indentured servants. Most of the indentured servants weren't of European extraction. A lot of them came from India, when it was still under British control. Until independence, the people down here felt like second-class citizens, and independence came during recent memory. There are plenty of people alive who remember the colonial days, and not with favor, in a lot of cases."

"I see your point," Rick said. "But doesn't that mean they'd identify with the indigenous people, rather than any outsiders? Fellow victims of colonial oppression?"

"Maybe so," Dani said. "But don't underestimate the pleasure they might find in seeing the notion of European discovery turned on its head. Whether they would have fared better under the Moors isn't what will shape their reactions, in my opinion."

"Liz, you haven't said much. What do you think of Dani's points?" Rick asked.

"I don't have Dani's background. She grew up with the people down here, so I trust her perceptions."

"That's a valuable insight," Rick said. "I'm not sure it changes our need to present an objective approach to our search, but it's worth some further thought. Certainly, it's something we need to pay attention to. You're right, Dani. We were making some assumptions about our audience that may not apply."

Dani nodded. "I don't have the connections here that I have in some of the other islands, but as we make our way north, I'll introduce you to some people who lived under colonial rule. You can see how they feel about the notion that Muslims got here way before Columbus."

"I'll look forward to that," Rick said.

"Me, too," Shellie said. "Interesting points, Dani."

"Speaking of making our way north," Rick said, "we need to talk about the map fragment. You don't by chance recognize the island?"

Dani and Liz both laughed.

"Well, I had to ask."

"Sure," Dani said. "Don't misinterpret our laughter. It's the kind of thing any sailor might sketch in a logbook, I think. Not intended for navigation, at least not in any long-range sense, anyway. Just something to jog their memory about local features."

"You mentioned there was some text that referenced it," Liz said.

"Yes, but Dani's comment is on target. The text doesn't lead you to a certain island. It deals with where the mullah I mentioned had set up camp ashore, relative to the indentation in the shoreline. We were hoping the shape of the shoreline might look familiar to you."

"It does," Dani said. "Too familiar. Given that we're missing the outline of the island itself, it's hard to narrow it down. There's not an indication of the orientation of the map, even. We can't assume that north is up; there were other conventions over the centuries."

"The text does give us a clue there, though," Rick said. "There's a description of the sun rising over the mountains, and burning off the fog over the harbor during the morning. It's almost poetic. But it does indicate that the shoreline in the fragment is on the western side of the island. Does that help?"

"A little. The leeward sides of most of the islands have a lot of similarities from one to the next, though. I'm sure you noticed that the sketch could fit this very harbor, allowing for the lack of detail in the drawing and the possibility of erosion and silting over centuries of storms."

Rick smiled. "Yes. The shape is a rough match. There were cliffs, though, according to the text. The camp was near the base of one that was of middling height. Mean anything?"

Dani shook her head. "Rocky cliffs? Or clay? You find both kinds. The clay ones are prone to mudslides, so they aren't as permanent."

"It doesn't say. There's mention of an overhang, if that helps."

"Not really. You find those with either kind of cliff, usually where they've been undercut by the sea. They're death traps; they're prone to collapse. But they're attractive because of the shelter they offer. The locals call them caves, sometimes."

"They're prone to collapse?" Shellie asked. "Even the ones under rock?"

"Less so than clay," Dani said, "but yes. Most of the islands are volcanic in origin, so much of the rock is porous."

"So you don't think it's Grenada?" Shellie asked. "In the sketch?"

"I don't know. Based on the rough shape, it could be. When you approach this harbor from the west, some people might describe the headlands as cliffs. It could also be any of a number of other islands to the north. In fact, it could be any one of several different stretches of shoreline on a given island. The text is going to be critical, I think."

"We should let you two read it," Rick said.

"It's in English?" Liz asked.

"Yes. We had it translated," Rick said.

"That's good for us," Dani said. "Do you read Arabic?"

"Some," Rick said. "I had trouble with this, though. It's archaic. The people who provided it to us had it translated by experts. Why?"

"Nuance may be critical," Dani said. "Will you be able to consult with whoever translated the original?"

"I think so, via email, but it'll be cumbersome."

"We may be able to narrow things down a bit before you do that," Dani said. "As long as we can ask if we need clarification."

"I'm sure we can do that. I'll pull up the text file on my laptop for you. It'll take you a while to read the whole thing. Any chance you could recommend a good tour guide? Shellie and I could use the time while you're reading to get better oriented ashore."

"We have just the person," Liz said. "I'll call him and set it up. How soon would you like to go?"

"Oh, give me a few minutes to organize the files for you. Say any time in the next hour? Okay with you, Shellie?"

"Yes, of course," Shellie said.

Liz nodded and picked up her cellphone.

6

"Looks like they're heading out to dinner," Ashley Stevens said. She and Leila were sitting in the shade of the cockpit awning on *Aquila*, the 44-foot boat they had chartered earlier. Ed and Bert had walked over to the grocery store across the street from the marina to buy provisions for a few days.

Their plan was to use *Aquila* as a mobile base of operations. It was an inconspicuous way to follow *Vengeance*, the yacht that the Everetts were using. A typical bareboat, *Aquila* was nondescript. With her ubiquitous white fiberglass hull and blue canvas trim, she was indistinguishable from all the other cookie-cutter yachts in the bareboat charter fleets that were based on many of the islands in the Eastern Caribbean.

"Should we wait until after sunset?" Leila asked.

"I don't think it'll make any difference," Ashley said. "The docks are lighted anyway. Probably best if we do it during the dinner hour. There'll be fewer people around. Besides, there's no telling how long we have."

"Makes sense to me. You going to do it? Or should I?"

"I'll do it," Ashley said. "You keep a lookout; call my cellphone if you see anything. I wish we knew what we're looking for, though."

"Documents from the Saudis," Leila said.

"Yeah, but that could mean anything. I'd hate to have to stand there and scan a whole sheaf of papers with my phone. That could take forever."

"You could steal them and return them," Leila said, "but if they came back before you were done, they might miss them. Then they'd know something was up."

"Maybe I can just get a good sample so we can see what's there. Then we can refine what we want to scan and go back another time. Or maybe he's paper-free. I'd have everything on my computer, if it were me."

"You got a thumb drive with *Bypass* on it?" Leila asked. *Bypass* was a utility developed by Quds Force's cyberespionage group to unlock password-protected computers.

Ashley smirked. "Of course. That would be too easy, wouldn't it, if he had it all in digital form?"

Leila shrugged. "You ready? They just got in a taxi. That's a good sign that they'll be gone for a while."

"Yeah. I'm on it," Ashley said, standing up and stepping onto the dock.

"Break a leg," Leila said. She watched as Ashley ambled down the dock, pausing every few steps, pretending to admire the boats tied up between *Aquila* and *Vengeance*.

When she reached *Vengeance*, Ashley turned onto the finger pier without pausing or looking around. Her hand in her pocket as if fumbling for keys, she swung a leg over the lifelines as most sailors did, ignoring the boarding gate in the lifelines. She'd look right at home if anybody saw her.

Leila nodded her approval and made a quick check to see if anyone was watching. Satisfied that Ashley was unobserved, she looked back at *Vengeance*. Ashley was crouched in the cockpit, bending over the companionway doors. Leila grinned as she saw Ashley straighten up and swing the doors open. Whatever kind of lock they had, it was no match for Ashley's picks. If anybody had seen her, they would have thought she used a key.

Ashley paused on the companionway ladder and looked around. Leila gave her a surreptitious thumb up and turned her attention to keeping a lookout.

"GO AHEAD AND GET US A TABLE," Dani said. "I'll just be a few minutes, but *Les Caribes* will be packed if you don't go now. I'll catch up with you; just order me a rum punch."

"What's wrong?" Liz asked.

"I forgot something; I need to check on why the bilge pump was cycling this afternoon."

"Won't it keep?" Liz asked.

"I'll only be a few minutes. I'm worried that the discharge hose on the forward head is cracked. The intervals between pump cycles were getting shorter and shorter. I meant to check it earlier. I want to close the seacock, just in case. If that hose lets go, I'm not sure the bilge pump will keep up with the leak. Go ahead."

Liz nodded and climbed into the taxi with Rick and Shellie. "We'd like to go to *Les Caribes*, on Grand Anse Beach," she said, as the driver closed the door behind her.

"What's up with Dani?" Shellie asked. "Shouldn't we just wait for her?"

Liz repeated what Dani had told her, explaining that there was a risk of flooding the bilge. She didn't mention the possibility of sinking, not wanting to alarm the Everetts.

"Won't that take her some time?" Rick asked.

"She's not going to try to fix it," Liz said. "She'll close the seacock; that's like a valve where the hose goes through the hull below the waterline. That way, if the hose splits, no seawater will come in. That'll only take her a few minutes."

"We could postpone dinner," Shellie said.

"Not at this place; they serve at seven. That's it. They open for cocktails at 5:30. It's first come, first served, and the tables fill up as soon as they open the door. It'll be all right. She should only be ten minutes behind us, if that."

"Well, if you say so," Shellie said. "But she might miss the sunset. I guess you two see spectacular sunsets every day, though."

"We do," Liz said, smiling.

"How much of the material did you get through while we were on our tour?" Rick asked.

"Most of it," Liz said. "Some parts were slow going. It wasn't easy to follow in several places."

"Right," Rick said. "I agree. I might be able to help with that. I think it was tough to translate, and some things probably just couldn't be put into English. I've run into that before with material as old as that. Do you have specific questions?"

"Yes, some. But we should wait until Dani joins us, to avoid your having to explain everything twice."

"Sure," Rick said. "Looks like we're here, anyhow. How much do we owe you?" he asked the driver.

"Jus' wait, mon. You pay me when we get back to the marina. Enjoy your meal; this place the bes' cookin' around', 'cept for my wife. And Liz. But this is special. I be right here when you finish, no problem."

Once they were seated and had ordered drinks, Liz asked, "How was the island tour?"

"Great," Shellie said. "But I got the feeling we just scratched the surface."

"You did," Liz said. "Grenada's a big island. It takes at least a full day to get a good feel for it, and even then, you won't see everything. I asked Felix to focus on the leeward side, since that's where your sketch map shows the Moors' base."

"That's what he told us," Shellie said. "He did a good job. We drove up the west coast and along the north shore, past a place he called Caribs' Leap. Do you think that story is true? About the Caribs?"

Liz shrugged. "I don't know, but almost every island has a cliff called Caribs' Leap. The story's always the same. Rather than surrender to be enslaved, they all jumped to their deaths. It must have happened somewhere, at least once."

"Yeah," Rick said. "Who knows? There's usually some substance behind tales like that. We talked with him a little about what Dani said, too."

"About the colonial days? Or about the idea of Muslims coming before Columbus?"

"Both. I'd say Dani nailed that one, at least in Felix's case."

Shellie glanced at her watch. "Speaking of Dani, it's been 20 minutes. Should we call her?"

"Sure. She'll probably walk in while I'm calling, but why not?" Liz took her cellphone from her purse and made the call.

"We're just checking on you," she said. "Call me when you get this." Putting the phone on the table, she said, "It went to voice-mail. That's unusual."

"Is she one of those people who can't stand to miss a call?" Shellie asked.

"No, but she always checks caller i.d. She would have answered if she saw the call came from me."

"You sound worried," Rick said.

"I am, a little bit. It really shouldn't have taken her but a minute, unless something went wrong."

"Do you need to go?" Shellie asked.

"I hate to do that to you," Liz said.

"Nonsense," Shellie said. "I'm worried, too. Can we skip dinner and do this another time?"

"I don't know. It's a *prix fixe, table d'hôte* arrangement. You two stay; I'll go see what's happening and call you."

"I'm exhausted from the day anyway," Rick said. "How about you, Shellie?"

"Let's go. Liz, you go ahead and take our taxi. We'll sort the bill out and come back to the boat."

"Are you sure?"

"I insist," Rick said. "Go."

"Thank you. I'm quite worried. This isn't like Dani at all," Liz said. "Excuse me."

VENGEANCE WAS dark as Liz approached. She walked all the way out on the finger pier, not stepping aboard. She saw that the companionway doors were open, which seemed strange to her since there were no lights on aboard. They were both careful about locking up when they left.

"Dani?" Liz called, almost shouting.

When there was no answer, she stepped aboard, careful not to rock the boat more than she had to. She opened a small locker in the steering pedestal and found a flashlight. Shining it into the companionway, she called Dani again as she swept the cone of light around the main cabin. She spotted Dani, sprawled face down at the foot of the companionway ladder. Seeing nothing else amiss, she descended into the darkness and switched on an overhead light.

Kneeling, she put two fingers on the side of Dani's neck, feeling for a pulse. She sighed with relief when she felt the strong, steady throbbing. She rose to a crouch and swung her light into the aft cabin, finding it empty. She moved forward and checked the rest of the boat to make sure they were alone.

Satisfied, she knelt beside Dani again, putting a hand on her friend's shoulder and shaking her gently. Dani groaned, and her eyelids flickered. Liz shook her shoulder again and rocked back on her heels as Dani rolled into a crouch, snarling like a wildcat. Liz fell backward to avoid Dani's clawed hands.

"It's okay, Dani. We're okay." Liz lunged toward her, wrapping Dani in her arms and pushing her backward, using her weight to pin Dani, who struggled for a second before she said, "Liz?"

"Yes. Take it easy. You're all right." She released Dani and sat up on her heels.

"What happened?" Dani asked, rubbing the back of her neck and wincing. "Who hit me?"

"I don't know. How do you feel?"

"Dizzy. Splitting headache, big knot at the base of my skull."

Liz looked around, spotting the big flashlight on the cabin sole. "Were you using the flashlight?"

"What?"

"The big flashlight." Liz picked it up and showed it to her.

Dani shook her head and doubled over, throwing up on the sole. "Shit," she said, after a moment. "What about the big flashlight?"

"Were you using it?"

"I don't ... what ... " Dani fell backward, sitting down hard, leaning back against the corner of the bulkhead at the nav station. "Dizzy."

"Take it easy. You've got a concussion. Do you remember coming back to the boat after the Everetts and I left to go to dinner?"

Dani stared at her for several seconds. "The bilge pump."

"That's right. You came back because you thought the discharge hose in the aft head was split. You were going to close the seacock."

"Did I?"

"It doesn't matter right now," Liz said. "Was somebody on the boat when you came back?"

"The companionway doors weren't locked. I thought you locked them."

"I did," Liz said.

"And they left the light on in the aft cabin," Dani said. "I remember that. But I thought I'd checked all the lights before we left."

Turning off unused lights was an ingrained habit among people who lived aboard boats, where electricity from batteries was precious.

"Did you come down the ladder?"

"I don't ... I remember calling out to see if anybody was aboard. I think I leaned into the companionway, and then somebody grabbed my shirt and jerked me off my feet. I remember falling headfirst, and that's it. How long have you been here?"

"Two or three minutes, at most. You were out cold when I found you."

"How long?"

"How long were you out?"

"Right. You know?"

"It must have been 45 minutes or so," Liz said.

"You didn't see anybody?" Dani asked.

"No."

"Did they take anything?"

"I don't know. I checked to make sure nobody was still aboard and then tried to wake you up."

"How long have I been awake?"

"Maybe three minutes. You just asked me that." Liz held up her right hand with three fingers extended. "How many fingers do you see?"

"Three. I'm okay. I see just fine. Where are Rick and Shellie?"

"They'll be here any minute. Why don't you stretch out on the settee and let me get an ice pack for that place on the back of your head? I think somebody brained you with the flashlight."

"Can't believe I was so dumb," Dani said, crawling up onto the settee. "I deserved it, but I'm going to kill whoever did it."

"Uh-huh," Liz said. "I'm sure of it, but I think you'd better wait until at least tomorrow."

"I don't know who to kill yet, anyway. Hurry up with that ice pack, okay?"

7

"Where's Ashley?" Ed asked as he and Bert set the bags of groceries in the cockpit.

"Aboard *Vengeance*. The people left a while ago like they were going out to dinner."

"Oh, shit!" Bert said. "Can you call her?"

Leila picked up her phone and touched the screen. "Sure. Why?" she asked, holding the phone to her ear. "What's up?"

"We just saw one of the women — the blonde with curly hair. She was getting out of a cab, heading for the marina entrance."

"She's not answering," Leila said. "Went right to voicemail."

"How long's Ash been aboard *Vengeance?*" Ed asked.

Leila glanced at the screen on her phone. "Half an hour, give or take a few minutes. Was the woman by herself?"

"Yes," Bert said.

"Good. Ash can handle that."

"Handle what?" Ashley's disembodied voice floated into their midst.

"Ashley?" Leila asked.

Ashley climbed onto the swim platform that was built into

the stern of *Aquila*. "You didn't call me," she said, anger in her voice. "I almost got caught."

"I just tried. It went to voicemail."

"When?" Ashley asked.

"Just now."

"Phone's off, now, in the waterproof case. How about when the woman came back right after I got there?"

"I didn't see her."

"Didn't see her! Where were you?"

"After you left, I came below to watch through the porthole. I was too conspicuous by myself in the cockpit."

"That must have been the split second when she came aboard."

"Slow down, you two," Ed said, in a calm tone. "What happened, Ash?"

"We saw them — all four of them — get in a taxi, obviously going out to dinner. We overheard enough of their conversation as they walked up the dock to put that together." She paused, making eye contact with each of the others.

"Okay," Ed said. "Then what?"

"Then I went aboard their boat. Picked the lock with no problem and went below. I did a quick search, saw that the Everetts were staying in the aft cabin. Checked their stuff — no files, but they had a fancy laptop. I opened it and plugged in the thumb drive with *Bypass* on it. Then I felt the boat shift, like somebody stepped aboard."

"And what did you do then?" Ed asked.

"Left the computer running *Bypass* and got into position beside the companionway ladder, far enough back in the passageway to the aft cabin so nobody could see me. As soon as she was far enough down, I hit her in the back of the neck as hard as I could with one of those big three-cell flashlights that was hanging by the ladder. She collapsed."

"And?" Ed asked.

"I grabbed the thumb drive from the computer. It was still trying to crack the password. Snatched a GPS and a handheld VHF marine radio so they'd think it was a theft, and hauled ass."

"How long ago was it that you boarded?" Ed asked.

Leila checked the time on the cellphone that she still held. "Forty minutes."

"Where have you been since she surprised you?"

"Under the dock, hanging on a piling. There were too many people around, strolling the dock, and I didn't know how long she'd be unconscious."

"Okay, good," Ed said. "Why didn't you snatch the computer, while you were acting like a sneak thief?"

"I knew I was going in the water. I didn't want to ruin it and lose the files that were on it. I figured tomorrow was another day; we'll get another chance at it."

"You sure she didn't get a look at you?" Ed said.

"Positive."

"What did you do with the GPS and the VHF?"

She opened the drawstring bag that was tied to her waist and handed Ed the VHF and GPS. "I figured they weren't good for anything. Just wanted to make it look like a petty theft."

"We might be able to get something off the GPS," Ed said. "Waypoints, routes. You never know. I'll stick these under the chart table in a minute. You put the computer back where you found it?"

"No. Left it on the berth in the aft cabin. They'll just think the sneak thief got interrupted."

"Okay," Ed said. "We need to tighten it up. We got lucky this time, but Lady Luck's fickle. Let's get some rest and get over our jet lag. Leila?"

"Yes?"

"You okay with keeping a lookout for four hours?"

"Sure."

"Good. I'll relieve you. Pay attention to what they're doing. You said the four of them left together?"

"Yes, why?"

"It's odd that the Everetts aren't back yet; they must have split up. Keep an eye out for them, and wake me up when they show. If they get out of a taxi, make a note of which one. It might be worth talking to the driver to see where they've been."

"WHAT HAPPENED?" Shellie asked, as she and Rick came down the companionway ladder.

"Are you okay?" Rick asked.

"Everything's under control," Liz said.

"We had a thief, apparently. Dani surprised him, and he knocked her out. But she's okay, except for a little concussion."

"A thief?" Shellie asked. "Did he steal anything?"

"I was just about to check. You might want to take a look in your cabin, while I look around the rest of the boat," Liz said.

Dani started to sit up. "I'll — "

"You stay put, Dani," Liz said. "Keep the ice pack on your head." She put a hand on Dani's chest, pushing her back onto the settee.

"Looks like our stuff's been plundered," Rick said, his voice coming from the aft stateroom a couple of minutes later. "But I don't think they took anything. My laptop's out on the bed, though."

"The handheld VHF and GPS are missing," Liz said. "I left them out on the chart table. There's no sign that they even went up forward."

"That's it?" Dani asked.

"Seems to be," Liz said. "It's odd that they left the laptop, though. That's the kind of thing I'd expect somebody to take."

"I can't log in," Shellie said, tapping on the computer. She'd brought it out into the main cabin.

"What?" Rick said. "Let me see ... hmm. It's not accepting my password. The keyboard's not responding."

"Try a hard reset," Dani said. "Reboot it from scratch. Hold the power button down until everything goes dark and then start over."

"Okay," Rick said. "I wonder if they were messing with it for some reason?"

"Why would anybody do that?" Shellie asked. "I'd think they'd just grab it and run. How long were they aboard?"

"We don't know," Liz said. "Dani came back and found the doors unlocked and a light on in your cabin. She called out and didn't get an answer, so she stuck her head below and somebody grabbed her by the shirt and pulled her below. I guess they hit her with the big flashlight we keep by the ladder."

"So that would have been right after we left," Rick said.

"Right," Dani said.

"Computer's up and running," Shellie said. "I just logged on — no problem. Everything looks normal on the desktop."

"That's a relief," Rick said. "Should we call the police, or something?"

"It won't do any good," Dani said. "I didn't get a look at whoever it was, and they're long gone by now. It is odd that they left your laptop, though."

"What about the GPS and ... what else was it?" Shellie asked.

"A handheld VHF radio — no big deal," Liz said. "They're easily replaced. The marine supply store across the street will probably have them in stock, or we can cope without them, if need be. We have both, permanently installed. We mostly used the handhelds for the dinghy."

"Does this kind of thing happen often?" Rick asked.

Liz shrugged. "It's not remarkable. It's a little unusual to have it happen in a marina; the security guy at the gate keeps an eye on who comes and goes."

"But kids swim out to boats, sometimes," Dani said. "It happens more often out in the anchorage outside the lagoon. I think somebody singled us out. Probably watched us leave and made their move."

"Why, though," Liz asked.

"You mean, 'Why us?'" Dani asked.

"Yes."

"Who knows? Maybe they were watching to see which boats were unattended and saw us leave. You sure you locked up?"

"Yes," Liz said.

"I watched her do it," Shellie said. "We were talking about the restaurant, and I stood there with you while you locked the doors, Liz."

"Can I get up now, Mom?" Dani asked.

"I guess," Liz said. "How's your head?"

"Sore. But the dizziness is gone. I want to check the doors; see how much damage they did."

"While you do that, I'll check the hose on the forward head," Liz said. "Excuse us for a minute."

Liz went forward into the cabin she and Dani were sharing, and Dani picked up the flashlight and climbed the companionway ladder. In under two minutes, they rejoined their guests at the table in the main saloon.

"You were right, Dani. It's the hose," Liz said. "We can pick up a couple of feet when we buy the new GPS and VHF in the morning. It'll only take five or ten minutes to replace it. What did you find with the lock?"

"If you're sure you locked it, then whoever broke in was a pro," Dani said. "There's no damage. They picked the lock, I'd say. Unless they had some kind of master key, but I can't imagine that."

"Is that hard to do?" Rick asked. "I know not all locks are

created equal."

"This is a good one," Dani said. "If somebody picked it, they had some skill. We've managed to lock ourselves out once and had to call a locksmith. He even had a hard time with it. It's one of those high security ones with the dimpled keys."

"That's strange," Liz said. "Usually, when kids or druggies break into a boat, they just pry the doors open with a crow bar and leave the wood splintered."

"Good thing for them they didn't do that," Dani said. "I'd have made them suffer before I killed them."

"What?" Shellie asked.

"Nobody hits me and gets away with it," Dani said. "Somebody's going to die. If they'd splintered the teak, I would make them suffer for it first, for sure."

Shellie laughed. Liz saw the color rise in Dani's cheeks and put a hand on her arm, shaking her head.

"She's angry," Liz said.

"I don't blame you," Rick said.

"Just be glad you're all right," Shellie said. "You could have been badly hurt."

Liz squeezed Dani's arm and winked at her, shaking her head again.

"Yes," Dani said, her teeth clenched. "You're right."

"Well," Liz said, "how about if I put together a light supper, since we missed dinner?"

"You sure?" Rick said. "After all this, we could just get a sandwich or something. The marina grill was still serving when we got back."

"I'm sure," Liz said. "I'd much rather cook. It'll give us all a chance to settle down, and I'll enjoy it. I can whip up a nice seafood pasta and some salad in no time. Dani, why don't you break out a bottle of whatever Rick and Shellie would like? A nice crisp white of some kind, I think. Tell them what we have on hand."

8

"How are you feeling this morning, Dani?" Shellie asked, taking a sip of coffee. Liz had just served breakfast at the table in the saloon.

"Much better than last night, thanks. I have just a hint of a headache, and that knot on the back of my head is tender, but other than that, I'm well enough."

"Don't you think you should go to the emergency room, just to be sure?" Rick asked. "Concussions can have some serious consequences."

"It's not my first time; I know what a serious one feels like. I was knocked unconscious for several days once. Last night barely qualifies as more than a bump on my head."

"She's got a thick skull," Liz said. "I mean that in the nicest way," she added, smirking.

Dani grinned. The cliché was a running joke between Liz and her. "I'm okay. Besides, in all the excitement last night, we didn't get to talk about your files. I'm eager to get on with your quest, if you'll forgive me for pushing my way into it."

Rick smiled. "You're welcome; the more the merrier. Liz did

say you had some questions, but she wanted to wait until both of you could talk with us. I guess now's a good time."

"Sure. Liz and I had a little time to talk about it while you were still on your island tour. My first thought is that Grenada's not the most likely place to start."

"Oh?" Rick asked. "Why's that? Something you saw in the translation?"

"No, it's more basic than that. It has to do with some fundamentals of sailing the North Atlantic — nothing peculiar to the Moors, or even Columbus. Just some natural phenomena."

"Tell us, then," Shellie said.

"If you leave from anywhere around the Straits of Gibraltar on a Soufrière vessel — that's just about any sailing vessel — you'll end up taking the same route to go west, almost no matter what you try to do. The prevailing winds and currents will take you down the coast to the tropics. Somewhere around the Canary Islands, you'll begin to make a little westing, but you'll really be fighting Mother Nature until you get to the Cape Verde Islands. Then everything changes. The currents begin to set you to the west, and you catch the trade winds."

"But was that always the case? What about the seasons, and climate change?" Shellie asked.

"It's a result of the earth's rotation, more than anything else. Seasons and changing weather patterns make some minor differences, but they get cancelled out by the time you get across the Atlantic. You're going to end up somewhere between the Bahamas and the equator, but the most likely spot is about midway up the island chain. Around St. Lucia or Martinique is the sweet spot."

"We were thinking that there'd have been no reason for Khashkhash to have deviated from the path of least resistance," Liz said.

"He would have had a good idea of the latitudes of the trading ports in Asia," Rick said.

"Yes, but they would have been in the same latitudes as the islands, for the same reasons," Liz said. "Just farther to the west, and on the other side of the Americas."

"That's why they became trading ports, and why they still are," Dani said. "The ones that you reach by sailing to the west end up in the tropics; the ones you reach sailing east are in the temperate zones, farther north or south. It's the way the winds and currents work."

"I never thought about that," Rick said. "What about the ports along the east coast, say Miami, versus New York?"

"Coastal sailing's a different game," Dani said. "The general rules in the northern hemisphere are that it's easy to sail north along an east-facing shore, or south along a west-facing shore. It's the opposite in the southern hemisphere."

"I actually should have tumbled to that," Rick said. "It's well known; I remember learning that about trade routes between Europe and America in the colonial era in my undergrad history courses."

"I'm sure there are exceptions, if you take land-based routes into account, but we're focused on sailing, with Khashkhash," Dani said. "And the descriptions of the mullah's base location referred to reaching other islands within a day's sail to the north or the south."

Liz said, "They mentioned that there was no landfall to the west unless they first sailed several days to the north or south, and then they were back to islands that were a day apart, strung out to the west."

"Okay," Rick said. "How does that match up with the sketch map?"

"Pretty well," Dani said. "I think whoever drew the map put those two mountains there for a reason. If you draw a line through the peaks and extend it to the north, it intersects the shoreline close to where a river flows into the harbor."

"That would have been important," Liz said. "The river, I

mean. They would have been looking for a place with fresh water."

"Right. I agree," Rick said. "And did you find some place that matches?"

"We found two solid matches, without even looking hard," Dani said. "One is in Soufrière, St. Lucia. The two big mountains are on a line with where the Soufrière River flows into the harbor."

"The other one's only a day to the north of that, on Martinique," Liz said. "It's a little harbor called Grand Anse d'Arlet. The river's more of a stream, judging from our chart. It may even be silted in by now, but both places fit."

"How long would it take to get there?" Rick asked.

"Soufrière is around 120 miles — less than 24 hours, depending on the wind. But Bequia's a good place to spend the night about halfway to Soufrière. It's a favorite place of ours, anyway. Well worth the stop, unless you want to push it. Either way's okay with us."

"I vote for a stop," Shellie said.

"Fine with me," Rick said. "And how far to Grand Anse d'Arlet?"

"Another 40 miles from Soufrière," Liz said. "There's a third possibility along the way to Grand Anse d'Arlet. It's not quite as good a match, but it may be worth a look."

"That's Rodney Bay, St. Lucia," Dani said. "It's an interesting spot. The harbor's much bigger. The British Navy used it a lot in the 18th and 19th centuries, when they were fighting with the French."

"Is it named after the admiral?" Rick asked.

"Yes. Fort Rodney's there. The admiral used to sit on top of the hill there with a telescope and watch for French ships to attack. On a clear day, he could see the approach to Fort-de-France."

"Let's do that one, too," Rick said. "As close together as they are, it'll be easy to do some serious comparisons. When should we leave?"

"We can leave later this morning and make Bequia by late afternoon," Liz said.

"But what about the stuff you need to buy? The GPS and what have you?"

"We'll have to clear customs and immigration at the yacht club before we leave. We'll go right by the marine supply store on the way. We can do it all and get under way in an hour or so, if you want."

"Sounds good, but there's not a rush. Let's enjoy the rest of our breakfast," Shellie said.

Liz smiled and refilled their coffee mugs. "There are more eggs. Help yourself, Rick."

"THEY'RE up and about on *Vengeance*," Leila said.

Yeah?" Ed asked. "What are they doing?"

"The two women who run the boat just headed out; they're in the dinghy, going to the dock at the marine supply store."

"Probably replacing the stuff I took," Ashley said. "Wonder when they're leaving? Everett's been here a couple of days, already."

Ed shrugged. "You put the tracker on the boat, right?"

"No, I didn't get a chance before that woman showed up."

"Shit," Ed said. "We'll have to hope we can con the customs and immigration people into telling us what their next port is, then."

"Think they're leaving today?"

"I don't' know. They're up and out bright and early," Ed said. "We should play it safe. Why don't you head over to the yacht club and get a cup of coffee? If they go to clear out, maybe you can overhear what they tell the agent."

"On my way," Ashley said, taking a final swig of her coffee. She climbed down into their dinghy and motored across the lagoon. As she was tying up to the club's dock, she saw the two women return to their own dinghy. She kept an eye on them as she walked up the ramp to the yacht club entrance. They were headed straight toward the club's dock.

"Good morning," Ashley said, as she walked up to the club's bar.

"Mornin', mornin'," the woman behind the bar said. "Coffee?"

"Please," Ashley said.

Cutting her eyes to the left, she saw the two women from *Vengeance* enter the club. They went into the customs and immigration office just as the woman set the coffee on the bar in front of her. She put a $5 E.C. note on the bar and said, "Keep the change."

"Thank you. Have a great day."

"Thanks," Ashley said, taking her coffee and moving to stand near the open door to the customs and immigration office. She took a sip of the coffee as she pretended to read the bulletin board on the wall. The board was located between the door to the club office and the door to customs and immigration.

She smiled to herself as she heard one of the women say, "Good morning. We need to clear out for Bequia."

"When are you leaving?" a man's voice asked.

"In the next hour or so," the woman answered.

"You have a beautiful day for your sail," the man said. "Nice breeze, wit' jus' a little south in it. Should be perfect."

Ashley took another sip of coffee and walked toward the dinghy dock. She had heard enough. She knew she'd been lucky; she still needed to plant the tracker on *Vengeance*. Maybe she could take care of that in Bequia. The people on *Vengeance* had missed their dinner out last night; perhaps they'd make up for that tonight.

Then she realized she didn't know how far away Bequia was.

She assumed that it wasn't far, but they would need to check the cruising guide and the nautical charts that they'd found in the chart table aboard *Aquila.*

She still wondered why the woman with the curly blonde hair had come back to *Vengeance* so soon last night. She shrugged off her curiosity; it couldn't have anything to do with her or her team. It was just bad luck. Fortune had a way of squaring things, though. She untied her dinghy and started the outboard, steering straight toward *Aquila*.

9

"This is so exciting!" Shellie said, as she watched Dani steering *Vengeance* through the channel leaving St. George's. "A new experience for me."

"You haven't done any sailing?" Dani asked.

"No, I haven't. Rick's done a little bit, but never out in the ocean. Nothing like this."

Dani smiled. "I hope it's fun for you. We've got near-perfect conditions for first-time sailors."

"What makes that so?" Shellie asked, as she watched Liz bustling about the deck, stowing the dock lines and fenders.

"The wind is blowing out of the east-southeast, so we'll be on what's called a beam reach most of the time. That means the wind's blowing at a right angle to our course. It may clock a bit and become more southeasterly, but that's okay. That will put us on a broad reach, which is still an easy point of sail."

"I would have thought the best sailing would be if the wind blew from behind us," Shellie said.

"That's a common misconception, that the wind pushes the boat along. The physics of sailing are more like the physics of flying. The shape of the sails, if you look down from the top, is similar to the shape of an airplane's wing seen from the end.

"On a beam reach, most of the wind's energy is providing lift, which is transformed into forward motion. The leading edge of the sail, that's called the luff, is splitting the wind. If the wind angle changes to the point where the luff doesn't split the wind cleanly, then some of the wind's force goes into trying to tip the boat over." Dani glanced over at Shellie. "I've probably told you way more than you wanted to know. Sorry."

"No, that's fascinating. I had no idea. I thought we were going to get blown along like a leaf in the wind, or something."

"Sailing requires balancing a lot of forces to make the boat go in the direction you want. If they get out of balance, the boat doesn't behave well; the ride gets uncomfortable, or she slows down, or something breaks."

"How long have you been doing this?"

"Sailing? Or running this charter business?"

"Sailing," Shellie said.

"As long as I can remember. My father's a sailor; he started taking me along when I was an infant, I guess."

"Did you ever get scared? When you were a child?"

"No. I always just thought the sea was something you had to accept and deal with, I guess. Does it frighten you?"

"A little, yes. It's overwhelming."

"What's overwhelming?" Liz asked, returning to the cockpit.

"The ocean," Shellie said. "Dani and I were just talking about sailing. She was explaining about being on a beam reach, going to Bequia."

"Speaking of sailing," Dani said.

"Is it time?" Liz asked.

"We might as well get the main and mizzen up, now that we're out of the lagoon."

"There doesn't seem to be much wind," Shellie said.

"No, we're protected by the land right now."

"Man, oh man," Rick said, climbing out of the companionway. "Look at all those boats." He gestured toward the anchorage off their port quarter, where 50 or more boats were at anchor in the calm, clear water off Pandey Beach.

"That's one of the favorite anchorages for cruising boats," Liz said. "It's calm under most conditions, and it's convenient to town and the yacht club."

"I can see the convenience part, but it doesn't look that protected," he said. "What if a storm comes out of the west? It's wide open."

"Yes," Dani said. "That's true of most of the lee-side anchorages in the islands. It's relatively rare to find a harbor like St. George's that offers all-around protection."

"This must be a little spooky at night," Shellie said. "Imagine sitting out here in the dark with nothing but the open sea behind you."

"It's what you're used to, I guess," Dani said. "I like the idea that there's nothing between me and Central America. It's exhilarating, somehow."

"I don't know if I could get used to that," Shellie said. "Is where we're going like this? Bequia? Is it open like this, to the west?"

"Admiralty Bay is Bequia's main harbor. It's more protected than this, but it's not as closed-in as St. George's. If the weather comes out of the west, it can get rough, but that doesn't happen often, not this time of year."

"In the summer, when you get thunderstorms, you can get some gusty winds out of the west," Liz said, "and then you need to be careful not to anchor too close to shore. But we're past that now."

"Let's get the main and the mizzen up, Liz," Dani said. As Liz went up to the mainmast and began to uncover the mainsail, Dani turned to Shellie. "Then I'll take up a course to the northwest until we're out of the wind shadow of the island. Once we're out far enough to have a steady breeze, we can roll out the headsails and shut down the diesel. Then you'll see what sailing's like."

"It'll take us right back to the time of the Moors' discovery," Rick said.

"Yes," Dani said. "Except they wouldn't have had the diesel to get them out of there. That's why the harbors that were open to the west attracted sailing vessels in the old days. Imagine trying to get a ship out of St. George's with only the little puffs of air that we had in there."

"That's what galley slaves were for," Rick said.

"Did the Moors' ships have oars?" Dani asked.

"I don't know," Rick said. "I should find out. That could influence where they set up shop, couldn't it?"

"I would think so," Dani said.

"Ready when you are, skipper," Liz called.

Dani turned the bow into the wind and she and Liz hoisted the mainsail and the mizzen.

"THIS IS MAGIC," Shellie said, a few hours later. She sat behind the helm, steering *Vengeance* as they rolled along over the swell. "I thought it would be rougher out here in the open water. These waves look huge, but they're gentle."

"These are swells," Dani said. "They just lift the boat and then lower it. If the wind were blowing harder, it might raise a chop on top of the swells that could make things a little rougher. And when the swells run into an island, they get twisted around and confused. That can be rough, too. But out in open water, it's usually like this."

"Nice," Shellie said. "It's not scary at all. And I thought we'd be out of sight of land, but we've had those little islands on the eastern horizon almost the whole way. How far are we from Bequia, now?"

"That's Bequia," Dani pointed at the dark smudge off their bow.

"It's much bigger than I expected," Shellie said. "From the chart Liz showed me, I thought it was small."

"It is small," Dani said. "You're seeing St. Vincent behind it. St. Vincent's a much bigger island. From here, you can't distinguish them. As we get closer, though, you'll begin to make out houses on Bequia, and St. Vincent will still be a dark mass in the distance. They're around 10 miles apart."

"Will we be there in time for us to take you and Liz out to dinner?" Rick asked, stepping into the cockpit. He had been below, reviewing an email he had received a couple of hours ago. "From what the cruising guide in our cabin says, there's a fine French restaurant there. It could be like a consolation prize for missing out last night."

"We should be," Dani said. "We're making great time. I'd say we'll have the anchor down in time to clear in before the customs office closes."

"We need to do more of this, Rick," Shellie said.

"More sailing?" he asked.

"Yes. I'm hooked."

"How long have you been steering?" he asked.

"I don't know. I could do this forever. The boat feels like it's alive. It's like nothing I've ever experienced. Is it always like this, Dani?"

Dani smiled. "No, but it's always magical. I told you that conditions were perfect for our trip today. Everyone should have a day like today for their first sail."

"Try it, Rick?" Shellie asked.

"No, you go ahead. You're having too much fun for me to take over."

"What was in the email?" Shellie asked. "Anything exciting?"

"No. Nothing related to the project; it was from the woman who's filling in for me this semester. Boring."

"Do you suppose the Moors had days like this? The sailing, I mean?" Shellie asked. "How different would their ships have been, Rick?"

"I don't know. Any ideas, Dani?"

"Not really. I thought there might be some references in the translated texts, but I didn't see any when I skimmed through yesterday. I confess that I was disappointed; I'm as curious as Shellie."

"I'm afraid I didn't spend much time on that part of the puzzle," Rick said. "I found a lot of references to their trading voyages around the Mediterranean. Once I was satisfied that they were good enough seamen for a transatlantic voyage to be possible, I moved on."

"What do you suppose happened to them?" Liz asked, joining them in the cockpit. "Is there any record?"

"You mean to the men who stayed in the islands with the mullah?" Rick asked.

"Yes. You said Khashkhash sailed back, laden with treasure, but I was wondering about the fate of the — what was it, a hundred men and three ships?"

"That's right. The short answer is we don't know for sure. The longer answer is that many years later, a man claiming to be one of the mullah's party made his way back to Palos. He said that their base had been besieged, presumably by the Caribs, although he just referred to them as the people of the islands. One of the three ships escaped and sailed to the north and west until they reached a large land mass. They sailed along the coast to the north until a storm blew them off shore, and they drifted at sea until some fishermen found them and brought them back to Europe, probably to the British Isles. There were only a few survivors, and they set out to return to Spain, first working as seamen on a trading vessel to get to the European continent. Two of them made it to what's now France, where one died. The survivor proceeded on foot to Palos."

"What a story," Dani said. "Let me guess; he wasn't given a hero's welcome."

"No, he wasn't. He was apparently not an educated man; most likely, he was a common seaman. He wasn't aware of the significance of his return; he was just trying to survive. Khashkhash and his sponsors were long gone by then, but eventually the lone survivor came to the attention of someone in authority. Whoever that was recorded his story and sent it to Cordoba. It ended up in the Caliphate's library."

"That wasn't in the material you showed us," Liz said.

"No, it wasn't," Rick said.

"Is that document still around?" Dani asked.

"No one knows where it is. There are a number of references to it, but the original is lost. What we know about it is best described as hearsay."

"About the sketch map," Dani said, "where did that come from? Was it from this lone survivor?"

"No. It was found with the papers of an historian and geographer who documented Khashkhash's voyage — with the papers that went into the translation that you read, in other words."

"So, you don't know with certainty where the mullah's base was at the time it was overrun?"

"That's correct. It's possible that it had been relocated, although it was in one place during the period of several years when Khashkhash was exploring the area. That's clear from Abul-Hassan's history. It seems unlikely that the mullah would have moved it after Khashkhash left. He didn't have much manpower, compared to the number of men who were around when the base was established."

"I couldn't tell from the files you shared with us what the base was like," Liz said.

Rick smiled. "No. There wasn't a description. It was in daily use for several years, but we have no idea whether it was a tent city or a fortress of some kind."

"I'd think a fortress would have left a trace," Shellie said.

"I don't know," Dani said. "The islands change. We're talking about almost a thousand years, in the tropics. Besides storms, there's volcanic activity, even an occasional earthquake. Wood rots and stone crumbles. If it was built on the shore of one of these harbors, there's no telling what happened to it — if it was even a permanent structure."

"The first step is to figure out which island they were on," Rick said. "Then maybe some other references will suddenly come into focus. That's the way these things work."

"Fascinating," Dani said. "Speaking of the way things work, I think I'll go replace that head discharge hose. Liz, can you and Shellie keep watch?"

"You bet," Shellie said. "I'm loving every minute of this."

Liz smiled and nodded. "Yell if you need an extra hand with the hose."

10

"I see now why you said Bequia is special," Shellie said, "and why you wanted to land the dinghy at the town dock and walk up here, instead of using the restaurant's dock."

"It's an attractive little town," Rick said.

"It's unusual," Liz said. "It's small, and the terrain isn't suited for agriculture. It was a fishing village in the old days."

"Fishing, huh," Rick said.

"Whaling, too," Dani said. "The whales migrate down through the islands every year. There's a long history of whaling here. One of the waterfront bars we passed is all decked out with whalebone. The barstools are vertebrae."

"Ugh," Shellie said.

"It works," Liz said. "It's not as macabre as you'd think. If you didn't know what they were, you might not notice. We could stop in for an after-dinner drink, if you like. It's not out of our way. Not much anyway."

"This looks like the kind of place where nothing's very far out of your way, " Rick said.

"That's so," Dani said. "If we had turned the other way when we left the town dock, you would have seen the main street just fizzle out. It's like it forgot where it's going, like it can't remember if it's a street, or a walkway, or a parking lot, or maybe an open-air market."

"Sounds like you know the town well, Dani," Shellie said.

"I spent a lot of my childhood here. One of my father's early partners lived here. While he and my father were off doing business, his wife took care of me."

"What about school?" Shellie asked. "Did you go to school here?"

"That was before I started school."

"Do they still live here?" Rick asked. "The people you stayed with?"

"She does. Her husband died years ago. He was a lot older than my father."

"Could we meet her? Would she be old enough to remember the colonial days?"

"Meeting her's no problem. She runs a little restaurant at the other end of town. And she loves to talk about the colonial days. We'd have to spend some extra time here tomorrow, though."

"I'd vote for that," Shellie said, "if you think we can spare the time, Rick."

"Background's important. You never know what you'll learn from somebody like her. Let's plan on it."

"Good," Dani said. "I enjoy introducing our guests to her. She's family; she's more of a mother to me than my own mother."

"Does she have children?" Shellie asked.

"Two sons. They're much older -- my father's age."

"How old is she?"

"Ancient," Dani said. "I've lost track, but you can ask her."

"She won't be offended?" Shellie asked.

"She's too old for that to bother her," Dani said, with a smile. "But she doesn't pay much attention to things like age. And she doesn't look her age, so don't be surprised."

"The whaling thing intrigues me," Rick said. "I always associate that with New England."

"Well, that's not wrong, but the Caribbean is full of whales at certain times of year," Dani said. "It wouldn't be unusual for us to spot some on our way north from here. Whale watching's a big business in Martinique."

"Are they making a comeback?" Shellie asked. "Because of the protection?"

"I can't judge that," Dani said. "But there seem to be plenty of them around here."

"They still hunt them here in Bequia," Liz said.

"Hunt them?" Shellie frowned.

"The International Whaling Commission allows them to take up to four a year," Dani said. "They do it the old-fashioned way. A few men in a tiny boat, sail-powered. When they spot a whale, they drop the mast and row, with rags to muffle the sound of the oars in the locks. They sneak up on the whale, and a man in the bow harpoons it, by hand. Then the fight begins. The whale can tow the boat for hours before they wear it down enough to kill it."

"What do they do with it once it's dead?" Rick asked.

"It's a community thing. They rarely get one, and when they do, the whole town shares the meat. They tow it back in and beach the carcass on a little island just north of Petit Nevis. The remains of an old whaling station are on Petit Nevis. That dates back to the 1800s, at least. To when whaling was big business. It's only a few hundred yards off the south coast. They used to use that, but it's privately owned, now. Somebody objected, so they butcher the whales on a tiny little sand spit called Sempler's Cay. That's between Petit Nevis and the main island."

"A whaling station? What's that like?" Rick asked.

"I don't know what it was like when it was in full swing," Dani said. "Now it's mostly the ruins of what's called a 'try-works,' where they rendered the blubber to get oil. There's a cradle that held a huge pot and some stonework chimneys."

"How old is it? Do you know?"

"No, I don't, but you should ask Mrs. Walker — the lady I was telling you about. Her family's been here forever — when you look at her, you'll see her Carib ancestry."

"So you aren't exaggerating, then?" Rick asked. Seeing Dani's puzzled look, he said, "About her family being here forever, I mean."

"No. She's a product of the Caribbean melting pot. You'll see when you meet her."

"Do you think she grew up hearing any of the oral history of the Caribs?"

"I'm sure she did. She has a lot of physical traits that came from the Caribs. Bequia's the kind of place where there weren't a lot of outsiders to dilute the gene pool. Why? What are you thinking?"

"I'm wondering if the Caribs hunted whales, and whether the use of that island as a whaling station might predate the Europeans."

"I don't know. Surely, they must have hunted whales. I thought all the indigenous people in the coastal Americas did."

"Probably so," Rick said, "but there's no evidence that the Caribs did. Not in any of the articles I've read."

"What kind of evidence would you expect?" Dani asked.

"Bones. The kind of stuff found in middens."

"Are there a lot of middens in the islands?" Liz asked.

"Yes. There are middens everywhere people lived — it's kitchen trash."

"I see. What do they find in the ones in the islands?" Liz asked.

"Mostly crab shells, shells from mollusks, fish bones. A few bones from small animals, but not too many of those. Most of the protein came from marine sources."

"Where are they found?" Dani asked. "The middens."

"They usually mark a site of habitation," Rick said. "Most are close to where people were living."

"Are many found along the shoreline?"

"Some, but I'd guess a lot of those got washed away, down here. Is that what you're thinking?"

"Well, that, and the size of whale bones. The whaling station at Petit Nevis has a ramp that they pulled the carcass up so they could cut off the meat and blubber. Then they shoved everything else back into the sea. People on Bequia have occasionally pulled some whale bones out of the deep water there to use for decoration, or even construction. It's not like killing a deer and carrying a joint of venison back to your camp. We're talking big, heavy stuff."

"Good point," Rick said. "It seems reasonable that the Caribs must have hunted whales, or at least dolphins. There have been some manatee remains reported in some of their middens, but not many. But they had big, seagoing canoes. They traded from island to island, so they had the wherewithal to chase down marine mammals."

"Manatees and dolphins are still pretty big to lug home. My bet's they butchered them where they killed them, or maybe towed them to a beach." Dani said. "That's what I'd do. That's what the locals do now."

"That makes a lot of sense, actually. It's not inconsistent with what happened with other primitive people who hunted whales. The Caribs might have just had a better way to get rid of the remains."

"An early form of recycling," Liz said.

Rick chuckled. "Right. I'm eager to meet this Mrs. Walker. Any chance we could see that whaling station?"

"Sure. That's easy," Liz said. "There's a nice little anchorage there, big enough for a few boats. With this settled weather, we could even spend the night there tomorrow night if you want, and get an early start to St. Lucia the next morning."

"I like that plan," Rick said. "Not to change the subject, but should we order dinner?"

All three of the women nodded.

"Thought you were going to starve us," Shellie said.

"I THINK you're in the clear, Ash," Ed said, lowering the binoculars. "All four of them got out of the dinghy and they've walked up the hill on the north side of town. This time of day, headed in that direction, my bet is they're out to dinner. The little map in the guidebook shows a fancy French restaurant up that way. They're probably gone for at least an hour, hour and a half."

"Okay, I'm on my way."

"Where are you going to put the tracker?" Bert asked.

"Since we've been here, I've had the time to study their boat. It's just as well I didn't do a rush job the other night. I think I've got the perfect spot, now."

"Where?" Ed asked. "Don't forget, it needs a clear view of the sky. Top of one of the masts would be perfect."

"Give me a break, Ed. You think nobody would notice me climbing the mast?"

He shrugged. "So, where, then?"

"See that rectangular box on the roof just forward of the mainmast?"

"Covered in canvas?" Ed asked. "Looks like a life raft in a canister."

"Yes, exactly. That's it. I'm going to put it right on top of that, under that canvas cover."

"What if somebody sits down on it?" Leila asked. "That looks like a perfect perch for somebody."

"That won't hurt anything," Ashley said. "Look at this thing." She held up a device in a white, high-impact-plastic case. It was about the footprint of an index card, but around 4 millimeters thick. "It's nice and flat; nobody's going to feel it, even if they do sit on it, especially under that canvas."

"Okay. Want me to run you over there in the dinghy?" Leila asked.

"No. Too much chance of being seen. I'll swim." They were anchored about 50 meters off *Vengeance's* port bow. "Should I give Everett's laptop another try while I'm there? I should have plenty of time."

"Skip it," Ed said. "No need; It's taken care of."

Ashley frowned at that as she got to her feet. She moved the cushion on which she'd been sitting and opened a cockpit locker underneath, pulling out a black neoprene wetsuit. "Camouflage," she said, wriggling into the skin-tight suit. She bent forward, flipping the zipper-pull lanyard over her left shoulder.

Standing up again, she reached into the locker and picked up a microfiber towel in a sealed, clear plastic pouch. "No wet footprints on their deck," she said, stuffing the pouch and the tracking device into the neck of her wetsuit. She grabbed the lanyard dangling over her shoulder and tugged it, zipping the suit closed along her spine.

Pulling a black neoprene hood over her blond hair, she said, "Back soon." She climbed down the boarding ladder that hung over *Aquila's* stern and slipped into the water. Using a smooth breast stroke, she barely rippled the surface of the water as she swam toward *Vengeance*.

"I'm surprised you told her to leave the computer alone," Leila said.

"Tehran's sending us copies of everything," Ed said. "They hacked into the foundation's email server. We should have it by morning. Besides, I took a look at the log from the *Bypass* thumb drive this morning. The hard drive on that computer's encrypted. It probably wouldn't have done us much good to clone it."

"She's out of the water," Bert said, a pair of binoculars pressed to his face. "She's creeping along the side deck. There. She's peeled the backing off the adhesive patch on the tracker. Lifting the edge of the canvas. She's done. Crawling back to their boarding ladder."

"I've got a handshake from the tracker," Ed said, fiddling with a touch-screen tablet computer. "And it's working. Great. Let's see if it goes to sleep ... yep. We're good." He took the tablet below and put it on the chart table.

As he climbed back into the cockpit, Ashley swam up alongside. "Before I get out of the water, would you check and make sure it's working?" she asked.

"Done," Ed said. "Good job. Come on up and get dressed. Dinner's on me."

"Where?" Leila asked, as Ashley stood on their boarding ladder and unzipped her wetsuit.

"Anywhere but the French place. Take a look at the guidebook while Ash gets dressed."

"ARE YOU STILL AWAKE?" Dani asked. She and Liz were in their cabin, having bid their guests goodnight half an hour earlier.

"Yes. What's on your mind?"

"This whole situation; there are some things that don't make sense to me."

"What, for example?" Liz asked.

"Well, the first thing that's off is the break-in last night."

"What about it?"

"I'm having trouble accepting that some junkie thief was able to pick a high security lock."

"Okay. What's the alternative explanation?"

"Well, the most likely is that we forgot to lock the doors."

"You know better than that, Dani. I checked them before we left, and Shellie watched me do it. She even asked if theft was a problem, when she saw me checking."

"She didn't mention that."

"No, but she did agree that I locked the doors and checked them."

"And I believe you. I just don't like the option that's left to explain the break-in."

"And what option is that?"

"It wasn't some common thief. It was somebody who had the skills to pick our lock. Or somebody with one of those high-tech electronic gizmos that does it for you."

"What kind of person would that be, Dani? Even the locksmith had trouble that time."

"Yes. That's what worries me. Why would somebody with that capability want to break into *Vengeance* and steal a GPS and a VHF? Both those things wouldn't bring enough cash to pay for one of those electronic lock picks. Remember, the locksmith said it was cheaper just to cut the lock out and replace it, and that's not cheap."

"I remember. But you interrupted them. Maybe they were going to take the computer, and whatever else they could find."

"I don't believe that. An ordinary thief wouldn't have left the computer after he knocked me out. I think they were trying to see what was in it; copy some files, maybe."

"Uh-oh. Your paranoia's showing. Why do you think that? The computer's password protected. Remember the trouble Rick had getting it to accept his password?"

"Yes. I'm thinking the thief was trying to hack into it, maybe trying passwords at random, and that caused it to lock up. Some computers will do that."

"But why not just steal it?" Liz asked. "Hack into it at their leisure?"

"Because then Rick would know somebody had his files," Dani said.

"What would be on the computer that would be worth all that? Rick's a history professor, not some kind of spy."

"As far as we know."

"Dani, get a grip. Where has that devious mind of yours taken you?"

"Who would stand to gain if Rick managed to prove that the Moors discovered the Americas hundreds of years before Columbus?" Dani asked.

"But it's all academic, Dani. It's not like that would give the Moors — or whoever they've been replaced by — any right to rule. We're not in the colonial era any more. The geopolitical boundaries are well-established now, don't you think?"

"Somebody's paying a quarter of a million dollars for us to sail Rick and Shellie around the islands for three months. That's a lot of money; I said before, there has to be a payoff."

"Okay, so what do you think is going on here?" Liz asked.

"I wish I knew."

"You said you liked Rick and Shellie the other day. Has that changed?"

"No, not really. They're nice."

"So you don't think they're involved in some nefarious plot to mess us up?"

"Not knowingly, anyway, but the more we learn about Rick, the less comfortable I am with him."

"Tell me, Dani, what has he done that's put you off?"

"It's not anything he's done, but he's not leveling with us."

"You think somebody's after him and he hasn't told us?"

"I hadn't thought of that angle."

"Oops! I should have kept my mouth shut. Now you have something new to fret about. What *were* you worrying about?"

"Think about this, Liz. What is he looking for, specifically?"

"I don't know. Evidence that the Moors were here before Columbus. Some kind of artifact, I guess. Like that dagger he and Shellie were talking about, maybe."

"Okay, say it is a dagger, then. Or something like that. One thousand years ago, somebody lost a dagger, somewhere on one of the islands. And that's kind of a best case."

"What do you mean, 'best case?'"

"The Caribs could have taken it when they wiped out that camp, or anything could have happened to it. It could have fallen over the side of a ship. And we don't even know it was a dagger; it could be almost anything that could be tied back to the Moors, and there'd still have to be some evidence that it wasn't brought here later, like the dagger they used as an example."

"Right. So what's your point?"

"Would you bet $250,000 that Rick, or anybody, for that matter, could find something — anything, because we don't know what it might be — that would prove someone from Europe came here 1,000 years ago?"

"Well, no. Even if I had that kind of money to play with. But whoever did has some other evidence; these documents Rick mentioned."

"You and I read the documents."

"But there might be more," Liz said.

"Might be," Dani said. "There are almost certainly more clues. I think he knows exactly what he's looking for. And he knows more about where it is than he's told us."

"If I say I agree with you, just for the sake of argument, will you tell me why any of that is our business? We're here to run the boat and help him find the right island. Maybe he's not at liberty to tell us more yet, even if he does know."

"It's our business because he's put us at risk. You're not the one with a goose egg on the back of her head. I could have been killed."

"Not with that thick skull of yours. I'm surprised the flashlight still works."

"You're right. Sit still and let me whack you with it; let's see if it can stand up to another impact without breaking."

"Okay, Dani. I understand what's got you wound up, now. You don't have to hit me over the head to make your point."

"You sure?"

"Yes, please. Now that you've talked through that, what do you think we should do?"

"I'm not sure. At some point, though, we need to confront him about it."

"Let's be cautious about that; it's possible that somebody's feeding him information a bit at a time. He may not know more than he's told us."

"Good point. I hadn't thought of that. But why would somebody do that, Liz? And why would he accept that?"

"Because the more he knows, the greater the risk of an inadvertent leak, maybe. And he could have a number of reasons to accept it; one being that somebody's funding some open-ended research. He does seem to have a genuine interest in the Caribs."

"Hmm," Dani said. "Maybe he's playing along with this foundation to get a free ride, trick them into funding his research on the Caribs. You've given me lots to ponder. Thanks for listening."

"My pleasure. Now think about breakfast with Mrs. Walker until you fall asleep."

11

"Now what," Leila asked, as she and Bert stepped out of the customs and immigration office in Bequia.

"I don't know; want to get a cup of coffee and look around? Get the lay of the land?"

"Yeah, okay," Leila said, inhaling and curling her lip. "Something stinks."

"It's this gutter," Bert said, pointing down as they stepped across the concrete-lined ditch that ran along the edge of the street.

"Gutter? It's more like an open sewer."

"It's just a storm drain, Leila."

"Well, it still stinks."

Bert stepped to where he could peer down into the ditch. "There's all kinds of stuff in there. Garbage, like. Probably comes in from the harbor when the tide's — "

His cellphone rang, interrupting him.

"Yeah?" he said, raising the phone to his ear.

"Where are you?" Ed asked.

"We just cleared in. Standing right outside customs. Why?"

"They just piled in their dinghy, headed to town. Keep out of their way, and keep an eye on them."

"Got it," Bert said.

"What's up?" Leila asked.

"They're coming to town. Ed wants us to keep out of their sight and see what they're up to."

"Okay," she said.

"Keep out of their sight," Bert said, shaking his head. "That dumb shit. They don't know who we are. What's the problem?"

"They don't know who we are now," Leila said. "But they might notice if they see us everywhere they go. It's early days, yet. Let's get that coffee. There's a place right across from the dinghy dock. We can sit in the shade and see which way they go."

Once they had settled at an outdoor table with their coffee," Leila said, "Ed's a pain in the ass, sometimes."

"He's the boss," Bert said. "Just suck it up. This is a pretty cushy assignment, you know?"

"I'd rather be back in the States."

Bert looked at her, his eyebrows raised. "Really? You've had enough? Ready to call it quits? I'd really miss you if — "

"No," she said. "That's not what I meant. I'd rather be assigned there; we could make more of a contribution there."

"You should be careful what you say. If that kind of comment made it back to Tehran, you'd be toast. They'd never accept that explanation. You got any idea what they'd do to you?"

"You aren't going to tell. And besides, you know what I meant."

"What makes you so sure I wouldn't tell? I could make points."

"Well, are you going to?"

"What do you think?"

"I don't think you are."

"I'm not, but what if I'm lying."

She studied him for a minute, frowning as she held his gaze. She shook her head. "You know what I am, don't you?"

He looked puzzled. "What you are?"

"What I was trained for? What my missions in the States were, before they put this team together and sent the four of us to Dubai?"

"No. Why would I?"

"I thought Ed might have told you. You're his second in command."

"What's that got to do with what you did in the States? I don't understand."

"It's why I'm on the team. You should know; Ed should have briefed you. I'm here in case there's a problem that requires a, um ... a permanent solution."

"You're the ... I don't ... I thought Ed was ... "

She held his gaze for a few seconds, watching as the beads of sweat broke out on his forehead. Smiling, she nodded. "Ed's not; I am. So don't think about spreading rumors about me. If I even think you might, I'll kill you. And you won't see it coming."

"But what about us? I-I thought we had something special g-going."

She laughed and shook her head again. "Men. You're such weaklings."

"I wouldn't tell them. I was just being a wiseass, that's all."

"You were being a jerk. That could get you killed. Now shut up. They just tied up their dinghy. Here they come."

"CAN WE WALK?" Shellie asked, looking at all the taxis waiting at the town dock where they had left the dinghy. "I want to get a feel for the town."

"Sure," Liz said. "There's not that much to see, but it's a nice morning."

"Besides, it'll save taxi fare," Rick said.

Dani and Liz laughed.

"There's no need to take a taxi," Dani said. "They're here for people who want to take island tours. You saw the north end of town last night." She pointed diagonally across the parking area. "The other end of town's only a few hundred yards south of here."

"Is that a market across the street from customs?" Shellie asked.

"Yes," Liz said. "T-shirts and local crafts. And a few yards farther, there's a produce market, but it's a little early for that. Most of the fruits and vegetables come on the ferry from St. Vincent, and it's not here yet."

"Can we look at the crafts?" Shellie asked.

"Yes, of course," Liz said. "We'll also pass some vendors set up along the walk from here down to Mrs. Walker's place. That's where you'll often find the model boats. Bequia's sort of famous for them."

"Model boats?" Rick asked.

"They're hand carved and beautifully finished," Liz said. "Real works of art."

"Are they models of real boats?" Rick asked. "Or *objets d'art*?"

"Both," Liz said. "A lot of them are scale models of the little whaling boats we were talking about yesterday."

"I'll definitely want to check those out," Rick said.

Ten minutes later, the four of them walked into a combination grocery store and restaurant at the south end of Bequia's main street.

"Good morning. Please make yourselves comfortable. I'll be right out," a woman called from what must have been the kitchen.

"What a lovely voice she has," Shellie said, in a soft tone. "It's so smooth and rich. Is that Mrs. Walker?"

Dani smiled and nodded. "Yes, — "

"Dani! What a wonderful surprise. And Liz." A tall, elegant-looking woman entered and wrapped her arms around Dani, lifting her off her feet in a hug. "And who are your friends?"

"Mrs. Walker, this is Dr. Michelle Everett," Dani said, "and her husband, Dr. Richard Everett."

"Please, I'm Shellie, and my husband's Rick. We've heard so much about you already, I feel like we know you."

"It's my pleasure to have you here. Please, let's sit down. Will you have some breakfast? My cook will be out in a moment to take your orders."

"I'm starving," Dani said.

"I don't believe a word of that, child. I know Liz can cook, even if you won't lift a finger in the kitchen."

Shellie and Rick studied the woman while she bantered with Dani and Liz. Her well-coifed hair was fine, straight, and coal black, with only a few strands of silver to show that she didn't color it. The *café au lait* skin over the finely chiseled bones of her face was as smooth as a baby's.

"I apologize for ignoring you, but I haven't seen my girls in far too long," Mrs. Walker said, turning to look at the Everetts. "How long have you been sailing with them?"

"There's no need to apologize," Shellie said. "We joined them in Grenada a couple of days ago."

"Ah, Grenada. And are Dani and Liz treating you well, I hope?"

"Of course," Rick said. "They're wonderful hostesses."

"What are your plans for your stay in Bequia, if I may ask?"

"We're just passing through on our way to St. Lucia," Shellie said, "but Bequia's lovely."

"You must stay and see our little island; I know you got here last night. I was about to be put out with you, Dani. You should have telephoned."

"Sorry. I wanted to surprise you. I should have known I couldn't." Turning to the Everetts, Dani said, "Mrs. Walker has spies all over the place. She's probably been tracking us since we left St. George's."

"Hush, child." Mrs. Walker glanced at the woman dressed in

white who had materialized beside her chair. "Are you ready, Maddy?"

"Yes, Mrs. Walker," the woman said.

"Do either of you have particular foods that you don't like?" Mrs. Walker asked.

"No, anything's fine," Shellie said.

"Good. I think we'll have a full English breakfast for the table. Maddy, bring us some coffee before you get started."

"Yes ma'am," the woman said. "Welcome home, Dani. Good to see you and Liz, and I hope you folks are enjoying Bequia." She nodded and turned to go, calling, "Coffee soon come," as she went into the kitchen.

"You say you are passing through?" Mrs. Walker asked.

"Dani and Liz are taking us to see the whaling station on Petit Nevis today," Rick said.

"I see. Do you have a particular interest in whaling?"

"Rick's a history professor," Dani said. She rattled off a short summary of his project, and then said, "He wanted to ask you some questions about whaling, and the Caribs, too."

"The Caribs?" Mrs. Walker raised her eyebrows.

"I told them that you'd been here since before the Europeans wiped them out."

"You are trying to vex me, child."

"I'm teasing. But you used to tell me about them. Some of the things you heard from your grandparents. And I've lost track of how old you are. The last birthday I remember celebrating with you was when I was little. I remember it was a big deal, and everybody came. But I can't remember how old you were."

Mrs. Walker chuckled. "You have a good memory, just like your father. I remember that birthday. It was a big event because that year I became the oldest person on the island. The only one older died that year. I decided that I was old enough, and I haven't gotten any older since. I don't care how old I am, so why should anybody else?"

Rick and Shellie laughed at that. "Dani thought you might know about the whaling, from family stories," he said.

"Yes, I know a bit. Petit Nevis was partly owned by some of my ancestors, way back. It was where my people butchered whales, back before the whaling people came and built the try-works. That was in the late 1800s. Not all that long ago, even though it was before my time." She chuckled. "What did you want to know?"

"Aside from my interest in the Moors coming to the islands before Columbus, the focus of my studies has been prehistoric cross-cultural contacts in the Americas."

Mrs. Walker nodded. "And prehistoric means before the Europeans came?"

"Basically, yes. On the mainland of the American continents, more artifacts survived, and the original inhabitants survived longer, as well. Their oral histories have been recorded, and in some cases, they're still passed down through the generations. But in the islands, the Europeans wiped out the original people much earlier, before many people had a chance to learn about their history."

"And nature took care of whatever the Europeans didn't destroy," Mrs. Walker said.

"Yes. One thing historians have wondered about is why there's no evidence of the Caribs hunting whales, just for example. It's been a puzzle, because almost all people who lived in a marine environment hunted marine mammals for food. When Dani and Liz mentioned the whaling station, it made me think of that. Obviously, there would have been whales here, and the Caribs had big, seaworthy canoes. They must have hunted whales, or dolphins."

Mrs. Walker nodded. "I'm sure they did, but the whaling you see in Bequia these days is a more recent development. A man came here in the late 1800s and started whaling to sell the whale oil. He was born here, the son of an English colonist, but he went away to sea. After many years, he came back and started the commercial whaling here.

"Before that, there was a legend that whales were hunted and beached on the little island, Petit Nevis. The people would butcher them for meat. Then there was slavery, and people didn't hunt whales so much. When that man came here, slavery had ended, but only a few old people remembered the stories of whale hunting. The commercial whaling went on for some years, maybe until about the time I was born. Then the whales became scarce, and people didn't need the oil for lamps any longer anyway.

"Some years after that, the whales recovered, and people began to hunt them again, but now it was more like the old days. They hunted for the meat, because they were hungry. And they began to use Petit Nevis again. I'm afraid I don't know much more about it."

"Dani told us they don't use Petit Nevis anymore," Rick said.

"That's right," Mrs. Walker said. "There were some disputes over who owned Petit Nevis in more recent times, I know that. In old times, before the Europeans, I think it belonged to everybody. Maybe that was better. Now they take the whales to Sempler's Cay to butcher them, but it's not as good a place. At Petit Nevis, the water is deeper and the current is stronger, so it washed away the remains. Now they rot and pollute the water around the Cay and even up in Friendship Bay." She shook her head.

"Thank you, Mrs. Walker," Rick said. "That's more useful to me than you can imagine."

"You're welcome. I see Maddy's about to bring your breakfast. Please excuse me for a moment. I should greet that couple at the table behind me; I didn't see them come in. I'll be right back."

"I WON'T HAVE to eat again for a day or two," Rick said, as the four of them ambled back toward the town dock and their dinghy. "That was some kind of meal. Thanks for introducing us to her; she's an amazing person."

"She certainly is," Shellie said. "How old do you suppose she is, really? She doesn't look like she could be out of her 50s, even."

Dani laughed. "I think she's close to one hundred."

"Get out," Rick said. "You can't be serious."

"Seriously," Dani said. "Her husband was older than my grandfather. They were in business together before my father came along."

"Wow! That's hard to believe."

"It's not that unusual," Liz said, "not down here. Dominica's famous for the number of people over a hundred years old. For a while, a woman there held the world's record as the oldest woman, but she finally died, maybe ten or fifteen years ago. Elizabeth Israel was her name, if you want to look her up. She lived to be 128."

"That's astonishing," Shellie said. "Why is that?"

"Who knows?" Dani asked. "I think she's the one who said her secret was moderation, that she only had a few ounces of rum and one cigar every day."

They laughed at that as they drew even with the town dock.

"If we're going to leave from Petit Nevis, tomorrow, I should stop in customs and clear out," Dani said.

"Good," Shellie said. "Rick and I can check out that market across the street while you do that."

Ten minutes later, they were in the dinghy, threading through the crowded anchorage. As Dani throttled back to approach *Vengeance*, Shellie said, "That boat was in the marina with us in Grenada."

"Which one?" Dani asked, as they coasted to a stop alongside *Vengeance*.

Shellie pointed at the yacht anchored several boat-lengths off their port bow. "*Aquila*," she said. "I recognize the name. I know it's Spanish for 'eagle,' but I like it because it reminds me of tequila."

"Do you like tequila?" Liz asked. "We may have some aboard, if you do."

"No, not particularly," Shellie said. "I just like the word. I have no idea why. What kind of boat is that?"

"A Beneteau 44," Dani said. "They must have made a zillion of them. They're popular with the bareboat charter companies down here. That one has the logo of the operation that's based in the marina we were in; that's probably where the people picked it up."

"Bareboat?" Rick asked.

"As opposed to a crewed charter," Liz said.

"Ah! So they just rent the boat and sail it themselves?"

"That's right," Liz said, as they climbed out of the dinghy.

"Let's just tow the dinghy," Dani said. "We're not going far, and it's all protected water." She climbed aboard and walked the dinghy aft until she could tie it off to one of the backstays.

"Can you get me online?" Rick said. "There are a couple of things I want to research, while I'm thinking of it."

"Sure," Liz said. "I'll power up the satellite access while Dani uncovers the sails."

"Don't get lost in the web, Rick," Shellie said. "You'll miss the sail; it's not far, is it, Dani?"

"Maybe an hour, anchor up to anchor down. We can do it all under sail, unless you're in a hurry. That might take a few minutes longer, but it's pretty shoreline for a lot of the way."

"Let's sail," Rick said. "I won't be long on the web, and then I can enjoy at least part of the trip."

"Good," Dani said, turning her attention to uncovering the mizzen sail. "Do you want to steer, Shellie?"

"Yes. Is that okay?"

"Sure," Dani said. "You and I can get started while Liz gets Rick set up on the internet."

12

"Hurry," Ed said, as Bert and Leila brought their dinghy alongside *Aquila*. "They're about to leave."

"Take it easy, Ed," Leila said. "They're just going around the corner. It's better if we don't follow them. We'll just attract their attention."

"How do you know where they're going?" Ed asked.

"We eavesdropped on them while they were discussing their plans. We followed them to a restaurant and got a table near theirs," Bert said. "Relax, and we'll tell you all about it. We can always check the tracker to make sure they're not skipping out."

They all sat in the cockpit in the shade of the awning, and Bert and Leila summarized the conversation they'd overheard. After about fifteen minutes, Leila said, "and that's about it, I think. Did I miss anything, Bert?"

"I don't think so, except that the woman who runs the restaurant seemed to know the two women that run *Vengeance* really well."

"True," Leila said. "She did."

"Why do you say that?" Ashley asked.

"She hugged the blonde one, and called her 'child,'" Bert said.

"And when we first went in and sat down, they were talking about a birthday party for the old woman," Leila said.

"Right," Bert said, "and the party was a long time ago, when Dani was a kid."

"Dani?" Ed asked. "She's one of the women on *Vengeance*?"

"Yes," Leila said. "The blonde. She seems to be the skipper. And the woman — they called her Mrs. Walker — "

"Wait," Ed said. "Aren't both of the women blondes?"

"The one that's the skipper's got blond hair with some curls. The other one's got reddish blond hair that she pulls back into a bun," Ashley said. "Right?"

"Yes," Leila said. "The strawberry blonde is Liz."

"Okay," Ed said. "Got it. Dani's the skipper, Liz is the other one. Use their names from now on, so we keep 'em straight. Go ahead, Leila. I interrupted what you were about to say about Mrs. Walker."

"Right. Mrs. Walker said Dani had a good memory, just like her father."

"Dani's father?" Ed asked.

"Yes, that's right," Leila said. "So she apparently knows, or knew, Dani's father. I'd guess Dani's in her mid-twenties, so if that party happened when she was a kid, we're talking ten or fifteen years. Maybe a little longer."

"Dani and Mrs. Walker acted like family," Bert said.

"They did," Leila said, nodding.

"You think they're related?"

Bert shrugged and looked at Leila.

"I kind of doubt it. Mrs. Walker's got some mixed blood. We mentioned the Carib ancestry, and she could also have some African slaves back there, too — hard to say, but her skin tone was darker than I would have thought for an Indian. But maybe they could be related by marriage. Are you thinking leverage?"

"Maybe," Ed said. "You never know what might come in handy. If they're close, it probably doesn't matter about a blood tie. We could still use Mrs. Walker to make Dani do our bidding, if it comes to that."

"If it comes to that, I'd go for Everett's wife," Leila said. "That's closer to the one we want to control."

"That's so," Ed said, "depending on what we need, either option could work. I get the questions about the Caribs, but any clue as to why Everett's interested in whaling?"

"None," Leila said. "Bert?"

Bert shook his head. "Think you can get Tehran to check up on that?"

"I'll try," Ed said. "I'd better go get a report together and send it off. Guess we'll be here tonight. They didn't say what they're planning for tomorrow?"

"Not that we heard, but they had a few minutes together with Mrs. Walker before we went inside," Leila said. "We watched from the street until they got settled — didn't want to be too obvious. So we might have missed that."

"No matter," Ed said. "We've got the tracker. Good work, you two."

"*Now* WE'RE GETTING BLOWN along like a leaf in the wind, as you put it the other day," Dani said. They were coasting along the south shore of Admiralty Bay under just the mainsail, running dead before the wind.

"It's a lot harder to steer than it was yesterday," Shellie said. "And we're rolling from side to side a lot."

"Imagine what the ride would be like in open water," Liz said.

"Not fun, I'll bet," Shellie said. "What's that place up on the cliffs?" She nodded toward a collection of structures high up on the hillside to their left.

"That's called Moonhole," Dani said. "Because there's a

natural arch up there that frames the moon sometimes. You can't make out the arch from down here, though."

"What is it? A resort of some kind?"

"Yes, of some kind. It was started in the '60s by an architect and his wife who dropped out of the rat race. It has a kind of strange history — almost like a commune, but for wealthy people, I guess," Liz said. "I'm not sure how it all worked. But from the pictures I've seen, it's interesting, architecturally. All the houses are built so they seem to grow out of the natural rock formations, and lots of the rooms are open to the outside — like missing a wall or two."

"Sounds wild," Shellie said. "Not my kind of place, though."

"What's not your kind of place," Rick asked, climbing into the cockpit and sitting down facing the shoreline.

"That place on the hillside," Shellie said. "What did you find on the web? You weren't gone long."

"Several articles, but I just skimmed them. I downloaded the best ones for later. Didn't want to miss the sailing."

"It'll get more exciting once we round the point up there," Dani said. "Then we'll fly the headsails and turn up close to the wind. We'll have to beat our way into the anchorage at Petit Nevis."

"Beat?" Shellie asked.

"That means we'll be working our way upwind," Liz said. "We'll sail at something less than a 45-degree angle to the direction the wind's coming from, and we'll change sides with the sails every so often, kind of zigzagging."

"I never realized a sailboat could go upwind," Shellie said. "That's fascinating."

"Some boats do it better than others," Dani said. "The ships Columbus sailed weren't very good at it. They were mostly square-rigged, meant to sail off the wind — like we're doing now. Some ships from that era had a few fore-and-aft rigged sails, like we have, but they weren't used for much except maneuvering."

"I've read that the Arabs developed sails that let them sail upwind," Rick said.

"They did," Dani said. "Those boats were referred to as 'lateen-rigged,' and they were around for maybe a thousand years before the people in Europe figured out how to marry them to their big, square rigged ships. It changed seafaring during the middle of the second millennium."

"What were you researching?" Shellie asked.

"A little bit on the Caribs, but there's not much available. I'm starting to get fascinated by the dearth of information. I don't think they've gotten much attention from academia. But I also had a quick look at the history of whaling. There's quite a bit of information on whaling in Bequia on the web. I downloaded several articles. A couple of things caught my attention. First, the way the people here go about it is almost identical to the approach that the Basques were using in the ninth century. They had lookouts posted on the high ground, just like here. When they spotted a whale, they used the same strategy to kill the animal, and then they towed it to a beach to butcher it."

"The ninth century, huh?" Shellie asked. "You think there was some influence? That would have been during the period the Moors ruled the Iberian Peninsula. Would they have picked up whaling from the Basques? Maybe brought it to the islands?"

"That's an intriguing theory," Rick said, "but there's nothing to support it. At least nothing I found. It's more likely that the Basques and the Caribs solved similar problems in similar ways, I think. Mostly, the approach was obvious. I wouldn't leap to any conclusions based on the similarities, but I thought it was interesting."

"What else caught your eye?" Shellie asked.

"Whaling in Bequia isn't looked upon with approval by a lot of members of the International Whaling Convention. The IWC sets quotas for what they call Aboriginal Subsistence Whaling. That means what it sounds like. They refer to it as

ASW, and there's a big faction that disputes Bequia's right to a quota."

"Why's that?" Dani asked.

"The argument is that Bequia's heritage of whaling doesn't derive from the aboriginal people. It grew out of the commercial whaling that Mrs. Walker told us about in the late 1800s. The AWS quotas are supposed to allow people like the Eskimos, for example, to continue doing what they've done for thousands of years. There's never been a claim raised by St. Vincent and the Grenadines that whaling in Bequia predates that commercial period."

"But it must," Dani said. "Bequia's not even the only place in Saint Vincent and the Grenadines where whales are taken. There are a couple of fishing villages along the west coast of St. Vincent proper that hunt smaller whales and marine mammals."

"Hmm," Rick said. "I don't know what the right or wrong of it is, but it doesn't appear that the local government has tried to make a case beyond saying they need the protein, and that it's been part of their heritage since the days of commercial whaling."

"Is the topic of whaling among the Caribs somehow relevant to your project?" Dani asked.

Rick looked at Dani for a moment, his brow wrinkling. "I'm not sure, Dani. Right now, any information on the Carib culture could be important, even if it just adds context to the question of interaction with the Moors. At this stage, I can't rule anything out. We know so little about the islands before Columbus — the smallest thing could be important in proving or disproving the notion that the Moors were here first."

"Beyond the academic questions, do you think the answer to the question of the Moors will have an impact on anybody's day-to-day lives?" Dani asked.

Rick grinned. "Hey, I'm an academic. That question's above my pay grade. Is knowledge worth pursuing for its own sake? Obviously, I think it is. What do you think?"

"Oh, I'm curious," Dani said. "Don't misread my question. I've been wondering what motivates people to fund research like this, though."

"Curiosity is one thing that motivates research. Wealth, and a long-term perspective are others. But I don't know what's behind our donors' interest. I've wondered myself."

Dani nodded. "Thanks, Rick. Sorry, but I just had to ask."

"It's a fair question. No need for an apology."

"It's time to come up on the wind and get the headsails out," Dani said. "That's where we're going, right up in there." She pointed to the east. "Swing the helm around, Shellie. Liz can sheet in the main and I'll raise the mizzen. Then we'll roll out the Yankee and the staysail."

13

"Mrs. Walker called while you were running them in to the whaling station," Dani said, as Liz tied off the dinghy and climbed aboard.

"What was on her mind?"

"Did you notice the couple who came into her place right after us?"

"The ones she spoke to when she excused herself for a few minutes?"

"Yes."

"I saw them, but that's all," Liz said. "What about them?"

"They cleared in right before we came ashore," Dani said. "They're on *Aquila*; there are four of them, Americans. Two couples."

"Okay, but — "

"They followed us to Mrs. Walker's. They were waiting at the coffee shop just down from customs, and when we passed by, they got up and followed us."

Liz frowned and shook her head. "Coincidence."

"I don't think so. They waited outside Mrs. Walker's for

several minutes before they came in, watching us visiting with her."

"Your overactive imagination is — "

"No, Liz. It's — "

"Dani, did Mrs. Walker get all of that from her chat with them?"

"No, she didn't. You know how the coconut telegraph works. The lady who runs the boutique up the way from her place watched them. She called Mrs. Walker after they left."

"Okay, but I meant did they tell Mrs. Walker about *Aquila* and the four of — "

"No. She called the customs office."

"Mrs. Walker called the customs office?" Liz asked.

"Yes, after her friend told her about them hanging around watching us. She even got their names from customs."

"It could still be coincidence, Dani."

"I don't think so. After that couple finished their breakfast, they stopped in the boutique and pretended to be shopping. They kind of casually mentioned having breakfast at Mrs. Walker's and wondered if the boutique lady knew whether we were regulars or something. They were subtle about it; didn't come right out and ask, but mentioned how nice it was to see the way Mrs. Walker visited with her regular customers, like we were family, almost. They were fishing, Liz."

"Well, knowing Mrs. Walker and her friends in Bequia, I'll bet they didn't catch anything."

"No, I don't think so," Dani said. "But they did ask the boutique lady about whaling, so they'd been eavesdropping on us."

"Maybe, but come on, Dani. Bequia advertises the whole whaling thing pretty heavily. Maybe they even came here because of that."

"I don't think so. They didn't know enough about it for that to be the case. The lady told them about the whaling museum in Friendship Bay, and they acted surprised."

Liz shrugged. "I still think you're reading too much into this."

"Liz, they went back to *Aquila* for a while after breakfast, but after we left the harbor, they went ashore again and took a taxi to the museum. They asked a bunch of questions about the Caribs and whaling. They had to get that from Rick's conversation with Mrs. Walker. They just now left the museum and walked up the hill to where they could see this anchorage. The woman had a camera with a big telephoto lens. They're probably spying on us, right now."

"Get a grip, Dani. Calm down. If they were following us, why would they have gone back ashore instead of tailing *Vengeance*?"

"Because they overheard us telling Mrs. Walker we were going to spend the night at Petit Nevis," Dani said.

Liz frowned and shook her head. "What are you thinking we should do, then?"

"Ask Rick if there's a reason why anybody would be following him, for one thing."

"Um, why don't you let me feel him out about that. You're kind of edgy, and we don't want to alarm the Everetts. I'll work out a way to do it without upsetting him. You know I'm good at that kind of thing."

"Okay, that's a good idea. While you're at it, see if you can talk them into going all the way to Ste. Anne tomorrow and then doubling back to Rodney Bay and Soufrière in a day or two. They wanted to go to Martinique anyway."

"Why? What are you planning?"

"If *Aquila* shows up in Ste. Anne, we'll know for sure that they're after us. No bareboat charter's going to pass up Soufrière and Rodney Bay; it's a long trip all the way to Martinique."

"But there are so many anchorages and so many boats in Martinique," Liz said. "We might never — "

"I'll get Sandrine to check the customs database."

Sandrine Davis was a senior officer with French customs in Martinique, and the wife of Phillip Davis, one of Dani's father's business associates.

"But Dani, *Aquila's* a common boat name, especially in the bareboat fleets. I've seen several different ones."

"I have their names, Liz. Mrs. Walker got them from customs."

"All right, then. I'll work on that change of plans."

"Are they going to call you when they're ready to come back aboard?" Dani asked.

"Yes. Thanks for reminding me. I left them the handheld VHF. Reach over and turn on the radio, would you? I hope I haven't missed their call."

"I don't think so. They're still wandering all over the island," Dani said.

~

"WELL, THAT WAS A WASTE OF TIME," Bert said. He and Leila had just left Bequia's whaling museum in Friendship Bay.

"Maybe, maybe not," she said.

"It was just a tourist place," he said.

"Yeah, but they said that we can walk up the hill over there and get a look at the whaling station on Petit Nevis."

"What good's that going to do?"

"We can see what they're up to," she said.

"Too far away," Bert said.

"Not with this." Leila tapped the telephoto lens on the camera that hung from her shoulder.

"Big deal. I'm starting to think maybe the Saudis cooked this whole thing up just to waste our time."

"Why do you say that?"

"How the hell is Everett supposed to find a campsite that was used almost a thousand years ago? They don't even know what island it was on, if there even was such a place."

"Correction, Bert. *We* don't know what island it was on. For all we know, Everett has an exact location — or the Saudis do."

"Yeah? Then why hasn't Tehran told us? They've got everything the Saudis have."

"And what makes you think that?"

"Ed said they did."

"No doubt that's what Ed was told. That doesn't make it so. The Saudis probably know we've got somebody on the inside. They're being cautious, to make sure we can't get there first and upstage them."

"So, you think Everett knows where he's going? All this is just for show? Or to throw us off?"

"He might."

"Is that why you and Ed were talking about snatching his wife?"

"That would be one way to find out what he knows," Leila said.

"Then why not do it?" Bert asked.

"They could be feeding him information a little bit at a time," Leila said. "If we snatch her and he doesn't know, then we've blown it."

They walked along in silence for a few minutes.

"Why wouldn't they just tell him where to find whatever it is they're looking for, if they know? Get it over with?" Ed asked.

"Credibility might be one reason," she said, looking over at him. "They want him to believe he really found the site; it'll make him a true believer. Then he'll be more persuasive. Let's face it. Nobody's going to want to believe that the Moors discovered America before Columbus did. Nobody outside the Muslim world, anyway."

"Yeah, I can see that," Ed said. "So, the harder it is to find, the more likely people are to believe it's real? That's what you're saying?"

"Pretty much."

"Okay. You said that was one reason they might be dribbling out the information to Everett. You got another one in mind?"

"Security. Say they suspect we've penetrated their operation. Then the less Everett knows, the better, from their perspective. He can't tell us what he doesn't know."

"You mean, if we were to kidnap his wife, or one of the women?"

"Exactly. Look, Bert, you need to cut out all this 'what if' bullshit and focus on the mission."

"Focus on the mission? But that is the — "

"No! Our mission is to follow Everett and see what he finds. Period. Not try to second-guess the Saudis, or our own leadership. Let's stop here. Now shut up and let me see what they're doing."

Leila had been checking the view over her shoulder as they walked. She raised the camera and put her eye to the viewfinder. There was a whirring sound as she zoomed in and focused.

"Perfect," she said, snapping a picture. "Dani and Liz are on *Vengeance* and the Everetts are poking around on shore. He's got a walking stick of some kind, stirring up the debris."

She handed him the camera. He watched the Everetts for several seconds.

"You don't suppose he thinks that's the camp, do you?" he asked.

"I don't know."

"There's lots of old stone walls and stuff," Bert said.

"Yeah. But remember the exhibits we just saw at the museum. That's all part of what was built after 1870. Remember the sketches they had?"

"I wonder if he's doing this to throw us off, then?" Bert asked.

"He doesn't know about us, Bert. Sometimes I wonder about you. Come on. Let's head back to *Aquila*. Maybe Ed got something new from Tehran."

14

"How was it?" Liz asked, as the Everetts came down the companionway ladder. Dani had just taken the dinghy ashore to pick them up while Liz started dinner. "Find anything exciting?"

"No, nothing exciting," Rick said. "Lots of interesting bits and pieces of junk there, but nothing that looked especially old. The oldest stuff we saw dates from the commercial whaling days. But it was still fascinating. My guess is that island's always been uninhabited."

"Why's that?" Dani asked, coming below deck after squaring away the dinghy.

"No source of fresh water and no signs of permanent habitation," Rick said.

"The small islands are dry," Dani said. "On the bigger ones, there's water, but even then, it's scarce compared to what we're used to. It's jokingly called Caribbean gold, a lot of times."

"How do people manage?" Shellie asked.

"Nowadays, there are desalination plants," Liz said, "but it's expensive to run them, so water's still precious. Before that, people had cisterns to catch rainwater."

"On a completely different subject," Liz said, "let's talk about tomorrow's trip."

"To Soufrière?" Rick asked.

"Well, that's what I wanted to discuss. While Dani was picking you up, I learned that some friends of ours from Dominica are going to be in Martinique for the next few days, and you had mentioned something about visiting someone at the *Musée Départemental d'Archéologie Précolombienne*."

"Yes, I did. There are several little museums in Martinique that I'd like to see. That's the one that I thought might be most helpful, but there's also a private collection that has some of the correspondence I mentioned."

"Between those missionary priests?" Liz asked.

"Yes," Rick said. "What about your friends?"

"You might like to meet them while they're there. He's the one who painted that sunset you admired, Shellie."

"The guy called Sharktooth?" Shellie asked.

"Yes. He and his wife are staying with some mutual friends of ours in Ste. Anne. Their house in Dominica was damaged by the recent hurricane. They'll only be there for a few more days, and both of them have a wealth of knowledge about the islands. He's well-acquainted with the whole of the Eastern Caribbean, and well-connected to a lot of government officials, too. I thought if you were interested, maybe we should sail straight up to Martinique while they're there. We can double back to Soufrière and Rodney Bay."

"That could actually be really helpful to me," Rick said. "I was wishing that I could see some of the pre-Columbian exhibits in Martinique before we got serious about trying to find the site where the Moors stayed."

"How long a trip is it from here?" Shellie asked.

"It's a long day," Dani said. "Around a hundred miles. Say twelve hours, give or take a little. We can leave early and get in around sunset. Liz and I would think nothing of it if it were just the two of us."

"How early would we have to leave?" Shellie asked.

"Dani and I are usually up at dawn," Liz said, "so we could sail out of here and you two can sleep in. You won't miss much, and I'll serve breakfast in the cockpit under sail whenever you get up. It'll be fun. That should put us in Ste. Anne around sunset."

"Sounds perfect," Rick said. "What about it, Shellie? You okay with it?"

"Sure. It sounds great. And I can't wait to meet somebody named Sharktooth."

"You'll like him," Dani said.

"I'm sure I will. Do we have time for a quick shower before dinner, Liz?"

"Sure. I'm just getting started. Take your time."

"I HEARD you get the computer out while I was in the shower before dinner," Shellie said. She and Rick had excused themselves after Liz had served dessert. Shellie wanted an early evening, so that she could make the most of tomorrow's sail.

"Yes, I did, but I just downloaded everything. I figured I'd look at it after dinner."

"You mean now?"

"Well, I don't want to keep you up if you're ready to go to sleep."

"I'm okay; it's early yet. I was just feeling a little tired after the day, and I am going to try to wake up when they do. I'd like to see them sail out of here without the engine. That's what Liz said they'd do. Did you get any interesting email?"

"I don't know. There's one from the foundation that said something about a revised translation."

"How could you stand to wait?"

Rick shrugged. "It's just work; I'm not complaining, mind you. It's a free ride, even if it's probably a wild goose chase. If nothing else, I'm learning some things I didn't know about the Caribs. That's worth it, to me."

"Still feeling that way? About the Moors?"

"Yes."

"I'm surprised you took this grant, Rick. It seems unlike you."

"Well, I was honest with the people at the foundation. They know how I feel about the likelihood that the Moors were here first; I told you that."

"I know you did. It just seems ... " She shook her head.

"Intellectually dishonest?" Rick asked.

"Well, that may be a little strong."

"That's actually the phrase I used during the interview. They said that was fine; that a healthy skepticism on my part suited their purpose. 'It will keep everybody honest,' is the way they put it."

"You really think it didn't happen?"

"I won't say it didn't. I just think it's unlikely that we'll find anything to prove it did. It's a seriously small needle in a huge haystack. But, longer odds have paid off, and I'm going to give it my best shot. Give me a second to skim this email, okay?"

"Sure."

"Hmm," Rick said. "That's interesting. They got somebody to go over some other documents in the archive. Something that they found when they were re-filing stuff. It mentions a cave in the mountains near the site. The Moors were using it for storage before Khashkhash sailed back to Spain."

"A cave?"

"That's what it says. I don't think of this as a part of the world where you find caves. It's pretty new, geologically. But who knows?"

"If there aren't many caves in the islands, that might narrow the search," Shellie said.

"It might, yes. I'll have to ask Dani and Liz about it tomorrow."

"Or their friend, this Sharktooth. Liz said he knew all the islands really well, remember?"

"Yes. Well, if you're getting up at dawn, let's turn out the light."

"G'night, Dr. Everett," Shellie said, as he put away the computer.

"Goodnight, Dr. Everett," he said, turning off the light by their berth and giving her a kiss as he crawled into bed.

"HOW'D you find out Sharktooth and Maureen are in Ste. Anne?" Dani asked, as Liz turned out the light.

"I thought that would be a good reason to go there tomorrow."

"The Everetts thought so, but — "

"I called Sharktooth to see if he could meet us there," Liz said.

"So you cooked this up? I'm impressed."

"Actually, I didn't. I was going to, but they were already there."

"Was their house damaged?" Dani asked.

"A little. They had some water damage from a roof leak."

"That doesn't sound like a reason for them to go to Martinique," Dani said.

"No, but it made a good story, I thought. They went mostly because Maureen wanted to go shopping with Sandrine. And Phillip and Sharktooth are doing a little fishing."

Dani chuckled. "Do they know you blamed their visit on the hurricane?"

"Yes. I didn't want them to blow my cover."

"Why not just tell the truth?"

"I wanted to make this seem time-sensitive — like as soon as their house is fixed, they'd be leaving. I didn't know Rick was going to be so eager, and I worried that he and Shellie might just say they'd rather wait."

"And you always seem so innocent," Dani said.

"I am. That's why I can get away with stuff like this."

"You've been spending too much time with Connie. She's a bad influence on you." Connie Barrera was a friend of theirs who had the skills of a born grifter.

"That's not so, Dani. I didn't mislead Rick and Shellie. Not about anything important, anyway."

"Of course not," Dani said. "Go to sleep, if your conscience will let you. We've got a long day tomorrow."

15

"Well," Shellie said, "if it's not Rip Van Winkle himself!"

Rick stood on the companionway ladder rubbing his eyes, looking out at the three women drinking coffee. He stifled a yawn. "Did I miss breakfast?"

"No," Liz said, pouring coffee from a thermal carafe into a mug and handing it to him. "We waited for you."

"I thought the engine would wake me up when you were raising the anchor."

"They showed me how to do that under sail," Shellie said, from behind the helm. "It's really cool, Rick. You should have seen it. Can we do that again?" she asked.

"Sure," Dani said. "It's easier in an uncrowded anchorage, though. We'll have to pick our spot."

"How long have we been sailing?" Rick asked.

"A couple of hours," Shellie said. "That's St. Vincent you see over the starboard quarter."

"Over the *starboard quarter*, huh," Rick said. "You're even starting to sound like a sailor."

"Oh, I'm hooked, Rick. We need to learn to do this."

"You're well on your way," Liz said. "Come on up and sit down,

Rick. You're blocking the ladder; I need to get breakfast going. Some of us have worked up an appetite."

"I'm starving," Shellie said. "I raised the mainsail; I had no idea how much of a workout it is to sail. Forget about going to the gym."

"Thanks for waiting breakfast for me," Rick said, with a chuckle. He stepped out into the cockpit, bracing himself with one hand as he made way for Liz to go below.

"While Liz is fixing breakfast, maybe you could tell us a little more about your friends we're going to meet," Shellie said. "All you told us about Sharktooth before was that he's an artist."

Dani laughed. "He'd be embarrassed to hear himself described as an artist. He does paint, but it's just a hobby for him."

"But you said his wife had an art gallery," Rick said.

"That's right, she does. But Sharktooth's interests are wide-ranging. He's an entrepreneur with his fingers in all kinds of things."

"How did you come to be friends?" Rick asked. "Did you meet them in Dominica?"

"I've known him as long as I can remember," Dani said. "He does business with my father — has since before I was born."

"You said Mrs. Walker's husband was a partner of your father's," Rick said. "But you never mentioned what your father did."

"Does. He's still active; he's a broker of sorts. He buys and sells heavy equipment internationally. He and his partners can provide skilled manpower, too. Back when I was little, I guess the islands were a ripe market. Or at least, more so than now."

"You said your dad lives in Paris," Shellie said.

"He does, now. Back then, he was still living in Martinique. He had two partners in the islands. One was Mrs. Walker's husband; I called him Uncle Leon, but I barely remember him. Sharktooth was the other one.

"The two of them were active in the Organization of Eastern

Caribbean States back then. They had a lot of high level government contacts in the islands that had been British colonies. They hadn't been independent countries for long, at that point. I think things were quite a bit less settled than they are now.

"The other man you'll meet in Ste. Anne is Phillip Davis. He was involved with them, as well."

"So he's somebody your father knew from when he lived in Martinique?"

"Well, no. Phillip lives in Martinique now, but back then, he was in the U.S. Army. He made a career of it. He was a military attaché for a lot of his career, and I think he was a conduit of sorts for development funds for some of the governments down here, so Papa and his partners worked with him. That was when I was too little to pay much attention to what they were doing.

"When Phillip retired from the military, he went into business with Papa, too. And there's another partner. My godfather, in fact. He lives in Miami.

"Phillip settled in Ste. Anne when he retired from the partnership. He married a woman who's a senior officer in the French customs service. Phillip's younger than the others; he was like a much older brother to me when I was in my teens."

"Is that who Sharktooth and his wife are visiting in Ste. Anne, then?" Shellie asked.

"Yes. And you remember us telling you about *Kayak Spirit*?"

"The boat you took Liz out on when you first met?"

"Yes, that's it. Phillip owns *Kayak Spirit*. She's an interesting old boat, what's called a Carriacou sloop. She was built in Carriacou, which is a little island that's part of Grenada. The man who built her was a smuggler; from the '50s until he died, he smuggled rum and cigarettes in and out of the French islands. He was based in Petite Martinique, another island, also part of Grenada. Petite Martinique has been a haven for smugglers from back in the early colonial days. Some people say it still is."

"Why is that?" Rick asked.

Dani shrugged. "I don't really know. I guess because it's useful for everybody. Evading inter-island customs duties is sort of a local sport, I think."

"What kind of tall tales are you telling now?" Liz asked, as she set a tray laden with scrambled eggs, saltfish patties, and fried potatoes on the bridge deck.

"Dani was just telling us a little bit about Sharktooth and Phillip and their wives," Shellie said.

"Shellie, I'm going to switch on the autopilot for you so you won't have to steer while you eat," Dani said. "Come on out here with the rest of us."

Liz folded out the cockpit table and passed plates to everyone. "You'll enjoy all of them," she said. "They're like Dani's family, but they always make me feel right at home. Nice people."

"I'm excited to meet them," Shellie said, sitting down beside Rick.

As they tucked into the food, a silence fell over the cockpit. After a few minutes, Rick pushed his plate away.

"Wonderful breakfast, Liz," he said. "Thanks."

"I'm glad you liked it. Can I get you anything else?"

"No, thanks. But while we drink our coffee, I wanted to ask if either of you knew of any caves in the islands."

"Caves?" Dani asked, shaking her head. "Only a few. They aren't really a feature of the islands. Why do you ask?"

"I got an email from our sponsor last night. They found some more documents related to the Moorish site. There was a cave of some sort near the camp. They used it as a storehouse."

"Is this at one of the places we're looking at already?" Liz asked.

"Yes, unless it forces us to reconsider," he said.

"The only one I can think of is the Bat Cave," Dani said.

"But nobody would store anything there," Liz said.

"The Bat Cave?" Rick asked. "Where's that?"

"Soufrière," Liz said.

"It's a cave in the cliff on the north side of the harbor. There's a huge colony of bats there — apparently has been forever. The tour guides take people there in small boats to watch them come and go. There's even a park mooring right outside it — like only a few yards away. We've spent the night there before. There are so many bats that you can hear them squeaking as you fall asleep."

"But it's flooded," Dani said. "I've never heard of anybody going in there. It's a narrow fissure that runs from below the water up — I don't know — maybe a couple of hundred feet. I don't know how far back into the cliff it goes."

"I don't think that could be it," Liz said.

"Unless it's changed somehow in the last several hundred years," Shellie said.

"The person to ask is Sharktooth," Dani said. "If there are caves, he'll know about them."

"Why's that?" Rick asked.

Dani shrugged. "He's a font of local knowledge. We'll ask him tomorrow."

"THEY'RE ALREADY MOVING," Ashley said, studying the tablet that showed the location of the tracker she had placed on *Vengeance.*

"No big deal," Ed said. "That's why you put the tracker aboard. Where are they?"

"Fifteen or twenty miles out to the northwest."

"So they've been under way for a while," Leila said. "What's out that way? Anything?"

"Nothing close," Ashley said, zooming out. "The Virgin Islands, but they're a few hundred miles away."

"Think they found out something yesterday?" Bert asked.

"Don't waste time on speculation," Ed said. "Let's get our act together and get on their trail. Figure they've had a couple of hours head-start; that puts them over the horizon. We can follow them without being seen, if we hold that distance."

Ten minutes later, *Aquila* was under way, motoring out of Admiralty Bay. "Let's get some sail up," Leila said. "The ride will be better, if nothing else. Ash, take the helm and just hold this course; we're pretty much aimed straight for *Vengeance*."

"Got it," Ashley said, sliding behind the helm and taking over from Leila.

"Come on, Bert," Leila said. "Let's unroll the main. You handle the outhaul; I'll get the sheet."

"Ready, Leila?" Bert asked, a few seconds later.

"Yeah. Go!" she said, and let the mainsheet run as Bert began to unroll the mainsail by pulling in the outhaul. With the mainsail flying, the boat heeled 20 degrees from the horizontal.

"Okay, Bert. Let's get the Genoa out. I'll handle the furling line and you take the sheet this time."

"Got it," Bert said. "Ready when you are."

"Go!" Leila said.

Bert pulled in the tail of the sheet hand over hand, rolling out a few feet of the big headsail. As the sail began to flog, he switched to cranking the sheet winch, and Leila belayed the furling line, releasing a foot or two at a time, letting the sail fill smoothly.

When the sail had unrolled completely, Leila asked, "How's the course?"

"Good," Ashley said.

"Kill the diesel, Ed," Leila said, her eyes on the Genoa.

She turned to look at Ashley. "How's the helm? Are you having to fight to hold our course?"

"No," Ashley said. "It's almost like I don't have to steer."

"Good," Leila said. "Let's put the autopilot on." She moved back behind the helm with Ashley and pushed a couple of buttons. "Okay," she said. "Get yourself a cup of coffee and relax."

Ashley dropped her death grip on the helm and shook the kinks out of her arms.

"Okay," Ed said. "So now all we have to do is make sure we don't overtake them."

"That's not going to happen," Leila said.

"Feels like we're hauling butt, to me," Ed said.

"Yeah, but their boat's faster, probably by a knot. Maybe two," Leila said.

"How do you know?" Ed asked.

"For one thing, it's ten or fifteen feet longer. The speed of a displacement hull through the water is a function of waterline length," Bert said.

"But ... " Ed shook his head. "Suppose we wanted to catch them?"

"The only way that could happen is if they decided to slow down for some reason," Leila said.

"We should have gotten a faster boat," Ed said.

"This is what was available," Bert said.

"A speedboat," Ed said. "We should have gotten a speedboat."

"There's a problem with that, Ed," Leila said. "A speed boat wouldn't blend in down here. This is sailboat country, if you haven't noticed."

Ed grunted and nodded. "You got a point there." He headed for the companionway. "Guess I'd better let Tehran know we're moving again."

"Anything back from them on the whaling question?" Bert asked.

"Not yet. They're checking."

16

"They've stopped," Ashley said, touching the screen of the tablet that showed the tracker's location.

"Where are they?" Ed asked.

"Hang on," Ashley said, swiping at the screen. "Let me get the sat nav app up." After half a minute, she said, "They're in Martinique, at the south end of the island, up in a big bay. Just a second." She zoomed in on *Vengeance's* plotted position. "The closest town is Ste. Anne. It says they're in an anchorage area."

"So maybe they've stopped for the night," Leila said.

"Probably," Ashley said. "Looking at the chart, there's no other reason they'd go into that bay. It's a dead end. They'll have to backtrack before they'll have a clear shot at anywhere else."

"Let me see," Ed said, reaching for the tablet. He stared at it for a few seconds, zooming out, then zooming back in. "I'd say that's their destination — not an overnight stop."

"Why's that?" Bert asked.

"It's way out to the east," Ed said. "There are plenty of other spots where they could have stopped. That one puts them maybe 20 to 30 miles out of their way if they were planning to head north again in the morning. They must have wanted to go there, for some reason."

"They had a couple of hours' head start on us," Ashley said.

"So what?" Ed asked.

"I was trying to figure out how long before we'd get there."

Leila took the tablet from Ed and fiddled with it for a few seconds. "Our ETA's in four and a half hours."

"Wait," Ed said. "That makes no sense. They were only ten miles ahead of us when we started. We're making eight knots or better. Four and a half hours would be almost 40 miles."

"I told you, their boat's faster," Leila said. "Plus, they knew where they were going, so they may not have wandered off course as much."

"But we were using the autopilot," Ashley said. "That kept us on course, right? I don't get your point."

"The autopilot just held us on a constant compass course," Leila said. "The current and the wind have both been pushing us out to the west for the last ten hours."

Ashley frowned. "That much?"

"Yeah," Leila said. "If you drew a line from Bequia on the chart to represent the course we steered, we'd probably be ten miles or more to the west of the line."

"Why didn't you take that into account, then," Ed asked.

"If we had known our destination, we could have allowed for it. We'd have been sailing closer to the wind, though, so it would have slowed us down. It kind of evens out. That's the way sailing works. It's not like land navigation. Cars don't go sideways; they go where you point them."

"Should we start the engine?" Ed asked.

"We're going faster under sail than we would with the engine on," Leila said.

"What about using both?" Ashley asked.

"It won't help," Leila said. "We're already making hull speed."

"What's that mean?" Ed asked.

"It's as fast as the boat will go," Bert said. "No matter how hard you push it, it won't go through the water any faster than hull speed. That's a physical limitation of a displacement vessel."

"Sounds like bullshit to me," Ed said.

"It's true," Leila said, "but if you don't believe it, go ahead and start the engine. Smell the fumes and listen to the noise; I don't care. You're the boss."

"Watch it, woman," Ed said. "Make yourself useful and fix us some dinner."

Leila locked eyes with him, her jaw clenched. His face flushed, and after a few seconds, he looked away.

"Come on, Leila," Bert said. "I'll give you a hand."

"GLAD YOU SUGGESTED DINNER UNDER WAY," Dani said. "I'm beat."

"I think we all are; I could see Rick and Shellie were fading," Liz said. "It was a long day. I wanted to take a hot shower and crash when we got in."

"You weren't the only one. I thought Rick was going to fall face first into that seafood curry before it was over."

"Shellie's serious about learning to sail," Liz said. "It's hard to tear her away from the helm."

Dani smiled. They were lying in their berths on either side of the forward cabin, conversing across the narrow space in quiet tones. "I really do like her," Dani said. "Both of them, actually. But her especially."

"Because she's hooked on sailing?" Liz asked.

"Well, that's to her credit, all right, but it's more than that. She's ... I don't know how to put it. She's easy company, I guess. She's a good listener; she encourages me to tell her stuff without making me feel like I'm being interrogated. Or patronized."

"She's a nice person," Liz said. "Rick is, too."

"Speaking of Rick," Dani said, "did you get around to asking him whether he could think of a reason why someone would be following him?"

"No. I didn't get a good opening earlier, and then we discovered that the people on *Aquila* were definitely following us, so I didn't see the need to bring it up. You disagree? I thought once we knew ... " Liz shrugged.

"Well, knowing whether we're being followed was part of it, for sure," Dani said. "But now that we know, the question is why. Are they following him? Or have we stepped into some other mess without knowing it?"

"Other mess? Like what?" Liz asked. "Montalba's on his way to prison, and we haven't crossed anybody else lately."

"Guys like Montalba don't give up easily. Prison's a minor nuisance to people like him."

"But it was Connie that he was after, anyway," Liz said. "Why would he have somebody following us?"

"Revenge, maybe," Dani said. "He's got a reputation to protect. And for all we know, he's got people following Connie and Paul, too. I still can't believe she had the drop on him and let him live."

"You need to let that go, Dani. It's not healthy. Besides, you wouldn't have killed him in cold blood; you know Connie wouldn't either."

Dani frowned. "It would hardly have been in cold blood. He was — "

"We weren't there," Liz said. "We don't really know. And it's over; there's nothing to be gained by rehashing it. You can't change any of it."

"Right. I keep telling myself that. Maybe I'll eventually believe it. But why's *Aquila* following us, then?"

"Well, maybe one of them is obsessed by *Vengeance,"* Liz said. "She turns heads often enough. Even Shellie's fallen under her spell, and she wasn't even a sailor."

"Come on, Liz. That's a stretch. They broke in and — "

"Why do you say *they* broke in? It could have just been a

druggie."

"We've been over that," Dani said. "It had the earmarks of a professional job, and you know it."

"True," Liz said. "It probably wasn't a druggie. You're right. But that doesn't mean it was the people on *Aquila*."

"Odds are it was," Dani said. "But we'll know for sure if they show up here tomorrow. There's zero chance that they'll come here by coincidence."

"My bet is that we've shaken them," Liz said. "How would they know we were here? There are too many places between Bequia and here for them to check them all."

"Yes, I agree. If they show up here in the next few hours, we'll know they're following us. And that would almost guarantee that they have some way of tracking us."

"You think they left a tracker when they broke in?" Liz asked.

"You said they weren't the ones who broke in, Liz."

"I just said we didn't know for sure that they did. If they've put a tracker aboard, that would change my opinion."

"Okay. Good for you, Pollyanna." Dani grinned when Liz stuck her tongue out. "If they do show up here, I'm going to ask Phillip to get somebody aboard to sweep for trackers or eavesdropping stuff."

"Makes sense," Liz said.

"Think you can keep Rick and Shellie occupied in the morning? Give me a little time to handle that without having to explain it to them?"

"Okay," Liz said. "But if I'm going to ask about whether Rick thinks somebody's following them ... "

"Maybe you should hold off on that," Dani said. "They might think we're paranoid or something."

Liz giggled at that.

"What's funny?" Dani said, scowling.

"Nothing. I'm punchy; let's turn off the light and get some sleep."

17

"Caves?" Sharktooth asked.

The group was finishing breakfast on the veranda at Phillip's house. Rick had described his project to the others in some detail, with Dani and Liz pitching in when he spoke about trying to identify the island where the Moors had been.

"That's the latest clue," Rick said. "The Moors supposedly used a cave for storage. It was in the mountains that were near their settlement."

"And you think the settlement was in one of those three harbors?" Sharktooth asked. "Why just those three?"

Dani explained her theory about St. Lucia or Martinique as the most likely landfall for the Moors.

Sharktooth and Phillip both nodded their agreement.

"But why only those harbors?" Phillip asked. "There are a number of other places on St. Lucia and Martinique that come to mind."

"There's a small fragment of a hand-drawn map," Rick said. "It shows the settlement, camp, whatever it was, on the shoreline up inside a distinct cove. And Dani and Liz pointed out that they would have chosen a spot with fresh water. Plus, the mountains." He looked at Dani and raised his eyebrows.

"To me, Soufrière is the most likely," Dani said. "The sketch chart shows two prominent, distinctive peaks."

"The Pitons," Maureen said. "Is that what you're thinking?"

"Yes. There are hills that match up in the other two harbors, but they're much less dramatic than the Pitons. The sketch almost looks like a child's drawing of the Pitons."

"What about Jalousie?" Sharktooth asked.

"That's what I was thinking, too," Phillip said. "It's more protected."

"Where?" Rick asked.

"Jalousie's between the Pitons," Dani said.

"You didn't mention it," Rick said.

"No, I didn't. There are two reasons. Whoever drew the sketch went to some trouble to render those peaks — made them distinct from the other high ground — and they form a range line that points to where the sketch shows the camp. The intersection of the range and the shoreline is right where the Soufrière River flows into the harbor."

"Did they draw a line through the peaks?" Phillip asked.

"No, but it was so obvious they didn't need to," Dani said.

"Plus," Rick said, "that fragment is a reproduction of something that was in one of the original documents. A scribe could have overlooked the importance of a sight line when he was transcribing it."

"That would put the camp underneath the town of Soufrière," Sharktooth said. "Even the river's probably not in the same place after all the development that's gone on over the centuries. You'll have a hard time excavating anything."

"I'm not sure there's anything to excavate," Rick said. "We don't have any indication that the Moors built anything permanent; they had some kind of shore base, but these were seamen, traders. They were exploring, not colonizing."

"But what about this mullah they left behind," Maureen said. "Was he a missionary or something?"

"That's doubtful," Rick said. "The Moors weren't into proselytizing, as a rule. There's no mention in anything I've read that would explain why he and his group stayed behind. My guess is they were trying to maintain a trading presence. Khashkhash may have been planning to send a fleet back after he returned to Spain. His ships were described as laden with riches, so he would have been able to find plenty of support for a second voyage, I'd think. But we really don't know. I have to admit, I was skeptical about the chance of finding anything."

"You say 'I was,'" Sharktooth said. "Are you less skeptical now, for some reason?"

"Well, the notion that they had a cave where they were storing things gives me a little more hope that we might find some sign of their presence," Rick said. "Especially if the cave isn't well-known. And from what Dani and Liz said, caves aren't a common thing in the islands."

"About that cave ..." Sharktooth said. "There was a slave rebellion in St. Lucia in the early 1700s. It persisted for quite a while, and the runaways hid in a network of caves and tunnels. They intermarried with the remnants of the Caribs. There's still a village up on the southern side of Gros Piton called Fond Gens Libre — Valley of the Free People. Back in the old days, it was called Unionvale.

"They were called Maroons, those people. There's been some effort to turn the area into a tourist attraction, with guided hikes. There's one place they call Brigands' Cave, but the rumor is there are a lot of unexplored tunnels and such in the area."

"But those would have been more recent, wouldn't they?" Rick asked. "The tunnels, I mean. You're talking about hundreds of years after the Moors."

"Yes," Sharktooth said. "That's so, but the Maroons hid up there because it was rugged country and there were at least some caves to begin with. How much they dug them out is a big question. Nobody's put any effort into researching any of that. The government's focus is on beaches and sport fishing — marine related tourism. That's where the money comes from. People don't come to a tropical paradise to study the history of the colonial era — certainly not about slavery and slave rebellion. Besides, the island people have conflicted feelings about that era — the days of slavery, and even colonialism. Some of it's too recent, too raw."

"That's interesting," Rick said. "Dani mentioned that, too."

"Rick, are you watching the time?" Shellie asked. "I don't want to interrupt, but ..."

"Thanks, Shellie. No, I'd forgotten. I emailed a contact at the *Musée Départemental d'Archéologie Précolombienne* yesterday. I've got an invitation to drop in late this morning; I'm supposed to call if I can't make it. Is it doable?"

"Sure," Phillip said. "Once traffic clears, it won't take long to get you there."

"Is it a taxi ride?" Rick asked.

"You can take my Jeep," Phillip said.

"But I haven't a clue where I'm going," Rick said.

Dani nudged Liz under the table.

Liz said, "I'll drive you in. I can stop by the big grocery store on the way back and pick up a few things."

"Can we go to the boat first?" Rick asked. "I need to get my presentation."

"Sure," Dani said. "Liz can take you. I was planning on going with Sandrine to her office to handle our clearance paperwork. Is that okay, Sandrine?"

"But of course," Sandrine said. "Or I can just — "

"No, I'd like to come with you. I wanted to ask you about something."

"Okay, then," Sandrine said. "We should go before I am late."

"I'll catch up with you later, Liz," Dani said, as she and Sandrine excused themselves.

"We should go, too," Liz said. "Will I see you when I get back from the store, Maureen?"

"Yes. I'm going to sit right here and do some sketching. I think Sharktooth and Phillip were going to the marine supply place in Marin for something."

"Great," Dani said. "Can I meet you there after I finish clearing in?"

"That'll work," Phillip said. "We're going to need a dinghy, though, if Liz has the Jeep."

"Take ours," Liz said. "I'll trade keys with you when I bring Rick and Shellie back from the boat in a few minutes."

"DID you find what you were looking for?" Dani asked, meeting Sharktooth and Phillip as they were coming out of the marine supply store in Marin.

"Fish hooks," Sharktooth said, brandishing a small bag.

"What was on your mind?" Phillip asked. "You seemed to want to lose your guests."

"Was I that obvious?"

"Not to them, I'm sure," Phillip said. "But you wouldn't normally have insisted on going with Sandrine. She's handled your clearance without you before, plenty of times."

"I had a favor to ask her," Dani said. "I'm pretty sure we're being followed, and I didn't want to discuss it where Rick and Shellie could hear."

"You t'ink they up to something?" Sharktooth asked.

"No, not really. Liz thinks I'm being paranoid, and I don't want to alarm them. I like them quite a lot."

"They seem like nice folks," Phillip said. "You wanted Sandrine to set up a trigger in the customs system?"

"Yes, that's it."

"So you know who's following you?"

"They're on a bareboat charter out of Grenada. I already have their names, even. Americans. The boat's a Beneteau 44 named *Aquila*, from Econo Charters."

"How'd you get their names?" Sharktooth asked. "From the charter company?"

"No. Mrs. Walker spotted them and called one of her friends in customs in Bequia."

"Why do you think they're following you?" Phillip asked, as they walked toward the dingy dock at the big marina.

"I haven't any idea."

"Let me rephrase that," Phillip said. "What makes you think they're following you?"

Dani told him what she had learned from Mrs. Walker. "I don't think there's much doubt," she said. "Liz tried to come up with innocent explanations, but they're pretty lame. You know what a Pollyanna she is. We'll know for sure if they show up here in the next few hours."

"You came straight from Bequia, right?" Sharktooth asked.

"Yes. It's one thing for us, but for a 44-footer, that's a serious push. Figure it would have taken them a *few* hours longer, at least. There's no reason for them to have passed up stopping in St. Lucia unless they're on our trail."

"How would they know where you were headed?" Phillip asked.

"There is that; that's why I decided to come straight to Martinique."

"I thought your guests made that decision," Phillip said.

"We talked them into it. I wanted to find out if these people are following us, for sure. If they show up here, can you ask Clarence to have somebody scan *Vengeance* for a tracking device?"

"Sure," Phillip said. "Maybe we should do that anyway, even if they don't show up. They could still be tracking you from afar."

"Thanks. I hadn't thought of that. Too bad Liz isn't here."

"Why do you say that?" Sharktooth said.

"She wouldn't think I'm paranoid at all compared to Phillip."

"Paranoids have their reasons," Phillip said, grinning.

"Yes, we do," Dani said. "It would be nice to get it done without our guests knowing."

"You don't think they're the quarry, then?" Phillip asked.

"I don't know. I wanted Liz to feel them out; see if Rick had any idea why somebody might be tailing him."

"And?" Phillip asked.

"She hasn't had an opportunity to do it unobtrusively, yet. Like I said, we didn't want to alarm them unnecessarily. If *Aquila* checks in today, then we'll know, so we'll pretty well have to tell them somebody's chasing us. Or them."

As Dani squatted down to unlock the dinghy, she asked, "Does either of you know much about those electric lock picks?"

"That's overkill for stealing dinghies," Phillip said. "It's easier just to cut the chain. They're only worthwhile for those high-security locks with the multifaceted dimpled keys, like the one we put on *Vengeance*."

"That's why I'm asking. Before we left Grenada, somebody broke into her."

"Using one of those automatic picks?"

"Well, they didn't do any damage, and all our keys are accounted for. That locksmith you got for us last time we were here said the only way to pick it was with one of those."

"Not just any one of those will even do it," Phillip said. "The ones that will open your lock are out-of-sight expensive. Did they steal anything?"

"I interrupted them. They took a handheld VHF and a GPS."

"Did you get a look at the thief?" Sharktooth asked.

"No, I was a dumbass. Went down the companionway and got knocked cold from behind."

"Think it's related to the people on *Aquila*?" Phillip asked.

"I'm trying to keep an open mind, but it's hard not to think that."

"It sure is," Phillip said. "Let's go back to the house, and I'll call Clarence and see if he's got somebody free this morning who can check out *Vengeance.*"

~

"DID you leave them at the museum?" Dani asked, when Liz joined them on Phillip's veranda.

"Yes. I went in with them for a few minutes and met the curator. He has a full day mapped out for them. He's giving them a tour of the museum, and then he has them set up with whoever has the diary of that missionary priest Rick told us about."

"When do you have to pick them up?" Dani asked.

"I don't. They're going to have dinner with the curator and his wife. He'll bring them by here around ten p.m."

"Great," Dani said.

"Why 'great?'" Liz asked. "I thought you were enjoying their company."

"I am, but we've got work to do."

"What's that? What work?"

"I'm not sure yet," Dani said. "Clarence sent Marie LaCroix out with a couple of techs to sweep *Vengeance.*"

"Sweep?" Liz frowned. "You mean for bugs?"

"That, too," Dani said. "But mostly for a tracker."

"So, *Aquila's* here?" Liz asked.

"Not yet," Phillip said. "But they could still be tracking you."

"I hadn't thought of that," Liz said.

"Nor had I," Dani said. "Phillip pointed it out."

"Hmm," Liz said. "Finding a tracker would just prove *somebody* is tracking us. It won't prove that it's *Aquila.*"

Dani rolled her eyes, and Phillip laughed.

"She's right," Sharktooth said. "Could be somebody else. You don' know for sure."

"Did you talk to Sandrine about watching for them?" Liz asked.

"Yes. She'll let us know. We're all going to meet her for lunch at the marina restaurant," Dani said.

Liz glanced at her watch. "What time?"

"Noon," Dani said.

"I could use a cup of coffee," Liz said. "Anybody else?"

"Yes," Phillip said.

"Me, too," Sharktooth said.

"I'll make a pot," Phillip said, standing up. "Want anything else?"

"Coffee's fine for me," Dani said, as her phone rang. "Sandrine," she said, touching the screen. "Behave. You're on the speaker," she said, answering the call.

"Who is listening?"

"Just us," Phillip said. "No guests."

"Maureen?"

"Taking a walk," Sharktooth said. "She wanted to sketch some of the street scenes in Ste. Anne."

"Okay. *Aquila* just cleared in at the internet café. The one in Ste. Anne," Sandrine said. "They listed their arrival time as eleven p.m. last night. The four people you told me about are aboard, Dani."

"Do you know where *Aquila* is?" Dani asked.

"*Mouillage de Ste. Anne.* That's all they put on the form."

"Thanks," Dani said.

"Are we still on for lunch?" Phillip asked.

"Yes, for sure," Sandrine said. "Bye-bye. It is busy now. See you soon." She disconnected the call.

"So," Liz said. "You were right, Dani."

"We need to find them and keep an eye on them," Dani said.

"Not a good idea. They know us by sight."

"Right. I forgot that."

"How?" Sharktooth asked. He saw their puzzled looks. "How do they know you by sight?"

Liz told him and Phillip about spotting two of the people from *Aquila* watching them from shore while they were anchored at Petit Nevis.

"I'll see if Clarence can arrange surveillance," Phillip said.

"While you're talking to him, tell him to warn Marie that they may be watching *Vengeance*," Dani said. "It would be better if they didn't see her people aboard."

"Roger that," Phillip said.

18

"Clarence thought I would find you here," Marie LaCroix said, as she walked up to the table where Phillip and Sandrine sat with Liz and Dani.

"Join us," Dani said. "We haven't ordered yet; we just sat down."

Marie pulled out a chair next to Dani and sat. "There is a satellite tracking device aboard *Vengeance*."

"I knew it!" Dani said. "Did you remove it?"

"No. Clarence and I decided not to. He called to warn me that we might be watched by these people who are following you. We put on a show of washing the decks and polishing the stainless steel to explain our presence. If you want, it is easy to remove, but we thought it might be better to leave it, depending on your plans."

"I think you and Clarence made the right call," Dani said. "Where is it?"

"On top of your life raft canister, under the canvas cover."

"I'm surprised we didn't see a bulge, or something," Liz said.

"It's not one of those cheap ones that all the yachts are using now," Marie said. "It's a type that I've only seen in the Middle East.

Four millimeters thick, with the footprint of a cigarette package. It was developed in Israel, by my former employers."

"What about battery life?" Phillip asked. "There can't be much room for a battery in a package that size."

"It depends," Marie said. "But they are very efficient. It sleeps unless it is queried, so the battery lasts a long time."

"Then somebody has to be close enough to query it," Dani said.

Marie shook her head. "It is queried by satellite. The people tracking you could be anywhere. Or there could be multiple people with access."

"Where would somebody get a device like that?" Liz asked. "Not something you order from the internet, I'm guessing."

"I don't know," Marie said. "But you are right about the internet. It's not like the ones that are sold all over the place for a couple of hundred dollars. These are quite expensive, and not only that. They require that someone has the ability and the access to program a satellite network. Unlike the commercially available ones, they don't come with a ready-made webpage that you log into for location tracking."

"What if we decide to disable it?" Dani asked. "How would we do that? It doesn't sound like there's an on-off switch."

Marie smiled. "No. The only reliable way is to physically destroy it. Or fasten it to a rock and drop it in deep water. Moving it to a randomly chosen vessel is another option."

"Did you find anything else?" Dani asked. "Bugs, video cameras?"

"No. You're clean except for the tracker."

"Were you able to spot *Aquila*?" Dani asked.

"Yes. They are anchored about 200 meters to your northwest. When I last checked with my people, one couple was aboard and the others were walking around Ste. Anne."

"So, they can see *Vengeance*?" Liz asked.

"Except for other boats in the way, yes," Marie said. "For sure, they can see you coming and going in the dinghy, even if they may have some trouble seeing what you are doing while you're aboard."

"Do you have time for this?" Phillip asked. "Clarence and I didn't discuss how long we might need surveillance."

"It is no problem. I am between assignments. I am happy to have this project; my team can use the experience. Best to keep them busy, so their skills stay sharp. Besides, this is easy duty. We are using another white sailboat with blue canvas as our base. We're anchored between *Vengeance* and *Aquila*. We look like another bare-boat charter."

"Let's order lunch," Sharktooth said, waving the waitress over.

"One last thing, Marie," Dani said.

"Yes?"

"If they leave *Aquila*, let me know, please."

Marie smiled. "*Bien sûr*. You are planning to visit, perhaps?"

"Perhaps."

"Let me know if you need help."

"Thanks. I think Liz and I can handle it, but I'll call if we need you. I'd rather have you watching to warn us if they're coming back unexpectedly."

"DID you see any sign of them in town?" Ed asked, as Bert and Leila tied up their dinghy alongside *Aquila*.

"No, but we were mostly scouting to get a feel for the place. We weren't looking for them specifically," Bert said.

"Why?" Leila asked. "Were they ashore?"

"Yeah. They've been busy since they went ashore while we were eating breakfast," Ashley said.

"Their dinghy was still tied up in the same place when Bert and I went ashore to clear in. What happened since then?"

"Liz brought the Everetts back to the boat not long after you went ashore," Ed said. "They only stayed a few minutes, and then they went back into town. All three of them."

"So Dani wasn't with them?" Leila asked.

"That's right."

"Wonder where she was?" Bert asked. "We pretty well covered the town. Looked in all the restaurants and shops and didn't see her."

"I don't know," Ashley said. "Maybe ten minutes after the three of them tied up, two men walked down the dock and took the dinghy. A white man, average build, maybe mid-forties, and a gigantic black guy, bald on top with dreadlocks to his waist."

"Could you see where they went?" Bert asked.

"They took off in the direction of Cul-de-Sac Marin, toward the marina and all the shops," Ashley said. "They came back maybe 45 minutes later with Dani."

"Back to the boat?" Leila asked.

"No, back to the dock. The three of them walked into town. The dinghy's still there at the dock."

"Yeah, we saw it," Leila said. "But we didn't know it had been moved. They must still be in town, somewhere."

"That's our guess," Ed said. "It shouldn't be hard to spot the three of them. That black guy's hard to miss."

"Sounds like it," Bert said. "We didn't see anybody like that, though."

"What's in town, anyway?" Ashley asked. "The guidebook makes it sound kind of touristy."

"It is," Leila said. "A couple of art galleries, lots of gift shops and restaurants. If it works out, there are some places we could try for dinner."

"That depends on what they're up to," Ed said. "It would be good if we could find out who those two men are, and where the Everetts are. We haven't seen them since they were in the dinghy with Liz."

"Nor have we seen Liz," Ashley said.

"So nobody's been back to the boat since she stopped by with the Everetts?" Leila asked.

"None of them," Ashley said. "There was a cleaning crew that went aboard mid-morning. They were — "

"A cleaning crew?" Leila asked.

"Yeah. Guess that's the way life is if you're running a million-dollar charter yacht. Two people. A man and a woman. They washed down the deck and polished all the metal," Ed said. "Then they took off, headed into Cul-de-Sac Marin."

"So those two women must bring *Vengeance* in here often," Leila said. "Cleaning crew, and the two guys you saw with Dani. Think they're boyfriends of Dani and Liz, maybe?"

"It didn't look like there was any romance there," Ashley said. "But they didn't look like they were strangers, either. I mean, the two guys took their dinghy; they must have had a key. Surely it was chained, and they went right to it — no looking around, trying to figure out which one they were supposed to take."

"Who knows?" Ed asked.

"I have an idea," Ashley said.

"What?" Ed asked.

"You and I should go in to town and see if we can spot any of them. We know they're there, and we know what the two men look like. Besides, I'd like to get off the boat and stretch my legs."

"That sounds reasonable," Ed said.

"Check out the restaurants," Leila said. "There are several where we could have dinner on a patio and keep an eye on the boats and the dinghy dock."

"All right," Ed said. "Let's go, Ash."

19

"Well, wherever they are, they aren't walking around Ste. Anne," Ashley said.

"They must have taken a taxi somewhere," Ed said. "Their dinghy hasn't moved all afternoon. We should have been ready to follow them this morning."

"This doesn't feel right for the kind of place Everett would be looking for," Ashley said.

"What do you mean? We can't tell a damn thing about what this place would have been like a thousand years ago," Ed said, frowning.

"I didn't mean the place itself, Ed. I was thinking about their behavior. When Everett came back to the boat this morning, he picked up a briefcase, remember?"

"Yeah. So?"

"He's been gone all day, with his wife."

"And Liz," Ed said.

"But not Dani, and she met up with those two men and went somewhere. This doesn't look like they're searching for something. My bet is Everett's doing some kind of administrative work.

Maybe getting a permit to excavate. Or maybe research, like at a library or somewhere."

"With Liz, though?"

"They could have rented a car. She probably knows her way around the island."

"But what about Dani?"

"I don't know, Ed. I'm just saying this seems like prep work, the way they're acting."

"Maybe so, but where the hell could they be? It'll be dark in another hour."

"Yeah, you're right. We should get Leila and Bert ashore and have an early dinner. We can see their dinghy well enough from here. When they come back, we'll be ready to go, or close enough, in case they leave the island."

They were sitting at the bar in a hotel that had a dining patio overlooking the anchorage.

"Okay," Ed said. "I'll get us a table. You go get Bert and Leila and bring them back. Listen up for your phone, though. If anything happens, I'll call you."

"On my way," Ashley said. "Call them and tell them to get ready, will you?"

"Yeah, sure." Ed took out his phone and made the call as he watched Ashley walking toward the town dock.

"Leila?"

"Yeah. You got something?"

"No. Ashley's on her way out to pick you and Bert up. We're going to have a quick dinner here. I'm getting a table where we can keep an eye out for Everett."

"Okay. There's been no activity aboard their boat, for what that's worth."

"Yeah, okay. See you soon."

He disconnected and turned to the bartender, making arrangements for a table for four that provided a view of the dock. He nursed his beer, watching as a waitress set up the table he'd chosen.

In a few minutes, the table was ready. He picked up his unfinished beer from the bar and took it to the table. He sat so that he could see *Vengeance's* dinghy. In the distance, he saw Leila and Bert climbing into their dinghy. He was surprised that Ashley wasn't in sight, but she appeared in the cockpit in a few seconds. He shook his head, wondering why she'd gone aboard the boat.

Less than ten minutes later, she walked in with Leila and Bert. As she pulled out a chair, Ashley said, "Sorry for the delay, but I had an idea on the way out there."

"What's that?" Ed asked.

"I snapped some pictures with the telephoto lens this morning while we were keeping watch."

"I don't remember that," he said.

"You were below, doing something on the computer. Anyway, I wanted to take a look at them; see what I got."

Ed shrugged. "Okay, but why now?"

"Take a look," she said, fiddling with her smartphone and handing it to him.

"I'll be damned," he said. "Any others?"

"Yeah. Swipe right to left."

"I wish to hell you'd remembered these earlier," he said, turning the phone so that Leila and Bert could see the photos.

"Those are the guys who took the dinghy? The one from *Vengeance*, I mean?" Leila asked.

"Yes," Ashley said.

"I thought Dani was with them." Bert said.

"No, that was later. The camera battery died as I was taking these, and I put it away and forgot about it. These were when they first took the dinghy."

"I see what you mean about the guy with the dreadlocks. He's one big man," Leila said.

"Yes," Ashley said, reaching for her phone. "Should I show these to the bartender and see if he recognizes either of them?"

"Go for it," Ed said.

Ashley got up and walked over to the bar, greeting the man who was polishing glassware. The others watched as he took the phone from her and studied it. After a moment, he shook his head and spoke to her in a soft voice. She nodded, and he called the waitress over. He showed her the phone and said something to her. She looked up at him, and then turned to face Ashley, shaking her head and shrugging.

Ashley smiled and thanked them. She put the phone in her purse and came back to the table.

"No luck?" Ed asked.

"No, but I think they may have been lying. He spoke to her in some kind of pidgin French, so I couldn't tell what he said, but I could read their eye contact and body language."

"I agree," Leila said. "I caught the look he gave her, too."

"Should we catch one of them later and put a little pressure on?" Ed asked.

"Yeah," Bert said. "We could — "

"No," Leila said. "I don't agree. Chances are we'd do more harm than good. It's not clear that those two men have anything to do with Everett's mission. Interrogating innocent locals to identify two men would attract attention that we don't want."

"We could make them talk," Bert said. "I think we should — "

"Tell him, Ed," Leila said. "I'm getting bored with him."

"Leila's our tactical operator; she decides the use of force, deadly or otherwise. Clear?" Ed locked eyes with him.

Bert dropped his gaze after a few seconds and looked at Leila. "Sorry," he said. "I didn't ... I only wanted — "

"Shut up and read the menu," Leila said. "Get a grip on yourself. I'm not going to hurt you. Not unless it's necessary."

~

"WHO CALLED WHILE I WAS INSIDE?" Liz asked, as she joined Dani and Phillip at the table on the veranda with Sharktooth and Maureen. "I heard your phone."

"Marie," Dani said. "She had a quick update on the surveillance. One couple spent the afternoon aboard *Aquila*, and the others searched the town, probably looking for us."

"Or the Everetts," Liz said.

"They're part of *us*," Dani said. She paused for a few seconds, looking at Liz. "Unless you've changed your mind about them. You think they're up to something?"

Liz chuckled. "No, I haven't changed my mind about them. They searched the town, did they?"

"Yes. Marie's people tailed them. They didn't talk to anybody, but they checked out all the shops. Bars and restaurants, too. The couple on *Aquila* took turns in the cockpit with binoculars, watching *Vengeance* and the dinghy dock."

"That must have been boring for them," Liz said. "Too bad all four of them didn't come to town."

"Yes. The day's not over, yet. Maybe they'll decide to go out to dinner. What time were Rick and Shellie expecting to be back?"

Liz shrugged. "Late. He said around ten o'clock, remember."

"Good," Dani said. "If they do leave their boat unattended, we can check it out without telling Rick and Shellie."

"Shouldn't we let Marie's team do that?" Liz asked.

"We're likely to spot something they'd miss," Dani said. "They're lacking context, and I don't know how to tell them what to look for, what might be important."

"What you t'ink you gonna find?" Sharktooth asked.

"That's the problem," Dani said. "I won't know until I see it."

Sharktooth nodded, and they were silent for a minute or two. Maureen had been looking out over the anchorage, sketching idly while they talked. She broke the silence. "Look at that sunset. You must sit out here every evening and wait for that, Phillip."

"As often as I can. It's not always this good, but it's rarely disappointing."

"Beautiful," Liz said. "It reminds me of your painting, Sharktooth. The one in our saloon."

Sharktooth looked away and began to pick at a hangnail. "You ver' kind," he said, almost whispering.

"Sharktooth," Dani said in a sharp tone.

He looked up at her from under his heavy brow. "Mmm?"

"Every guest we've had aboard has admired that painting. Quit being so hard on yourself. It's a — "

She was interrupted by the ringing of her cellphone. Glancing at the screen, she said, "Marie." She got up and moved away from the group to take the call. In less than a minute, she came back to the table. "We got our wish," she said.

"What's going on?" Sandrine asked, coming from inside the house. "Have I missed the cocktail hour? It was very busy at — " she stopped when she caught the expression on Phillip's face. "Sorry, I am interrupting something. Please, Dani?"

"It's okay. Marie just called. The people on *Aquila* are all ashore, getting ready to order dinner. Liz and I need to get moving. Phillip can fill you in."

"Do we need to go to *Vengeance* first?" Liz asked. "For tools?"

"No," Dani said. "My rigging knife should be more than a match for the companionway lock on that boat."

"Want a ride to your dinghy?" Sharktooth asked.

"No, that's another problem," Dani said. "They're sitting where they can see the dinghy dock."

"I've got a dinghy in the marina, with *Kayak Spirit*," Phillip said.

"If they can see the dinghy dock, they might be able to see their boat," Dani said. "We'd be better off swimming out from the beach down the hill. Do you have snorkel gear and wetsuits?"

"Sure, let's go downstairs," Phillip said.

"How about a dry bag?" Dani asked. "I'm going to steal whatever I can find, like phones, computers, whatever."

"I've got you covered," Phillip said. "Sharktooth, tell Sandrine what's happening, would you? Come on, Dani, Liz."

20

"You have the makings of a thief," Liz said, as she and Dani made their way up the path from the beach toward Phillip's villa.

"You sound surprised," Dani said.

"I expected you to take the computer, but what else is in that dry bag? It's bulging."

"Come on, Liz. Remember how suspicious it was that they didn't take Rick's computer when it was left in plain view? I took everything a druggie might take. Even an envelope full of cash."

"How much cash?"

"I didn't stop to count it. Leaving all the valuables when they hit *Vengeance* was an amateurish mistake. These people are idiots."

"Nobody's going to say you were an amateur, but why did you say '*these people* are idiots?'"

"They're the ones who broke into *Vengeance*."

"You don't know that for sure," Liz said.

"Yes, I do. I found our VHF and GPS under their chart table."

"You didn't say anything about that. Why not?"

"I just did; we were in a hurry to get out of there, remember?

And since we got ashore, you've been ragging on me. I never got a chance to tell you what I found."

"Okay. So now that we're safe and dry, what else did you steal, you little thief?"

"Hey, don't make out like I'm the only guilty one; you were an accessory, or whatever they call it. Standing lookout's just as bad as breaking and entering."

"I don't know about that. And speaking of breaking, you went out of your way to damage the companionway doors. That was unnecessary."

"I wanted it to look authentic. Besides, I'm still pissed off about the knot on my head. I hope the charter company makes them pay."

"You know they won't; they're insured for theft, I'm sure. Now, answer me. What else did you take?"

"I got a laptop, our stuff, *their* handheld VHF, a satellite phone, a little bag of burglar's tools, including that automatic lock pick. Plus, a bunch of stuff that was in the drawer with the money and their passports. I just scooped all that out. I did a quick check in the cabins, but I didn't find anything there, so I ... oh yeah. I got their camera. It was in one of the cabins. The one with the telephoto lens we saw them using to spy on us at Petit Nevis."

"I can't wait to dump the dry bag and see what you got. Sorry to pick on you, but it was too tempting to pass up."

"Sure. Like you never get a chance to pick on me. There's one other thing."

"That you stole?"

"No. About the people. The two women are sharing the aft stateroom, and the men each have a forward cabin. And the forwards are both doubles, for what it's worth."

"So they aren't couples, then," Liz said.

"Well, I don't know about the women, but the men look to be single."

"You think the women are a couple?"

"Who knows? I just thought it was kind of odd, that's all. There are two double berths in the aft stateroom. There's no reason to think the women are a couple, but they could be."

"Were there only three staterooms?"

"Yes."

"Maybe they drew straws, and the women lost," Liz said.

"Or maybe there's some kind of male prerogative at work. We may discover more when we get a look at this stuff." Dani opened the gate into Phillip's yard. "What time is it?"

"It's still early," Liz said, checking her watch. "Seven thirty-five. Why?"

"I just wondered how much time we have before Rick and Shellie get back."

"Should we tell them what's going on?" Liz asked.

"I don't know," Dani said, knocking on the door into the villa. "I thought we might have a better feel for that after we went through all this stuff."

"Looks like you made it back okay," Maureen said, opening the door. "Come on in. The boys are in the kitchen with Sandrine. She and Sharktooth are cooking dinner."

"Thanks for waiting on us," Liz said. "Have we got time to lose the wetsuits and rinse off the saltwater?"

"Sure. I put some fresh towels in the downstairs bathroom. Phillip said you both kept some clothes in the cupboard in there. Just come up to the kitchen when you're ready, and don't rush. There's plenty of time. Sharktooth and Sandrine are arguing about how to season the curry."

"ED!" Leila called, as she stepped into *Aquila's* cockpit.

"Yeah? I'll be up in a second. Let me lock the dinghy."

"Somebody broke in while we were gone," Ashley said, joining Leila in the cockpit.

"Broke in?" Bert said, as he stepped over the coaming. "Shit, I'll say. Busted the door."

"Careful," Ed said. Using his cellphone's flashlight, he examined the damage. "Nothing subtle about that."

"I didn't see anybody on the boat," Leila said. "I kept an eye on her the whole time we were at dinner. No dinghies even came close to her,"

Ed knelt, running a finger over the nonskid fiberglass surface of the bridge deck. "Wet. They swam out and climbed aboard."

"But I didn't see anybody," Leila said, again.

"No. Somebody that was sneaky enough could slither under the lifelines and roll into the cockpit without silhouetting themselves against the skyline."

"I'll check below," Leila said, "and make sure nobody's still here. You wait here until I call."

"Go," Ed said. "But if you catch somebody, don't kill them before we question them."

Leila nodded and slipped down the companionway ladder.

"You think this is related to our mission?" Ashley asked.

"I don't know. It might be, but probably not."

"Clear below," Leila called. She turned on the lights and the others joined her below deck. "Spread out and check to see if anything's missing."

"I'll do the nav station," Ed said, lifting the top of the chart table. "Bert, take our cabin. Leila, you and Ash check your cabin."

Three minutes later, they gathered in the main saloon.

"Bert?" Ed asked. "What about our cabins?"

"They went through everything. Tossed all our stuff on the floor. It's a mess, but I don't think they took anything. Not that there was anything worth stealing."

"Leila?" Ed asked.

"Same in our cabin, but they took the camera."

"I think I left it out when I transferred those pictures to my phone," Ashley said.

"No matter," Leila said. "They would have found it anyway."

"Yeah," Ed said. "They were thorough. They got everything worth taking from the nav center, except the built-in electronics."

"Everything?" Leila asked.

"Yeah. Our handheld radio, the sat phone, that radio and GPS that Ashley stole from *Vengeance*. Our computer, and — "

"The computer?" Leila interrupted. "That's not good. At least it's encrypted, right?"

"I guess," Ed said. "I don't know. It's however it came. Password protected. And all our papers — passports, the emergency cash. They cleaned us out."

"Shit!" Bert said. "Can we call Tehran on a cellphone?"

"We can, but only in an emergency. They aren't encrypted," Ed said. "Why?"

"We need passports; we're stuck without them," Bert said.

"Tehran's not going to help with that. They could do forged ones, but the ones we had are real. It's too risky to use forged ones down here. Most of these islands are able to scan for chips. It's okay — "

"How the hell is it okay?" Bert asked.

"Calm down, Bert," Leila said. "We're U.S. citizens, remember? We'll call the consulate and get replacements. Not that big a deal."

"Yeah, but we can't go anywhere until we — "

"It doesn't take long. Relax," Ed said. "We've got the tracker if Everett leaves. Leila's right. This looks like a typical theft from an unoccupied yacht. We just need to act like typical tourists. Leila?"

"Yes?"

"You want to be a typical tourist and call the cops? Report this? We may need something from them to get replacement passports."

"Yes. I'll call from on deck; you keep our village idiot quiet, okay?"

"Hey! I outrank you, you mouthy bitch. Don't you — "

Leila appeared to flinch, barely moving. Bert doubled over and gasped for breath, collapsing to the deck. Leila rubbed the knuckles of her right hand and nudged him with her foot. "He's a liability."

Ed nodded. "I'll talk to him."

"I warned him once before. If this doesn't convince him, I'll kill him next time. I'd do it now, but we're already short-handed. Let him know he's on borrowed time, please."

"I will," Ed said. "Ease up. The cops may want to visit. We don't have time to deal with a corpse right now."

Leila nodded and went up on deck to make her call.

21

"So what did you find out?" Phillip asked, as Liz and Dani came into the kitchen.

"We haven't had time to look, yet," Dani said, setting the dry bag on the island in the middle of the kitchen. She unrolled the folded-over top and unzipped it. Upending the bag, she let the contents slide out.

"Laptop," Sharktooth said. "May I?"

"Sure," Dani said.

He opened the lid and the screen came to life, asking for a user i.d. and a password. "Looks like a job for Marie's bunch," he said, closing the lid. "No point messing with it; we'd risk it wiping the disk if it's secured well. Shall I call her, see if she got somebody can pick it up?"

"Sure," Dani said. She fanned out the four passports out on the counter.

Sandrine picked one up and examined it with a practiced eye. "I think this is real, but I will take them to the office tomorrow and see if they scan."

"But they already checked in, didn't they?" Liz asked. "Wouldn't they have been scanned already?"

"Yes. But at the internet café, remember?"

Liz frowned.

"They do not scan with the machine. They only make a copy of the first page."

"Okay," Liz said. "What does the machine do, then? I thought it just read the barcode."

"More than that; it records the information on the chip; these are chipped passports. Very easy to spot a forgery, unless they are stolen and modified. Even then, if the theft has been reported to the issuing agency, we would know."

Dani had arranged the remaining items on the countertop. She picked up a bulging envelope and shook out the contents. There were several stacks of $100 bills, held together with rubber bands. She thumbed through one of them.

"Used, but still fresh and crisp," she said. "The serial numbers aren't sequential, either."

"How much?" Phillip asked.

"Twenty bills, ten stacks. Looks like $20,000, if each stack's the same."

The others each took a bundle and flipped through it.

"Twenty," Sharktooth said.

"Yes," Sandrine said.

Maureen and Liz and Phillip nodded, their counts agreeing as well.

Dani had counted the remaining four packets while the others were working. "Twenty thousand, then."

"A lot of money for innocent tourists," Sandrine said. "But divided among the four of them, less than what must be reported on the clearance forms."

Maureen held the camera. "Look," she said, turning it so the others could see the screen on the back. "Pictures of *Vengeance*, somewhere." She scrolled until they saw Dani and Liz sitting in the cockpit. "Tough to see you in the shade," she said.
"That you?"

"Yes. We saw them up on the hill over Friendship Bay," Liz said.

"We were anchored at Petit Nevis," Dani said.

Maureen scrolled again. "Looks like Rick and Shellie, walking around ashore. Are they at the old try-works, then?"

"Exactly," Liz said.

Maureen scrolled through several more shots of the same subjects, stopping when she saw one of Sharktooth climbing down into a dinghy. Phillip was already seated, twisted at the waist to start the outboard. A few more shots showed clear images of their faces.

"This morning," Phillip said.

"Mm-hmm," Sharktooth said. "That explains the phone call."

"What phone call?" Dani asked.

"While you were out robbing yachts, I got a call from the bartender at the hotel where they're having dinner," Phillip said. "One of the women showed him and the waitress pictures of Sharktooth and me. Asked if they knew who we were."

"Of course they didn't recognize you," Dani said, grinning.

"No, of course not." Phillip winked. "But the bartender stepped into the kitchen and called us, just in case somebody else might mistake those two in the pictures for us."

"DID YOU GET BERT STRAIGHTENED OUT?" Leila asked.

"Yeah. He threw up once he came to," Ed said. "He's sacked out for the night."

"Where's Ash?" she asked.

"In your cabin. She's done for the day, too."

"What the hell's the matter with Bert, anyway?" she asked.

"He mumbled something about being second in command, and I explained to him that you only report through our chain of command for admin stuff."

"He should have already known that."

"I agree. But he's got this gender role thing firmly fixed in his mind."

"Doesn't he get that we can't play those games in the outside world? If I wear a hijab and walk behind you guys, it'll blow our cover."

"I explained that to him. But he's like a lot of guys. One of the attractions to going back to Iran is that whole world view. Keep women in their place."

"Yeah. That's why I'm here. If I were living in Iran, I'd be throwing bombs at assholes like him."

"You should be careful saying stuff like that. Word could get back."

"You're not going to tell; I've got you by the balls, and you know it."

"I'm not your problem."

"You think Ashley is?" she asked.

"She could be," Ed said.

"No, she's with me." Leila smiled.

"As long as we're leveling with each other, why did you go back if you feel that way? You could have stayed in the States and had an easy life. Why take on this whole thing?"

"Because, Iran is my country, and I and a lot of other people like me are going to take it back."

"Back to the days of the Shah, you mean?"

"That wasn't perfect, but they had some things right. These pinhead mullahs running things now are nuts, with their ultra-conservative bullshit."

"Why are you working for them, then?"

"I'm not."

"What are you saying? Are you ... "

She shook her head. "I'm loyal to my country; not to Islam. When the time is right, we're going to change things."

"Your country? Which one?"

"You don't need to ask, do you?"

"Why do you trust me, Leila?"

"We covered that. You'd be stoned to death if I showed those pictures to Rahimi."

"But I'd have to be back in Iran before what happened could come into play. I could ... "

"If you keep talking like this, you and Bert may both have an accident."

"You know I won't say anything, Leila. I'm just curious."

"Enough with your curiosity."

"What did the cops say?" Ed asked, after an uneasy silence. "You were on the phone for a long time. I take it they aren't coming out here?"

"No. The four of us need to go to their office in Marin in the morning and make a formal report. They'll give us some paperwork that we can take to the U.S. Consulate in Fort-de-France; it's only a short taxi ride, they said. The Consulate will work with the U.S. Embassy in Barbados, and we should get replacement passports in a day or two. This happens often enough so they have a regular process."

"Really?" Ed asked. "It's that common?"

"Yeah. They said the sneak thieves target bareboat charters because tourists are careless with their belongings."

"What *about* our belongings? Any chance of recovering anything?"

"Oh, the guy I talked with gave me a song and dance about how if we had the serial numbers and so forth, they'd be on the lookout, check out the people known to receive stolen property, that kind of thing. When I pressed him, he admitted that was bullshit, especially here."

"Here? In Martinique?"

"In Ste. Anne. In Martinique, too, but especially in Ste. Anne. It's only 20 miles across the channel to St. Lucia. People do the trip all the time in little fishing boats. He said most of the thieves come over here from St. Lucia because the pickings are better."

"Tomorrow morning, huh?" Ed said.

"Yeah."

"Here's hoping Everett doesn't decide to leave tomorrow."

"We've got the tracker. Good thing Ash had the tablet in her purse. Speaking of that kind of thing, what about Tehran?"

"I sent an email from my phone. There's a computer store in Fort-de-France run by a guy who's supposedly from Pakistan. He'll be expecting me. Besides the computer, he'll have a sat phone and some cash for us."

"Good. So we're set, once we get the new passports. I'm beat. See you in the morning."

"How was your day?" Liz asked, as she answered the knock on Phillip's door to find Rick and Shellie.

"Great," Rick said. "Thanks for all your help. Sorry we're so late."

"Oh, that's no problem. We just finished dinner ourselves. Come on in." Liz swung the door wide and stepped out of their way.

As they came in, Dani and Marie LaCroix entered the foyer from the living room.

"Call me as soon as you crack it," Dani was saying.

Marie smiled at the newcomers. "Good night, Liz. Dani, that may be as soon as a couple of hours. Maybe two or three a.m. You do not wish for me to wait until morning?"

"No. I'd rather know who the hell they are as soon as we can. We may need to take action of some kind, even if it's just to ditch the tracker and run for it."

"Very well," Marie said.

"Run for it?" Rick was frowning as he stared at the laptop in Marie's hand. "Excuse me, but what's going on?"

"Sorry, Rick, Shellie," Liz said. "Meet our friend Marie LaCroix." Marie nodded at the Everetts, and Liz said, "Rick and Shellie Everett, Marie."

The three shook hands, and Marie said, "Well, I must hurry, then." She nodded again and walked out the door.

"We need to talk," Dani said. "Come into the living room and have a seat."

"Would you like an after-dinner drink, coffee, or anything?" Liz asked, as the Everetts sat down on a couch. "We may be here a little while."

Rick looked at Shellie. "No thanks, I'm okay," she said.

"I'm fine," Rick said. "Did something happen?"

"I'll bring you up to speed, and then we can discuss what you'd like to do," Dani said. "Okay?"

"Sure," Rick said. "Is this about my project, somehow?"

"We aren't sure, but it may be. We're still working on that," Dani said. "let me tell you what we know so far." She gave a three-minute summary of what had happened since *Vengeance* had been broken into. "Now, I think that's everything that you don't already know," she said. "Questions?"

"Wow!" Rick said, shaking his head. "That's a lot to take in. So who are these people, anyway?"

"We have their passports, so we have a good start on that. Sandrine will find out more in the morning after she verifies that the passports are real. And who knows what Marie may find on their computer? Sometime tomorrow morning, we should know a lot more about them."

"Who is Marie? Really?" Shellie asked. "Is she some kind of cop?"

Dani looked at Phillip. "She works with a former business associate of mine," Phillip said. "They do contract work for the government. Forensics, and so forth."

"They're helping us out as a favor to Phillip," Dani said. "Plus, Liz and I have gotten to be friends with Marie; she sails with us when we're all three not busy. And she and her people are between assignments right now, so they offered to keep an eye on *Aquila*."

"I can't believe you broke into their boat," Shellie said.

"They're spying on us," Dani said, "and they broke into *Vengeance*, and attacked me in the bargain. It's personal, at this point."

"How do you know they're the ones who broke into *Vengeance*?" Rick asked.

"They had the stuff that was stolen from us," Dani said.

"Weren't you scared?" Shellie asked. "Suppose they had come back?"

"Scared? No. Liz was with me; she was in the cockpit, keeping watch. And Marie's people are on a boat that's anchored between us and *Aquila*."

"Still," Rick said, "these people sound dangerous."

"I can take care of myself," Dani said, "as long as nobody blindsides me. And I'm not about to let that happen again."

Shellie frowned.

Rick shook his head. "So, what now?"

"Now that you know what we know," Liz said, "we want to ask you a question."

"Okay," Rick said. "Shoot."

"We have to wonder if there's something about your project that might cause these people to be spying on you," Liz said. "What do you think?"

Rick stared down at the floor for a moment. "Well," he looked up, making eye contact with everybody. "I don't know. Have you and Dani told them what you know about the project?"

"Yes. We thought that would be all right, given the situation that's developed."

"Sure. Of course, it's fine. You can imagine that there could be some, uh, let's just say, *political* implications to finding out that the Moors discovered the New World, right?" Rick looked around the group again.

Everyone nodded, and he continued. "I can only guess that there might be any number of people, countries, religious organizations, what have you, who would prefer not to stir up this kind of speculation. On the other hand, there are probably an equal number who would think it was a fine turn of events. But I don't know of anything specific. I've had no indication that anyone's interested in what we're doing."

"Who knows about it?" Dani asked. "The foundation you mentioned, but anybody else?"

"The department head at the university where I teach, but she's sworn to secrecy, and I trust her. We both worried that this could go either way. We'd either make an earth-shaking discovery, or we'd look like crackpots. We agreed to keep it quiet until we knew which."

"Anybody else?"

"The charter broker," Shellie said, " Elaine, um ... "

"Elaine Moore," Liz said. "She never discloses information about charters. Discretion is important to a lot of clients: she trades on her reputation for protecting clients' privacy. We're on the low end of her portfolio. She books for a lot of yachts that go for over a hundred thousand a week, and people who have the means to do that ... well, let's just say they want their plans kept quiet. Anyone else that you can think of?"

"I mentioned to you that the documents came from the archives of a foreign government that wanted to remain anonymous, at least for now. But I think it's in their interest for you to know, in case it's somehow connected to them. Will you keep this among us?"

He looked at each person in the group, holding eye contact until they all agreed. "Okay," he said. "Saudi Arabia has an extensive archive of ancient Arabic material. Manuscripts, official documents, artifacts — if you can imagine it, they probably have it. They're my main source. And you can see why they would want that kept quiet."

"Thanks, Rick," Dani said. "Does anybody have anything else?"

When no one spoke up, Liz stood up. "It's getting late. Shall we go home to *Vengeance*?"

Rick, Shellie, and Dani nodded and got up from their seats.

"Breakfast here in the morning at 7:30," Sandrine said, as they walked to the door.

22

"Good morning; come in," Phillip said, as he opened the door for Dani and Liz and the Everetts. "Sandrine's in the kitchen; she started the eggs when we saw you get in the dinghy. Did you hear from Marie about the computer yet?" he asked, while he escorted them through the house to the outside dining area.

"Yes," Dani said, "but shouldn't we wait for Sandrine?"

"Sure. Have a seat and let Sharktooth pour you all some coffee. I'll go give her a hand. We'll only be a minute."

"Mornin', mornin'," Sharktooth said, filling mugs with steaming, fragrant coffee and handing them to Maureen, who set one in front of each of the vacant chairs.

"How are you?" Maureen asked.

"Great, thanks," Rick said. "We're trying to figure out our next stop."

"I been thinkin' 'bout that," Sharktooth said. "You said somethin' 'bout a cave."

"Yes, that's right," Rick said.

"When I was involved wit' the Ministry of Tourism at home, I met people from some of the other islands in the EC."

"The EC?" Rick asked.

"Sorry," Sharktooth said. "EC's short for the Organization of Eastern Caribbean States."

"What did you do with the Ministry of Tourism?" Shellie asked.

Sharktooth looked down at his place mat, and Maureen said, "He was the Minister of Tourism for a while. He doesn't like to tell anybody he was involved in politics."

Sharktooth shook his head. "Tha's not important. Anyhow, what I was goin' to say is, the only island that was tryin' to play up caves as a tourist attraction was St. Lucia."

"You said something about that yesterday," Rick said. "Brigands' Cave?"

"Tha's right. I haven't come up with any other caves in the Lesser Antilles. There mus' be a few, but most of the caves are in the Greater Antilles — Cuba, Jamaica, like that. Mebbe I heard of one in Antigua."

"Okay," Rick said. "But everything points to this area, around Martinique and St. Lucia."

"Mm-hmm," Sharktooth said. "I t'ink the mention of the cave points to Soufrière, out of the three places you mentioned yesterday. I called the tourism person I know from St. Lucia. He gave me the name of a mon who runs tours 'roun' Soufrière. He takes people to Brigands' Cave."

"I can't imagine that if it's a tourist attraction, there'd be anything left for me to look at," Rick said, "but I guess it's a starting point."

"Mebbe he knows 'bout some other caves," Sharktooth said, handing Rick a scrap of paper. "Here's his cellphone number. He lives in Soufrière."

"Randolph Mercer," Rick said, looking at the note. "I'll call him when we get there. Thanks, Sharktooth."

"The plates are hot," Sandrine said, balancing a large tray with both hands.

Phillip used potholders to put a plate in front of each of them. Sandrine set the tray aside and Phillip held her chair for her before he took his own seat.

"Please," Sandrine said. "Eat, before the eggs become cold."

A few minutes passed in silence, and then Dani, having washed down her last swallow of eggs with a sip of coffee, said, "About that computer. Marie's people were able to get past the password protection without much trouble. The bottom line is, it looks like these people are following you, Rick. Some of the files appear to be translations of those old manuscripts you described."

"Who are they?" Rick asked, eyes wide. "How could they have gotten their hands on the translations? The foundation ... " He shook his head, frowning.

"They got the files as attachments to emails from someone in Iran. Marie said the IP address was in Tehran."

"Iran? But that doesn't make sense. I told you the Saudis had the originals. They aren't exactly friendly with Iran."

"That was mentioned in some of the emails, too," Dani said. "Marie's take is that the Iranians have hacked into this foundation's servers, and they either have an inside source in Saudi Arabia or they've hacked into some server there. Maybe both. They even had the latest update, the one about the cave."

"But Iran?" Rick asked. "I thought the people on *Aquila* were Americans."

"That's what their passports show; U.S. born, all four of them," Sandrine said. "Unless they are forgeries. But I will find out when I get to the office." She glanced at her watch. "Come, Phillip. You drive me to work now?"

Phillip nodded and pushed his chair back.

"I will call soon," Sandrine said. "You will stay today? Or go to Soufrière?"

"I don't know," Rick said. "We'll have to think about that. Can we let you know when you call?"

"Yes, certainly," Sandrine said. "I will talk with you soon, then."

"HOW FAR IS IT TO SOUFRIÈRE?" Rick asked, after he took a sip of coffee.

"Around 35 miles," Dani said. "An easy four-hour sail."

"And to this Petit Anse d'Arlet? It must be closer," he asked.

"A little, yes," Dani said. "It's just around the western corner of the island from us — 15 miles. And Rodney Bay's around 24 miles. We'd go right by it on the way to Soufrière."

"My intuition says we should go to Soufrière," Rick said.

"Then that's where we should go," Liz said. "It's easy. We can leave after lunch and be there before dinner."

"Maybe I should call your friend, Sharktooth. If we left now, he could take us to the cave this afternoon."

"Mebbe. But I don't know this mon. I got his name from a mon who used to be St. Lucia's tourism minister. I don't even know if he knows this Randolph Mercer fella. So you mus' start fresh wit' him. He won't know any of us. But don' worry; he's in the tourist business."

Rick nodded. "Okay. Thanks for the background. Excuse me while I call him." He went inside the house.

"If we leave today," Dani said, "*Aquila* can't follow us."

"Because of the passports?" Shellie asked.

"Right. Unless they skip clearing out," Dani said.

"Or manage to clear at the internet cafe without showing passports," Liz said. "Based on Sandrine's comments, they're pretty lax. Then they'd have the problem of trying to clear in somewhere with no passports, though. I guess you're right; they're stuck here. But they've got the tracker, anyway."

"We could leave it here," Dani said. "But then they'd know we'd discovered it. I wonder ... "

"What?" Liz asked.

"I was wondering if they were using the laptop to track us."

Rick came back in. "You're talking about *Aquila*?" he asked.

"Yes," Shellie said. "What did you learn? Did you talk to Randolph Mercer?"

"Yes, but he was working, leading a tour. He can take us tomorrow; he's tied up for today. He says it takes the better part of a day."

"It must be a big cave," Shellie said.

"I don't know," Rick said. "The problem is, it's a couple of hours' hike each way to get to the one up on the side of Gros Piton."

"There's more than one cave, then?" Sharktooth asked.

"Yes, he says there are several places called Brigands' Cave. But the one he will take us to is the real thing."

Sharktooth laughed and shook his head.

"What?" Rick asked.

"This mon, he mus' be a hustler."

"You don't believe him?" Rick asked. "About several caves being called the same thing?"

"Oh, tha's mos' likely true. Jus' the idea that he's goin' to show you the *real* one. Tha's what made me laugh."

"So should we look for someone else?"

"No, I don' t'ink so. You mus' start somewhere. This mon, he sounds like he may know about some caves. Jus' be sure you ask the right questions."

"Okay. I did book with him for tomorrow, by the way."

"When would you like to leave?" Dani asked.

"I vote for sometime this afternoon," Shellie said. "Our hosts from last night said there were some interesting shops in Marin. I'd like to walk around and do a little shopping, if we have time."

"Sure. Why not? I don't suppose it matters what time we get to Soufrière, does it?"

"No," Dani said. "We won't be able to clear in there until

tomorrow morning, anyway. The customs office there has short hours; they don't have much commercial traffic — just tourists."

"Great! Can I get a taxi to Marin, then?" Shellie asked.

"Nothing's open yet," Liz said. "Phillip should be back any minute. Maybe we can ... hi, Phillip."

"Hi. What's up?"

"I was about to suggest to Shellie that we might be able to borrow your Jeep to go shopping in Marin later this morning."

"Sure. That's no problem. So you're not leaving?"

"This afternoon, sometime." Rick said.

"Did Sandrine call yet?" Phillip asked. "She was going to — "

The ringing of a cellphone interrupted him. Dani pulled her phone out of her pocket.

"Hi, Sandrine," she said. "You must be psychic. Phillip just asked if you had called."

"So he is home, already. Good. I have scanned the passports. I have some news."

"Are they forged?" Dani asked.

"No, they are genuine, issued by the U.S. passport office. But what is interesting is that they were already in our system here."

"From when they cleared in the other day?" Liz asked.

"No, remember they cleared at the internet cafe. Those entries are uploaded in batch mode; there's a delay. Sometimes as much as a few days, depending on the business and their hours. The scanned entries from our offices are updated immediately. But what is interesting is that these four people arrived here on a flight from Dubai in the early morning, four days ago."

"From Dubai," Rick said. "But they're Americans."

"Yes," Sandrine said. "Four days ago, they came here, to Martinique. A few hours later, they left on a flight to Grenada."

"Can you tell how long they were in Dubai?" Dani asked.

"For nine days, on their most recent visit. From the stamps, they travel there often, mostly from Europe. I could have someone go through the passports and analyze their travel, perhaps."

"That's probably not worth doing," Phillip said. "Let's get those passports to Marie. Clarence has people who can do that research if they need to. First though, we should see what he can find out about them from the U.S."

"Okay, then," Sandrine said. "Have you decided when you will leave, Shellie?"

"We were thinking after lunch sometime," Shellie said.

"Ah! This is perfect. I have the rest of the morning free. Would you be interested in a little bit of the shopping?"

When the laughter died down, Sandrine asked, "I have said something wrong?"

"No," Liz said. "Not at all." She told Sandrine about Shellie's request.

"Great minds are thinking the same thing," Sandrine said. "So, Liz, you and Shellie, you come now? To my office?"

"Ten minutes," Liz said.

"I will be waiting in the car park. Phillip?"

"Yes?"

"I will leave the passports in an envelope for Marie to pick up at the counter outside my office, yes?"

"I'll tell her."

23

"Look, Ed." Leila nudged him as they walked down the street in Marin. They had just left the *Mairie*, where they reported the previous night's theft to the policeman on duty. She gestured with her head, and said, "Don't be too obvious, but that's Liz, from *Vengeance*. She and Everett's wife just went in that dress shop. There's another woman with them, but I don't recognize her."

"What's going on?" Ashley asked. She and Bert were walking a step behind Leila and Ed.

Leila shook her head and kept walking. In a few steps, they came to a café with two small tables on the sidewalk. "Let's grab a cup of coffee," Leila said. She sat where she could see the door of the shop the three women had entered.

Ed said, "Looks like self-service. Everybody have a seat; I'll get it. Four coffees?"

Everybody nodded. Leila took out her cell phone and appeared to be reading something on the screen.

"Why'd we stop?" Bert asked. "Shouldn't we hurry to get our passports replaced?"

"Yeah," Ashley said. "We're stuck here without them."

"Everett's wife and one of the women from *Vengeance* just went in that dress shop," Leila said. "There's a woman with them; I'd like to get a picture of her."

"Everett wasn't with them?" Ed asked. He set a tray holding four cups of coffee on the table and took the remaining chair.

"No," Leila said. "There they are." She snapped away with her cellphone.

"Did you see the way that woman was dressed, Ash?" she asked. Shellie was dawdling, window shopping as she meandered up the sidewalk. Liz and the other woman followed her, talking to one another.

"Yeah. Business attire, like she just came from an office somewhere."

"She looks like she's showing them around," Leila said. "That makes three local contacts here. Her, and those two men from yesterday. I think I'd like to follow them."

"Worth doing," Ed said. "It would be nice to know why Everett came here. How about if you and Ash keep an eye on them? Bert and I can go see the man at the computer shop and pick up our stuff. After we take care of that, we'll give you a call and see where things stand. We can always meet up at the consulate in a couple of hours."

"The guy at the consulate told you he'd be there from three until six, right?" Leila asked.

"Yeah, so there's no big rush, anyway." Ed slugged down his coffee and stood. "Come on, Bert."

Ashley watched them walk away. When they were out of earshot, she said, "Bert's a loser."

"He's a warm body; we're short-handed," Leila said. "But you're right. That's why Ed and I don't leave him alone."

"You don't trust him? I thought he was the second in command."

"Yeah. Well, that's what you get with a bunch of misogynists calling the shots."

"You think he's a double agent?" Ashley asked.

"Why?" Leila fixed Ashley with a cold stare. "Has he said or done something?"

"No, not really. But he asks strange questions, sometimes."

"What kind of questions?"

"About you and Ed. He thinks maybe you're fooling around, like."

Leila laughed at that and shook her head. "What a moron."

"You mean Bert?"

"Yes. Bert. Ed's a lot of things, but stupid isn't one of them. Bert's too dumb to be a double agent."

Ashley looked at Leila for a few seconds. "I've wondered about you and Ed, too. He defers to you quite a bit."

"Because he's seen me in action. We worked together on a mission in the States once. That's enough questions. And watch what you say around Bert. Let me or Ed handle him. You understand?"

Ashley swallowed hard at the look Leila sent her way. She nodded. "Sorry. I — "

"Shut up. They're coming this way. Finish your coffee. Let them get about a half a block away, then you follow them. I'll hang back for a while and we'll tag-team them, okay?"

Ashley nodded. She took a deep breath and sighed. After several seconds, she got up and began following their quarry.

"HELLO, MARIE," Phillip said, answering his cellphone. "Hang on; I'll switch to the speaker; it saves my repeating everything." He set the phone on the table. "Marie?"

"Yes. Who else is listening, please?"

"Rick and Sharktooth and Dani. Maureen is outside, sketching, and Liz and — "

"I know Liz and Sandrine are showing Shellie the shops. I

have a team following the people from *Aquila*. The two women from *Aquila* are following Liz and Sandrine and Shellie."

"What?" Dani asked.

"Following Liz and Sandrine and Shellie?" Phillip asked.

"That is correct. They picked them up about ten minutes ago. My people called to ask for instructions, because the people from *Aquila* split up. The men are in a taxi, going to Fort-de-France. Before that, all four of them went to make a police report on the break-in last night. From what they told the police, they have an appointment at the U.S. consulate this afternoon about replacing their passports. My people think it was an accident that they saw Liz and Shellie and Sandrine."

"Did you get the passports okay?" Phillip asked.

"Yes, we have them. We are in the process of making an inquiry through Interpol, but it might be a good idea for you to ask your friend at the Miami Police to check them out, too. Interpol will eventually get whatever the U.S. has, but it can take some time."

"Luke Pantene," Phillip said. "Yes, I'll call him when we're done. Good idea."

"You have the passport information?" Marie asked.

"Yes. We made copies last night."

"Marie?" Dani asked.

"Yes, Dani?"

"About their computer — was there software on there to monitor the tracker? Or does that happen via the web?"

"No, there was no app for that. And no, it is not done over the web. They must have another device for that, or perhaps they use a smartphone. This is possible."

"Okay, thanks. So as best we know, they can still track us."

"Yes, that is correct. Are you planning to move soon? Or destroy the tracking device?"

"I think we're better off letting them track us," Dani said. "If we ditch the tracker, it might push them to take a more aggressive approach."

Marie laughed. "You? You are worried that *they* might become aggressive? You're the one who always provokes people. What has happened to you?"

"They already know all the background from the files they've hacked," Dani said. "If we got rid of the tracker, they would probably still be able to find us. It might be more work for them; that's all."

"Yes," Marie said. "But why make it easy for them?"

"Because," Dani said, "if we get rid of the tracker, they'll know we're on to them. As things stand now, they think we don't know they're after us. That puts the advantage on our side, to my way of thinking."

"I see," Marie said. "What do you think they will do? Only follow you and report back to Tehran? They must plan some action, or this effort would not be worthwhile."

"Oh, I expect at some point, they'll make a move against us," Dani said. "But we'll be ready for them, and they won't expect that."

"Rick?" Phillip asked.

"Yes?"

"How do you feel about this?"

"I'm not sure. I can't imagine that these people would attack us. We're not talking about finding buried treasure here, only things that are of academic interest."

"There's strong rivalry between the Saudis and the Iranians, though," Phillip said.

"Yes, but I don't see how this would benefit one over the other. I mean, okay, they could one-up the Saudis, I guess, but that's about all I can see as a reason. The Iranians probably just want to know what the Saudis are up to."

"Nothing related to the Middle East is that simple," Phillip said. "And I'm not sure any of us can guess what their motivations are."

"We only know that these Americans are in correspondence with the Iranians," Marie said. "We don't know why, or what their relationship to Iran is. Is it possible that these people on *Aquila* could be academic rivals of yours, Rick?"

"I suppose they could be," Rick said. "If we had more information on them, we'd be in a better position to judge that. You think maybe the Iranians are sponsoring these people? Is that it?"

"We've drifted away from the key questions, here," Dani said.

"What're the key questions, then?" Rick asked.

"The first one is whether you're still committed to your search."

"Okay," Rick said. "Nothing has happened that makes me want to drop it. So these people are spying on us for some reason we don't understand. What are they going to do? Swoop in and snatch whatever we find? That's assuming there's even anything to find."

"We don't know what they plan to do," Dani said. "But you want to go ahead, even in the face of that uncertainty. Is that correct?"

"Yes," Rick said. "You had other questions?"

"Should we ditch the tracker? Or make it easy for them to follow us?"

"I liked your logic," Rick said. "It's probably to our advantage that they don't know we know about them. At least for now."

"Liz mentioned earlier that *Aquila* can't leave here until they replace their passports," Dani said. "Anybody have an idea as to how long that'll take?"

"Yes," Marie said. "Our source in the police says this is routine. If they are lucky, perhaps late tomorrow they will have replacements. If not, then almost surely the next day."

"That's what Sandrine said, too," Phillip said.

"This is all I have," Marie said. "I will call Phillip when we hear from our Interpol inquiry. Phillip, please let me know what you learn from your friend Luke, yes?"

"I will. If we're done, I'll call him right now. Thanks, Marie."

"You are welcome. Goodbye for now."

Phillip excused himself to make the call to Luke Pantene. While he was gone, Dani got a call from Liz. She and her companions were wrapping up their excursion and wanted to meet for lunch at the marina restaurant in thirty minutes.

"Ed?" Leila asked, when her call was answered.

"Yeah, Leila, what's up?"

"Ashley and I are having lunch at the marina restaurant. Where are you and Bert?"

"We're about to get a sandwich at one of the stalls in the market here in Fort-de-France. We gave up on you when we didn't hear from you. I didn't want to call, in case ... well, you know. We found the computer store and got our stuff. I'll tell you about it later. Why are you at the marina? Still following those women?"

"Yeah, you got it."

"Are you where you can talk?"

"Yes. I'm outside, on my way back from the ladies' room. I left Ashley watching them. Sorry I didn't call earlier, but I couldn't manage it. The three women hit almost every shop in the town, and then headed back here. They got a big table, and the one we don't know made a phone call. Pretty soon, the two guys we saw yesterday showed up with Rick Everett and Dani and another woman. They're all at the same table, having a grand old time."

"So that woman goes with the two guys, huh?"

"Yeah, my guess is she's the white one's wife, from the way they acted."

"Okay. What about the other woman?"

"Oh, no doubt there. She's clearly married to that giant with the dreadlocks."

"So, let's see. We have four locals here linked to either Everett or the women from *Vengeance*. What do you think? Which is it?"

"It may not be either/or. The four locals seem to know one another, but the woman we saw shopping?"

"Yeah, what about her?"

"She and Dani excused themselves and went in the customs office. It was busy enough so that I could follow them in. Dani's clearing out, but she — "

"What about the other woman?" Ed asked.

"That's what I was going to tell you. She runs the customs office."

"Runs it? How do you know?"

"It was obvious; the people working there were all over her, getting her to sign stuff, asking her questions, you know. She handled it all like it was nothing unusual, and she and Dani went into her private office. Her name's Sandrine Davis; I got it from one of the notices on the bulletin board out front. Had her picture on it and everything."

"Interesting. So *Vengeance* is leaving?"

"Yeah. Dani got VIP treatment. Sandrine called one of the agents back to her office, and he came out with a handful of papers and passports and did his thing for a few minutes at his computer. Then he took it all back to the office and Dani and Sandrine left and went back to the restaurant."

"Good work. I'm not sure what to make of it, though."

"I don't know either, except somebody's connected. You know how the French are about their paperwork. The police barely gave us the time of day."

"Think it's Dani? Or Everett? Maybe that foundation's pulling some strings. You sure they're leaving, and this wasn't some other kind of permit, or something?"

"We overheard enough to know they're going somewhere this

afternoon, but I hadn't really thought about that. I jumped to the conclusion that they were handling clearance paperwork, because we knew they were leaving. What are you thinking, Ed?"

"Maybe they're moving to somewhere else in Martinique and the paperwork was some kind of work permit. I don't know. It seems odd that French customs would roll out the red carpet for a charter boat skipper."

"Yes, but they're socializing — the whole crowd of them."

"It'll be interesting to see where they go this afternoon," Ed said. "That may give us a clue. But I wonder about the other couple."

"The giant and his wife?" Leila asked.

"Yeah. We're going to be stuck here for another day, at least. Maybe we can do a little digging on the Davis woman and the others. If nothing else, it'll make the time pass."

"Unless *Vengeance* stays in Martinique," Leila said. "Then we can follow them."

"Yes. Or split up and do both. It's closing in on time for you and Ash to get a taxi and come downtown, speaking of splitting up."

"It's only a few miles," Leila said. "We've got time."

"It's only a few miles, but the traffic is a mess. It took us 45 minutes, and the driver said the later it is, the heavier the traffic. We should hit the consulate as early as we can; maybe it'll get us out of here sooner."

"All right. I'll settle our check and get Ashley. See you in a bit. Want to just meet at the consulate?"

"Yeah. If we're early, we can hang out until they open. Bye."

"Bye," Leila said. She slipped the phone back in her pocket and walked into the restaurant, stopping at the cash register to ask for their check before she joined Ashley at their table.

"Ready?" Leila asked.

Ashley nodded. "If the waitress will just bring — "

"I took care of it. Let's go."

24

"This is fantastic!" Shellie said. "What do you call it? Sailing like this?"

"This point of sail is called a broad reach," Dani said. "That's because the wind is 'broad', or well behind the beam."

"It feels like we're flying."

Dani reached up to the touch screen above the helm. "Ten knots," she said. "Close enough to flying, at least for *Vengeance*."

"Is *Vengeance* a fast boat?" Shellie asked.

"Yes. On a short race course where you're changing direction often, a lighter boat may be a bit faster, because it accelerates more easily, but on most points of sail in open water, they're not as fast as traditional designs like *Vengeance*. Nor as comfortable."

"Interesting. You've used the term 'point of sail,' often when we're talking about sailing. Is that the direction of the boat relative to the direction of the wind?"

"Yes," Dani said. "Good for you for picking that up."

"I really want to learn to do this. It's like magic, the way we glide along with nothing but the wind."

"Yes. Magic, for sure," Dani said, leaning back against the

windward cockpit coaming and stretching her arms out. "And you're learning quickly."

"You're teaching my wife magic?" Rick said, coming into the cockpit from below.

"Sailing, Rick," Shellie said. "Sailing's magic."

"Hey, everybody," Liz said, poking her head up through the companionway. "I just got off the phone with Marie."

"What's new with her?" Dani asked.

"The two women who were following us left the restaurant before we did," Liz said.

"I guessed those two were probably your tail when I saw them leave," Dani said. "They don't look much like their passport photos, do they?"

"I did, too," Liz said. "And no, they don't look anything like their passport pictures. But who does?"

"How did you spot them?" Rick asked. "I never saw anybody watching us, even after Dani told us they had followed you while you were shopping."

"Practice," Liz said. "Their behavior was just a little off for two women out for a ladies' lunch."

"What else?" Dani asked. "Any word on the Interpol query?"

"No, not yet. But she did have something else. While the women were following us, the men took a taxi into Fort-de-France and went to a shady little back-alley electronics store. They were in there for quite a while, and it wasn't the kind of place her people could follow them into. They came out carrying a laptop bag and a shopping bag. When they stopped for lunch, they unboxed a satellite phone and transferred it to the laptop bag after they made a call on it."

"Did they ditch the shopping bag, then?" Dani asked.

"No, but they ate at a place in the market, and after lunch, they bought a duffle bag from one of the stands and put the shopping bag in it. Marie said they acted like whatever was in the bag was valuable — kept it close, never really set it down."

"Odd that they'd go to a hole-in-the-wall place to buy a computer and a sat phone," Dani said. "There are all kinds of shops closer than Fort-de-France that sell that kind of stuff.

Liz grinned. "That's what Marie thought, too. She had somebody check up on the shop with the police. They know the place. They're pretty sure the man who runs it deals in contraband from time to time, but they've never managed to catch him at it."

"What kind of contraband?" Rick asked. "Like stolen goods? Or maybe valuable antiquities? People that deal in stuff like that are often back-alley operations."

"If they knew for sure what he was dealing in, they'd bust him," Dani said. "But I suspect it's more along the lines of stolen stuff. It still seems odd that they'd go somewhere like that to replace the things I took."

"Marie agreed," Liz said. "After the women left the marina, they took a taxi to the U.S. Consulate and met the men there. They found a bar nearby and killed an hour and a half, then went to the consulate. They're back aboard *Aquila*, now."

"Anything else?" Dani asked.

"She thinks she may have some preliminary information from Interpol later this evening. She'll call us."

"Shellie," Dani said.

"Yes?"

"It's time to put a little more south in our course, now. We're far enough past the north end of St. Lucia so that we can start to head for Soufrière."

"Okay. Is there a compass course I should steer to get there?"

"Not just yet. What we're going to do is swoop around kind of gradually. We'll go several miles out to the west before we take up a course directly to Soufrière. That way, the hills won't block our wind, at least until we get a lot closer to where were going."

"So what do I need to do, then?" Shellie asked.

"Liz and I will sheet the sails in a little. You'll feel the pressure through the helm as *Vengeance* tries to come around so that the wind's a bit closer to the beam. Just let her go. Pay attention to how the helm feels, and she'll tell you what to do. If you let her come around too far, the sails will begin to flutter along their front edges. That's called luffing. If that happens, turn her back away from the wind until it stops. You'll be able to tell. Okay?"

Shellie nodded, and Dani moved to the headsail sheet winches and cranked them a few turns, first trimming the Genoa sheet, and then the staysail sheet. Liz watched the main and mizzen and trimmed them slightly as they began to luff.

"Looking good," Dani said. "How's the helm feel, Shellie?"

"About the same as before you trimmed the sails, I think."

"Good. That's as it should be," Liz said.

"You could almost steer that way," Rick said.

"You can steer that way," Dani said. "We just did. No almost about it."

Rick studied the sails for a moment and then put a hand on the helm. "May I? I just want to feel it, Shellie — I'm not trying to take over."

She smiled and dropped her hands to her lap, letting Rick swing the helm back and forth a few degrees as he kept an eye on the sails.

"Amazing," he said, gesturing for Shellie to take over. "I see what they mean about 'balancing the helm.' I never understood what that meant."

"You've done some sailing?" Liz asked.

"Oh, once or twice, with friends. But I never really understood how it all worked. I see how you could get wrapped up in this."

"That's a good thing," Shellie said. "Keep that in mind."

"Yes, ma'am," he said.

"Now, Dani," she said, "when you touched the screen to see how fast we were going a few minutes ago, did I see something that said ETA on the screen?"

"Yes," Dani chuckled. "Did you catch what it said?"

"I thought it said 16:23. Could that be right?"

"That's what I saw, too," Dani said.

"But I thought you said it was a four-hour trip," Shellie said. "We didn't leave until a little after one. That would put us in after five."

"Yes," Dani said. "But we're going faster than I expected. And we're not there yet. A lot can happen in the next few hours. Wind shifts, a thunderstorm, or ... maybe we'll keep flying at 10 knots. That's part of the magic, too."

"WHAT HAVE you found out about Soufrière?" Ed asked, looking over Leila's shoulder as she scanned the screen of their laptop.

She had tracked *Vengeance* using the tablet after they got back from the consulate. Watching over a period of about an hour as they gradually settled onto a course that pointed straight toward the westernmost point on the island of St. Lucia, she had zoomed in to see more detail. There was a natural harbor on the south side of the point, and a town called Soufrière.

Meanwhile, Ed had downloaded their files onto the new laptop from a cloud backup and was reviewing them. She had asked if there were any references to Soufrière, and he had shrugged and given her the laptop, saying, "I don't know. I was just making sure we had everything. Help yourself; I'm cross-eyed from staring at the screen."

She had gone online to see what she could learn about *Vengeance's* destination. Then she had scanned the files they had, looking for an indication that Soufrière might be significant to Everett's quest.

"Think that might be the place?" Ed asked, when she didn't answer after several seconds.

"Sorry," she said. "I was lost for a minute, there. It could be. It's hard to make sense of that scrappy little piece of map in the file. The photocopy of it's lousy. But it kind of fits. The harbor's there.

The two mountains, definitely. And there's a cave, called Brigands' Cave. Plus, there's one right in the harbor, called the Bat Cave. But it looks like it's only accessible by boat. I doubt that's the one, but maybe Brigands' Cave is. There's not much real information about it, though."

"This is the first time they've gone somewhere that looks like it could be the place," Ed said.

"Wonder why they swung so far out to the west, instead of going straight?" she asked.

"Who knows?" Ed asked. "But Soufrière might be a match, huh?"

"Yeah, but I'm not so sure, Ed. The cave's a tourist attraction. They're not going to find anything there; it's bound to have been picked over. Did you get Rahimi on the phone earlier?"

"I did. I didn't want to say anything while Bert was around. I've spoken to him a couple of times."

"Is that why you put Ashley up to uh ... whatever?"

He chuckled. "Yeah. What a dumb bastard. Did you see how easy he was? She should be ashamed of herself, hustling the poor fool."

"Ashley's good at that, Ed. It's what she's trained for. And a guy like Bert? He probably doesn't get many offers. How long did you tell her we needed?"

"She's got a room at that hotel on the beach south of Ste. Anne. She's going to keep him occupied until sometime in the morning."

"All night? Poor Ashley; she'll be bored silly."

"Hey, like you said, it's what she's good at."

"Better her than me, I guess."

"Don't speak too soon," Ed said, grinning as she turned to look at him. "Depending on how well she does with him, you may be next."

"Don't even joke about that."

"I'm not," he said, suppressing laughter.

"That's not what I do, Ed. I'd just kill him and be done with it."

"Exactly."

"What?" Leila's eyebrows rose. "Are you serious? Then there'd only be the three of us."

"Yeah. Depending on what Ash gets out of him. Rahimi thinks he's a plant."

"A plant? She's going to question him? Who does Rahimi think he's working for?"

"Yes. Distracting him while we work this out is just an added benefit. Rahimi thinks he's working for some U.S. agency. Probably the CIA."

Leila shook her head. "I don't know. You'd think the CIA could have found somebody with a brain if they were going to the trouble."

"That could be part of his cover, playing dumb."

"How's Ashley supposed to decide? Any guidance from Rahimi on that?"

"As you said, it's what she does. Drugs, maybe? I don't want to know."

"Did Rahimi have anything else? You said you talked to him a couple of times."

"Yes. They got some more info from Riyadh. They think whatever Everett's looking for will put an end to Shia Islam."

"What could it be? It would almost have to be ... "

"Ancient documents. Written by the Prophet's own hand."

"So has our mission changed?"

"Yes and no. It's no longer vague, now. We're to stay on Everett until he finds whatever it is. That much hasn't changed. Once he finds it, our job is to eliminate everybody and destroy it."

"Destroy the prize? We're not even supposed to see what's in it?"

"It's too dangerous, according to Rahimi. There been rumors about the existence of something like this for a thousand years, he said. The mullahs and the Ayatollah don't want it around."

"Okay. If that's our mission, it would be nice if we had weapons to work with. Something besides knives and fists."

Ed grinned again. "Would a MAC-11 do it for you?"

"Better than nothing, but not my first choice. Do you have one?"

"Not yet. But the guy in Fort-de-France is getting them. He should have them tomorrow."

"Does Bert know about any of this?"

"No. I kept it from him."

"That must have been a challenge, with him in that shop with you."

"Not really. He got wrapped up in some video game. You don't like MAC-11s?"

"No. Those .380 rounds don't have much stopping power."

"Oh," Ed said. "There may be a MAC-10 or two in the lot, but he's trying for the MAC-11s. He says they're more popular with his regular clients."

"His regular clients?"

"Drug runners. He says they favor the MAC-11."

"That figures. They're easy to conceal, but I'm not sure a whole magazine of .380s would stop that big man with the dreadlocks. A MAC-10 in .45 caliber would give us a better chance. Can you call him back?"

"No. He has to take what he gets from his supplier."

"We'll work with that, then. Maybe we'll get lucky."

"Speaking of getting lucky, how are you feeling about good old Bert?" Ed asked.

"I don't understand what you're asking. I told you — "

"No, hang on. I'm not comfortable with him, no matter what Ashley finds out."

"Are you suggesting that we make our own decision on him?"

"We could. Even if Ashley says he's clean, we could still take him out, make it look like an accident. If you and I decide, she'll go along with it, don't you think?"

She locked eyes with Ed until he looked away. "Is this personal, Ed?"

His face flushed, a scowl spreading over it. "What the hell kind of question is that? Neither one of us trusts him, Leila. I thought we could — "

"I know the two of you have a ... let's just call it a history, of sorts."

"It's not what you think, Leila," Ed said, still red in the face.

"You have no idea what I think. We'll see what Ashley learns from him. Then I'll make the decision. Remember what you explained to Bert? Violence is my specialty, and my call. That's why I'm along on this mission. Now leave me alone. I want to finish reading these files."

25

"Are you supposed to call this cave man?" Shellie asked, as they sat around the cockpit table after breakfast, drinking coffee with Dani and Liz.

"Caveman," Rick said, laughing. "I like that."

"Well?" Shellie asked, smiling. "I didn't even realize what I said. Are you?"

"No, the way I left it with him, he's going to come by around nine this morning. He'll give us a ride ashore, and he's got a friend with a taxi who'll take us to the trailhead."

"Are you going with us?" Shellie asked, turning to Dani and Liz.

"You're welcome, if you'd like," Rick added, seeing the looks they exchanged. "I kind of assumed you knew that."

"I have to go get us cleared in," Dani said. "That needs to be done before anybody goes ashore, technically." She glanced at her phone, checking the time. "They don't open until 8:30. If it's busy, I may not be back until after 9:00. Besides, I've got a few little maintenance projects to keep me occupied. I'll pass, if it's okay."

"Sure," Rick said. "Whatever suits you. Liz?"

"I'll stay here with Dani. Thanks, though. I want to try some sketches of the town from out here. Soufrière's one of the places that looks like what I imagine the Caribbean towns were like at the height of the colonial era."

"It almost has the look of a movie set," Shellie said. "I'll look forward to seeing your sketches."

"Excuse me, please," Dani said. "I'm going to go to the customs office; maybe I'll beat the rush. It looks like quite a few boats came in last night." She went below to gather up their papers.

"It's hard for me to remember that we can sail four hours and be in a different country," Shellie said. "You must spend a lot of time clearing in and out with the authorities."

Liz smiled. "You get used to it."

"It's time consuming, though," Rick said. "Isn't it?"

"Well, yes," Liz said. "It is, but it's just part of sailing down here. A lot of people find it frustrating."

"I can understand that, I guess," Shellie said, picking up the carafe of coffee and refilling her mug. "Liz? Rick?"

Both nodded.

"Thanks," Liz said, as Shellie filled her mug.

Shellie smiled. "About bareboat charters, do people have to reserve them in advance?"

"Most people do," Liz said. "But if you're not picky about what kind of boat you get, sometimes you can just walk in and rent one. It's sort of like car rentals. In the busy places, you're less likely to find something on short notice. Why? Are you thinking about it?"

"Well, yes. Do you have, like a driver's license for boats, or something? How do they know you won't wreck it?"

Liz laughed. "There are all kinds of licenses and certificates; it varies from country to country. Dani and I each have a commercial captain's license. Hers is from the U.S.; mine is from Belgium. But you only need a commercial license if you're carrying passengers for hire or operating a commercial vessel. The bareboat companies accept all kinds of credentials, depending on their own rules. Some want to see a sailing résumé, some look for certificates from recognized courses. They also require damage deposits, most of them."

"So, those people who rented *Aquila*, for example," Rick said. "What do you suppose they used? Anything that might tell us something about them?"

"Good question," Liz said. "I don't know, but it may be that we can find out. I'll pass that along to Phillip and Marie in a little while."

"I wanted to ask about Marie," Shellie said. "She comes across like a — "

"Hello, *Vengeance*!" A man in a brightly painted 24-foot speed boat called, interrupting Shellie.

He slowed his boat and hung fenders over the port side, then brought the boat in alongside *Vengeance* and handed Liz a bow line. As she tied it off to a midship cleat, he tied a stern line to one of the lifeline stanchions.

"Good morning," he said. "I am Randolph. You are the captain?"

"The mate," Liz said. "I'm Liz. The captain's at the customs office."

"Ah. Okay. I am here for Mr. Everett and his wife, but I t'ink they mus' be below."

Thinking they were in the cockpit, Liz glanced over her shoulder. She was just in time to see Rick climbing into the cockpit, backpack in hand.

"Hi. I'm Rick Everett. My wife will be right up. We were gathering our stuff."

"No problem, Mr. Everett. I am Randolph. Nice to meet you. Welcome to Soufrière. You have been to St. Lucia before?"

"No, this is our first time. And just call me Rick."

"Thank you, and welcome to St. Lucia. Ah! You must be Mrs. Everett," Randolph reached for Rick's backpack and lowered it into the boat.

"Yes, but call me Shellie, okay?"

"Yes, ma'am. Come on aboard, both of you. And will you and the captain be joining us?" he smiled up at Liz.

"Not today," she said.

"Don' worry, then. I will take extra good care of your guests for you. We will be gone mos' of the day, I t'ink."

"All right. We'll be here when you get back. Have a fine time, and good luck with your project, Rick." She cast off the bow line as Randolph untied the one from the stanchion. He put a hand on *Vengeance's* toe rail and shoved his boat away, giving Liz a wave as he shifted into forward gear and headed for town.

Liz was still watching them when she saw Dani walk out onto the town dock and crouch to unlock their dinghy. She went back into the cockpit and retrieved her steaming coffee mug. Climbing out of the cockpit again, she stood on the side deck sipping coffee, watching Dani as she worked her way through the boats that were swinging on moorings in the harbor.

"DID THEIR GUIDE SHOW UP?" Dani asked, bringing the dinghy alongside and tying it off.

"Yes. You just missed them. I didn't notice where they went, once I spotted you. Are we legal now?"

"Yes," Dani said, climbing aboard. "All set."

"What are you going to tinker with today? Varnish?"

Dani smiled and shook her head. "I thought I'd catch up on my reading. The idea of hiking two hours to get to some dank, dark cave didn't appeal."

"Not to me, either," Liz said. "Besides, I really have wanted to try to capture the feel of Soufrière in a painting ever since the first time I came here."

"Have you ever done any spelunking?" Dani asked.

"No. Why?" Liz frowned. "Have you?"

"Enough to know I don't like it. I didn't know the meaning of claustrophobia until I got stuck in a cave one time."

"Where were you?"

"In Jamaica, up in the mountains. It was one of those times I tagged along with Phillip when my folks thought I was at Mrs. Walker's."

"And you got stuck?"

"Not literally. But I've got to say the idea of that's almost enough to bring on a panic attack."

"So how *did* you get stuck, if not literally?"

"Some corrupt soldiers were chasing us, and we hid out in the cave, way back up in this chimney. We shimmied up it and wedged ourselves in. They came in looking for us but they didn't see the opening to the chimney."

"So they left?"

"Eventually. First, they gassed the place with CS."

"What's CS?"

"Tear gas. It was pretty awful, but we managed to wait them out without giving ourselves away."

"They didn't hear you gagging or anything?"

"Like I said, it wasn't fun."

"What happened after they left?"

"We followed them and ambushed them the next day. Made short work of them, too."

"So that's why you didn't want to go today? The tear gas attack?"

"No. The cave. Tear gas, I can handle, but I'm petrified by the idea of being in a cave. I never knew it until then, but caves spook me. So I didn't want to go. Besides, I was feeling the need for some downtime."

"Me, too. I'm looking forward to idling the day away, for a change."

~

"WHAT DID you do to him, anyway?" Leila asked Ashley.

Ashley had brought Bert, semi-coherent and complaining of a hangover, back to *Aquila* as Leila and Ed were finishing lunch. Bert had stumbled below and crawled into his berth, beginning to snore within a minute.

"Drugged his drink, to start with. He's not going to remember what really happened, but he'll think we had a great time, given the hangover — and a few other things. He's going to have some soreness and bruises in interesting places to further the illusion." She laughed.

"Did you learn anything?" Ed asked.

"Nothing we didn't already know. He's dumber than dirt, but there's no sign he's working for anybody but us. He's okay, except for being stupid. We need to watch what we tell him, though. He could blow our cover without meaning to."

Leila stared at Ed, but he wouldn't look her in the eye. After a few seconds, he said, "While you two babysit him, I'm going back to see our contact in Fort-de-France. He should have our weapons by now, and I'd rather Bert didn't know about them. Not just yet, anyway."

"Weapons?" Ashley asked.

"Leila can fill you in. I talked to Rahimi again; there's a new twist to our mission. If I hear from the consulate about the passports, I'll call you and you can meet me there. They've got my cellphone number."

"What about the dinghy?" Leila asked.

"What about it?"

"Want me to run you ashore and bring it back? So Ashley and Bert and I will have it to get ashore if the consulate calls?"

"No, that's okay. I don't need it," Ed said. "I asked the water taxi that brought Ash and Bert back to swing by and pick me up. I just now saw him leaving the town dock; he'll be here in a minute." Ed stepped onto the side deck, and the water taxi came alongside.

"Keep your phones on," Ed said, as he stepped down into the boat.

Once they were alone, Leila looked at Ashley and asked, "Are you sure about Bert?"

"Yes. Why?"

"Ed wants to get rid of him."

"Get rid of him? You mean ... " Ashley frowned. "But he's not spying on us."

"Ed all but asked me to kill him anyway. He thought you'd go along, if he and I were in agreement."

"Well, are you?" Ashley asked.

"In agreement? No," Leila said. "I don't see a reason to kill Bert. So he's an idiot; he might still be useful."

"Why did Ed think you should kill him?"

"I'm not sure. I have some suspicions, but I don't want to gossip about Ed."

"That's funny," Ashley said, frowning. "Bert said something about Ed when he was under."

"What did he say?"

"It was pretty garbled, and I didn't pursue it because I was focused on something else related to Bert. But he mumbled something about compromising photographs of Ed from 'before.' He was laughing about it."

"Before? Before when?"

"I don't know, Leila." She shook her head. "What's this about our mission changing?"

Leila told her what Ed had learned about the ancient documents that Everett was hunting.

"So that's why the weapons," Ashley said.

"Yes. Are you okay with that?"

"Yes," Ashley said. "It's a first for me, but I'm okay with it. You've done that kind of thing before, right?"

Leila nodded.

"What about Ed?" Ashley asked.

Leila shook her head. "I don't think so. That mission I mentioned that we were on in the States?"

"You and Ed?"

Leila nodded.

"What about it?"

"It was pretty bloody; Ed lost it."

"Lost it? How?"

"Fainted. After he pissed his pants. So I figure that was his first time, and he wasn't even conscious once the shooting started."

"Men," Ashley said, laughing.

"Speaking of men, how long is Bert going to be out of it? If Ed calls about the consulate, we're going to have to rouse him. They won't give us his passport unless he's with us."

"Yeah." Ashley glanced at her watch. "He's been under for about 12 hours. I'll go ahead and give him something that'll bring him around. He may say some strange things at first. Don't be surprised. Just let him ramble. He should be okay in 45 minutes or so."

26

"How was it?" Liz asked, passing glasses of dry white wine around the cockpit table. Rick and Shellie had been back from their hike long enough to get cleaned up for cocktails and dinner.

"It was okay," Rick said. "Randolph's a good tour guide, but the cave was a disappointment."

"That was predictable, though," Shellie said. "We knew it was a tourist spot to begin with."

"Yeah. I didn't have much hope for it; it's too popular," Rick said. "Still, I thought maybe there'd be some hidden caverns. You know, off to the side, cut off by a collapsed tunnel or something. But no such luck."

"How about other caves?" Dani asked. "Did he know of any?"

"No. I don't think he's really knowledgeable about the geology of the island. He's a tour guide; he knows what to show people. The Brigands' Cave is just one of his attractions. He tells a good tale about it, but that's it."

"What's your plan, now?" Dani asked.

"We're here," Rick said. "I'd like to at least walk around the town a little, try to get a feel for what it might have been like before it was settled by the Europeans. I know, I know. It's probably futile, but you never know. The translations of the documents and the sketch map both seem to point here."

"You can't wait for inspiration," Shellie said. "You have to run it down and grab it by the scruff of the neck."

Liz laughed. "I like that, Shellie."

"It's not original. Not the idea, anyway. But I like it, too," Shellie said.

"Excuse, please," a soft, low-pitched voice interrupted.

They all turned toward the source of the words, peering into the gathering dusk. A tall, thin man, his face devoid of expression, peered back at them. At first glance, he appeared to be standing on the glassy surface of the water, both hands on the starboard lifelines, just forward of the cockpit.

"Yes?" Dani said, vaulting to her feet and stepping onto the side deck. She dropped to one knee in front of the apparition, noticing that he stood on a beat-up surfboard.

"Good evening, ma'am," he said, his voice just above a whisper. He ducked his head and tugged at his forelock in a deferential salute of sorts. "I am Gerald. So sorry to intrude, but I wish to welcome you to Soufrière."

"Thank you," Dani said, conscious that Liz and the Everetts were watching in silence.

"Yes," he said. "I am glad you come here. I been waiting for you, I t'ink."

Dani took in his matte black skin, the surface dusted with fine crystals of salt. He was painfully thin, but looked strong and wiry. His muscles rippled under his skin like writhing snakes as he held steady against the slight movement of the surfboard under his feet. His tangled, salt-matted dreadlocks hung to his shoulders. Pop-tops and other small bits of metal were braided into his hair and reflected the ambient light.

"Waiting for us?" she asked, looking into his fiery red eyes, noticing the pupils were dilated as she caught a whiff of ganja wafting from his hair.

"I t'ink so, ma'am. Don' worry. I will not harm. I heard them talking. They said you be here soon." His voice was low. Dani strained to hear him.

"They?" Dani asked. "They, who?"

"The men. They say you look for the cave."

"Look for the cave," she said. "Which cave?"

"The cave." He looked past Dani, studying the varnished teak eyebrow along the edge of the coachroof. Then he spoke in a normal tone. "She is beautiful, your ship. Like in the old days. I don' like the new boats so much. A boat like this one, she make me want to go to sea an' not come back. Beautiful."

Dani studied his hands, clutching the lifeline as he spoke. They were large, too big for the rest of him. His fingers were gnarled and scarred, ending in long, thick yellow nails. The nails were splintered, dirty. More like claws.

"Thank you, Gerald," she said, when he stopped talking. "Tell me more about the men."

He looked back at her, making eye contact, panic flickering in his eyes. He shook his head.

"What men?" she asked. "They told you we would look for the cave?"

"I ... " he shook his head again and coughed. "Ver' thirsty. Most sorry. Excuse, please." He released the lifeline and dropped into a crouch, about to paddle away.

"Gerald?" Dani said.

He froze and turned his shaggy head, looking up at her. "Yes, ma'am?"

"I have some Guinness. Would you like to sit with us and have some?"

He frowned, chewing his tongue. "Is all right for me to come on your beautiful yacht? I am ... " he looked away, down at the water.

"Yes, it is all right. You are welcome. Come and sit with us and drink a Guinness, please. It would be our pleasure to get to know you."

"You are ver' kind, ma'am. Is okay wit' your frien's, you t'ink?"

"Yes, I'm sure it is. You can tell us about Soufrière."

"Well, all right then, you say so. Is ver' nice." He stood again, his balance unerring. He handed Dani a frayed, thin piece of twisted-fiber cord that looked as if he'd made it from coconut husks. "Tie, please?"

Dani flipped a round turn and two half-hitches around the lower lifeline, noticing his look of approval at her marlinspike skill. He grasped the top lifeline with his oversized, scaly hands. With effortless grace, he came over the lifelines and stood waiting, his head bowed slightly.

"Welcome aboard, Gerald," she said motioning for him to go ahead of her to the cockpit. "I'm Dani. Please, go ahead."

He stepped into the cockpit's narrow footwell and waited for her to introduce him to the others. When he had met everyone, Liz said, "Please, have a seat, Gerald. Thank you for visiting us."

"You are ver' nice people," he said. "I welcome you to Soufrière."

"I'll get you that Guinness," Dani said, "Unless you'd like some wine."

"Thank you, ma'am. Guinness be fine. I don' use alcohol — I am Rastafarian."

Rick said, "But — "

"You like your Guinness cold? Or not?" Dani interrupted, with a look at Rick and a shake of her head. "We have it whichever way you like."

"I like cold bes', thank you, ma'am."

"Tell us about yourself, Gerald," Liz said. "Is Soufrière your home?"

"Yes, ma'am. I am born here. I never go away, except to

Jalousie and Unionvale. Or Fond Gens Libre, some people call now. Was Unionvale for long time. Same place."

Dani handed him a Guinness and sat down next to him. "I saw a spear gun on your surfboard. Do you fish?"

He grinned, showing a mouthful of large, straight teeth that were a dazzling white in the dark of the evening. "Yes, ma'am. Is how I make my living. I bring you some fish. Tomorrow, prob'ly. All finish for today. I take to town already this afternoon. To the market."

"That would be nice," Liz said.

"Is my pleasure." He took a swallow of the Guinness. "The leas' I do to repay your kindness. You have good day in Soufrière?"

"Yes," Rick said. "We hiked up Gros Piton and saw Brigands' Cave."

"Mm-hmm. I did see you wit' the mon, Randolph. I camp in forest up there."

"We didn't see you," Shellie said. "Or a camp."

"No, ma'am. Nobody see me, 'cept when I show them. Is bes' that way. Mos' people don' like me, so I stay out of the way. You like the cave?"

"We were a little disappointed in the cave," Rick said. "We were hoping to find a cave that not so many people have been into. A more natural one, if you know what I mean."

Gerald nodded and took another sip of his Guinness. "You stay here tomorrow?"

"Yes, we'll be here tomorrow," Rick said.

"Good. I show you cave tomorrow. This cave, people like Randolph, they don' know 'bout, mebbe."

"That would be great," Rick said. "Where is it?"

"There," Gerald gestured toward Petit Piton. "Many cave, but all connect together. This one, people use long time. Draw on walls. People before us, you see?"

"I think so," Rick said.

"Good. I mus' go now. Tomorrow, I show you."

"Where will we meet you?"

"Miss Dani?" Gerald asked.

"Yes."

"You know beach between two mooring place? Mebbe halfway Petit Piton? Little reef?"

"Yes."

"You bring there, Miss Dani. Go to road, walk to Pitons. I meet you, no problem."

"What time?" Rick asked.

Gerald shrugged, "When you come, I am there. Don' worry. Tomorrow. Thank you for Guinness, Miss Dani."

He stood and stepped over the lifelines onto his surfboard, untied it, and paddled away into the darkness, all in a matter of seconds.

"It's almost like he disappeared," Shellie said. "What a strange man."

"Welcome to the islands," Dani said. "Soufrière isn't exactly on the beaten path, but that was a little unusual, even for here."

"What was going on with the alcohol thing?" Rick said.

"I don't know. A lot of the Rastas we run across will drink a little beer. Especially Guinness. But they say they don't use alcohol, if you offer them rum or wine."

"That whole experience was a little creepy," Shellie said. "It almost sounded like he'd been spying on us. Do you think it's safe for us to go off with him?"

Dani shrugged. "He's different, but not that different. I think you'll be fine. He invited you; people here take hospitality seriously. I don't think he would have taken the trouble to paddle out here and introduce himself if he meant any harm."

"But he's odd," Shellie said. "Do you think he was in the woods, watching us when we were out with Randolph?"

"I don't think there's any doubt," Dani said. "He may live in the woods somewhere up there, that camp he mentioned. I'll go with you, if that makes you feel better."

"Oh, you're welcome, but you don't have to," Rick said.

"I'd feel better if you and Liz were here on the boat," Shellie said. "That way, if we don't come back on time ... " She shook her head. "You could call the police, or something."

"Whatever makes you comfortable," Dani said. "You don't have to decide now."

"Speaking of now," Liz said, "I should get dinner on the table. It's getting late."

"They're still in Soufrière," Ashley said, looking at the tablet. "That must be a good sign."

"Why do you say that?" Ed asked.

"Because, from looking at the guidebook, there isn't much there, once you've seen the town and the Bat Cave." She grinned and faked a shudder. "Some tourist attraction. Bats."

They sat in *Aquila's* cockpit, sipping iced tea and recovering from their trip into Fort-de-France. Bert had gone straight back to his cabin when they returned to the boat, still complaining about his head.

"Leila, I think we should go," Ed said.

"Let's do," Leila said.

"But ... " Ashley shrugged.

"But what?" Leila asked.

"Soufrière's not a very big place."

"You're worried they might recognize the boat?" Ed asked.

"Yes, exactly," Ashley said.

"All these rent-a-boats look alike," Ed said.

"To you they do," Ashley said. "But you're not a boat person. Those two women do this for a living. They probably know a lot of the other boats by sight, especially ones that are based in their neighborhood."

"Can we anchor around the corner, or something?" Leila asked. "In Soufrière, I mean."

"That's what got me worried," Ashley said. "The whole area around there's a marine park. They don't allow anchoring; you have to tie up to a mooring buoy. Every boat's going to be visible to anybody who looks."

Ed frowned and shook his head. "So, do you have an idea, Ash?"

"We could sail to Rodney Bay. That's only around twenty or twenty-five miles. If we left the boat there, we could rent a car and drive down to Soufrière. There are resorts there, places we could stay. Or we could take a water taxi down there if we don't want a car."

"I like having the boat for a base of operations," Ed said. "What other ideas do you have?"

"We can go check out Soufrière and see where they are. There are two places where they have moorings. Most of them are in the main harbor, but there are a few between the two mountains. We could see which place they're in and we'd stay in the other."

"How far apart are they?" Leila asked. "These two places?"

"A mile or two, max," Ashley said, "But it looks like there's no line of sight between the two areas. The smaller of the two mountains is between them."

"I like that," Ed said. "Is there a downside?"

"Yes," Ashley said. "The downside is that we may not be able to get a mooring, depending on how crowded it is."

"Are there other places near there?" Leila asked.

"There are some along the coast north of Soufrière, but nowhere close by on the south side. The problem with that would be shore access, if we want to tail them. It wouldn't be easy — go ashore, try to get a taxi, maybe in the middle of nowhere ... "

"Yeah," Ed said. "Okay. Let's head for Soufrière. If we can't find a spot, we'll double back, take the closest place, and move in the morning. If it's like you said and there's not much there, the moorings probably turn over pretty quick. How's that sound?"

"You're the boss," Leila said. "You want to leave now?"

"How long will it take us?" Ed asked.

"Four or five hours," Leila said. "We might be better off motoring, with Bert out of commission. We'll rotate every two hours, keep a fresh set of eyes on deck, since it's nighttime."

"Let's do it, then," Ed said.

27

"Done?" Leila asked, as Ashley sat down on the bench beside her. Leila had been pretending to snap photographs of the boats while Ashley handled their inbound clearance.

"Yes. We're all checked in. Any activity on *Vengeance*?"

"Your timing's perfect," Leila said. "The Everetts just now climbed in the dinghy with Dani. They should be coming out from behind the boat any time, now."

"How's the new camera?" Ashley asked.

"No complaints. I think this zoom lens is way better than the one that was stolen."

"Good," Ashley said. "I thought it would be. Here they come."

"Should we get out of sight?" Leila asked, handing Ashley the camera. "Want to put this in the bag?"

Ashley took the camera and held it in her lap while she opened the camera bag. Taking out a pair of hats, she said, "Baseball cap? Or sun hat?"

Leila took the baseball cap and pulled it down, shading most of her face. "You need the big hat to hide your blond hair."

Ashley zipped the camera bag closed and put on the wide-brimmed canvas hat. She reached back and tugged a Velcro strip free, unfurling a lightweight cloth screen for her neck and upper shoulders. "I think we're okay here. Let's see what they're up to."

"They're not coming this way," Leila said. "Looks like they're heading down toward Petit Piton."

"There's a beachfront restaurant down there. I saw it marked on the sketch chart in the cruising guide," Ashley said. "That's about the only thing I'd think would attract them to that area. Let's move."

"Yeah," Leila said. "Let's follow the road down that way."

"Look," Ashley said, five minutes later. "There goes the dinghy, headed back out to *Vengeance*."

"Only one person in it," Leila said. "You think the Everetts are having breakfast at that place?"

"No," Ashley said. "I saw the ad for it. They're only open for lunch and dinner. Besides, I don't think they had time to get that far."

"Shit," Leila said. "If they're heading south, they've got a good half mile on us."

"Jog?" Ashley asked.

"May as well. If we see anybody coming our way, drop back to a walk. You go ahead. I'm going to give Ed a quick call, let him know what's happening. I'll catch you."

"WHAT'S your bet that Gerald is a no-show?" Dani asked. She had just returned from taking Rick and Shellie ashore and was sitting in the cockpit with Liz, finishing the coffee left from breakfast.

Liz shrugged. "Why would he have bothered to paddle out here last night, then?"

"I don't know. I keep asking myself that."

"But you encouraged them to go, Dani. I don't understand what you're thinking."

"There wasn't much risk in their going. And I'm intrigued by something he said last night, too."

"Gerald?"

"Yes. Who else?"

"What did he say?"

"When I was crouched on the side deck right after he came up, he was mumbling half the time."

"Yes. We couldn't hear most of what he was saying, until he commented on *Vengeance*. What was that all about?"

"I don't know. At the time, I thought he was high as a kite, hallucinating, maybe, from the look in his eyes. I caught a strong whiff of ganja, but it dissipated before he came up."

"I saw his eyes," Liz said. "They were bloodshot and dilated. I thought he was probably high on something."

"I guess he'd been partaking of the sacrament," Dani said, smiling. "It's hard to know how 'with it' he was. That's why I wondered if he would show up this morning."

"Oh, well. Rick wanted to walk around town, anyway. They'll call us when they're ready to come back, either way. We got off the subject, though. What was it that Gerald said that intrigued you so?"

"Right, it keeps slipping my mind, because it was so confusing, with his mumbling. I decided I'd misheard, but looking back on it, I don't think I did. He said something about how he'd been waiting for us. Something like, 'Welcome. I been waitin' for you, I t'ink.' And I wasn't sure I'd heard him correctly. So, I said, 'waiting?'"

"That's strange," Liz said. "How'd he respond?"

"More mumbling, but something to the effect that he'd overheard some men saying that we would be here looking for the cave soon."

"You mean like somebody knew we were coming?"

"That's what my first thought was, but it didn't make any sense, and I thought he was out of it. I asked him what cave he was talking about, and he said, 'the cave,' and then went on to how pretty *Vengeance* looked. I tried to get him back on the subject of the men — like, 'What men, Gerald?' And he got this panicked look and shook his head like druggies do when they're freaked out."

"But you still invited him aboard?"

"He was about to cut and run at that point. He was muttering about being thirsty, and he let go of the lifelines and dropped into a crouch on his surfboard, like he was going to paddle away. I wanted to know more about the cave, in particular. So, yes. That's when I offered him a Guinness."

"You didn't say anything to Rick and Shellie about this. Why not?"

"Once he came aboard and started talking with us, he said he'd seen them with the guide when they went to Brigands' Cave. His conversation with me before that had been so muddled that I thought maybe he was just confused. He seemed harmless enough, so I put it aside."

"You think he was talking about Rick and Randolph when he mentioned 'the men?' Is that it?"

"Yes. I just thought he'd been high when he saw them, maybe. And Rick was definitely hooked on the cave thing, so I decided to let it go. You think I should have said something? I mean later, to Rick and Shellie?"

"I don't know. It doesn't matter, now. Like you said, he's not exactly a threatening sort. Quite the opposite. But it will be interesting to hear how Rick and Shellie get on with him."

"If he shows up," Dani said.

Liz poured them each another mug of coffee. "On a different topic, I'm surprised we haven't heard from Marie or Phillip," Liz said.

"Me, too," Dani said. "Let's call them."

"I did, while you were running Rick and Shellie ashore. I left a message on Phillip's voicemail."

Dani looked down through the companionway, peering at the ship's clock on the forward bulkhead. "He's probably taking Sandrine to work. He'll call in a few minutes."

Liz nodded. "That's what I thought."

"How was your sketching yesterday?"

"Okay," Liz said. "I got distracted by the cliff face over there, though." She pointed at the rocky outcroppings on Petit Piton a few hundred yards away. "I spent most of my time on that."

Dani twisted in her seat, looking over her shoulder. "There are some interesting contrasts in the textures there."

"Yes. All that green scrub, and the rocky parts peeking through. And in the afternoon sunlight, this long, almost vertical crevice pops out at you. It stretches from that big oval of exposed rock down through the underbrush, all the way to the base of the cliff. It reminds me of the Bat Cave, but it's longer and narrower, and it runs at more of an angle."

"I'm not seeing it," Dani said.

"No, not yet," Liz said, "It'll show up in a few — "

Her phone interrupted her. "Phillip," she said, touching the screen. "Hi, Phillip. You're on the speaker with me and Dani."

"Good morning," Phillip said. "Sorry I missed your call. I was driving Sandrine to her office. Your guests aren't around?"

"They're ashore, exploring," Liz said. "We were wondering if you or Marie had heard anything from Luke or Interpol about the people from *Aquila*."

"Not yet, but I was about to call you when I got your voice-mail. Sandrine checked first thing when she got in to work. *Aquila* cleared out late yesterday afternoon, headed your way."

"They got their passports, then," Liz said.

"Yes, I guess so," Phillip said.

"They're headed for St. Lucia?" Dani asked.

"Listed their next port of call as Soufrière."

"When did they leave?" Liz asked, standing up and scanning the boats in the harbor.

"I don't know, but they're not in the anchorage off Ste. Anne now. I looked before I called."

"Okay," Dani said. "Thanks for the heads up. Anything else?"

"Not right now. I've got a call in for Marie; I was going to ask if they saw when *Aquila* left. One of us will be in touch soon."

"All right, then," Liz said. "We'll talk later." She disconnected the call. "They're not in the harbor here," she said, sitting down again.

"I think I'll take the dinghy around to the other side of Petit Piton and see if they picked up one of those moorings," Dani said. "Do you want to ride with me?"

"No, thanks. I'll stay here. If they're not here yet, I should be able to spot them approaching. Besides, I'm more comfortable if we have somebody aboard while we're here."

"Worried about petty thieves?" Dani asked.

"Yes. The websites both say they've had a recent increase in thefts here. But only from unoccupied boats. No sense tempting anybody."

Dani nodded, rubbing the back of her head. "I agree. Once is enough."

"Still have a knot?" Liz asked.

Dani snatched her hand away from the site of her recent injury. "No. Guess that was subconscious."

"Take the handheld radio with you," Liz said, as Dani moved to untie the dinghy. "If Rick and Shellie phone me for a pickup, I'll give you a shout." She passed the radio to Dani.

"Back soon," Dani said, taking the radio and climbing down into the dinghy.

LEILA WAS HOLDING the phone away from her ear because of Ed's shouting. When he paused for breath, she interrupted. "Look, Ed. I'm sorry we've got the dinghy and you're stuck on the boat, but that's the way it worked out. Where do you and Bert need to go, anyway?"

"Nowhere right now, but suppose the women on *Vengeance* decide to go somewhere? Or we get hungry? It'll be lunchtime soon."

"It's Everett we need to worry about," she said, "not the women on *Vengeance*. But if it makes you feel better, take a water taxi in and retrieve the dinghy. You remember the combination for the lock?"

"Yeah, okay. Maybe I'll do that, unless we decide to make sandwiches. Any idea where they're going?"

"None, right now. I stopped walking to call in. Ashley's following them. I need to get moving and catch up with her, okay?"

"Yeah, go ahead." Ed disconnected the call.

Leila slipped the phone in her pocket and started jogging at an easy pace. After she'd covered a few hundred yards, she rounded a gradual bend in the road and saw Ashley stopped another two hundred yards ahead. As she dropped back to a walk, she saw Ashley raise the camera and focus on something back in the direction of town.

"What's up with the guys?" Ashley asked, when Leila was within speaking distance.

Leila rolled her eyes and shook her head. "They're bored, I guess."

"That's no surprise, given who they have for company," Ashley said. "Dickheads."

"Did they go in there?" Leila inclined her head in the direction of the restaurant near the end of the road. They were standing next to a sign marking the entrance. The building was visible through the trees, on the other side of the parking area.

"No," Ashley said. "When they got to within a couple of hundred yards of where we're standing, someone stepped out of the woods and waved to them. I didn't get a good look at whoever it was, but they went on into the trees, right over there." She pointed to an ill-defined path.

"Where does it go?" Leila asked.

"It skirts along the base of the cliff. I followed them in there for a little way, but I came back out. There are too many breaks in the foliage after you get past the restaurant; there's not enough cover to follow without being seen."

"Any idea where it leads?"

"Yeah. I heard people working in the restaurant and went in and asked them. It peters out after a few hundred yards and turns into a climb up the cliff face. They said it's a goat trail, not safe for people."

"So, is the restaurant open?" Leila asked. "Think we could hang out here for a while and see if they come back?"

"Yeah, it's actually a perfect spot. Once you go in, there's a patio that opens up on the other side where the tables are. There's a great view of the cliff face in one direction, and the main harbor in the other. The people were really nice. They said we're welcome to take a table and relax. The kitchen's not open for another hour, but I asked them to make us a pot of coffee. They said it's not busy, and we can spend the day enjoying the view if we'd like to. They said it's a great spot for watching birds on the cliff. Popular with nature photographers."

"Let's do it, at least for a while," Leila said.

"Yeah," Ashley said. "While I was talking with them, I could catch a glimpse of the Everetts through the leaves every so often. If what I was seeing is the rest of the trail, they should come out in the open before too long."

"Great," Leila said. "Lead on."

"You going to call Ed and Bert? They could join us for lunch or something."

"No. To hell with them. Let 'em eat sardines and crackers. Assholes."

"I won't ask," Ashley said.

"Wise of you. No need in both of us being pissed off."

"*Aquila's* THERE," Dani said, as she tied the dinghy to *Vengeance* and climbed aboard. "The two men were lounging in the cockpit, but the dinghy's missing. No sign of the women, but I guess one of them could have been below."

"Or they may have both gotten ashore without us realizing they were here," Liz said. "Marie called. She said they noticed *Aquila* leaving around nine o'clock last night."

"Why the delay in telling us?" Dani asked.

"There was a new boat that anchored between them and *Aquila*. They didn't realize the boat that left was *Aquila* until this morning, when there was enough light to make out what happened. Last night, they thought it was a different boat that got under way."

"I don't suppose it matters," Dani said. "We wouldn't have done anything differently if we'd known."

"That's what I told her," Liz said, "but she didn't agree. She pointed out that this left *Aquila* able to spy on us without our knowing they were in the neighborhood. She thought we should warn Rick and Shellie, once I told her what they were doing."

"What do you think about that?" Dani asked.

"I don't know," Liz said. "It might just worry them; what would they do about it?"

"That's so, but if we don't, and something happens ... "

"You're right," Liz said. "I'll call them right now."

"While you do that, I'm going to make a quick run by the town dinghy dock and see if there's an Econo Charters dinghy there."

"Why?" Liz said.

"I'll tell you when I get back." Dani dropped back into their dinghy and roared away.

Liz called Rick and told him what they had discovered. By the time she'd explained everything to him and gotten a report on their excursion so far, Dani was back. She tied their dinghy and climbed aboard.

"Well?" Liz asked.

"It was there."

"How do you know there's not another Econo Charter boat here?"

"It had *Aquila* painted on it," Dani said. "And it's losing air. It'll be sunk in a few minutes."

"Do you think they hit something sharp?"

"Yes, my rigging knife," Dani said, grinning.

"Why did you do that?"

"Because they weren't around. Nobody was."

"Because they weren't around? I don't get — "

"For me to punch out. I owe them some pain and suffering for knocking me out in Grenada. Sinking their dinghy seemed like the least I could do to even the score. Besides, it'll slow them down, whatever they're up to."

Liz shook her head and chuckled. "But they'll just think they hit something."

"Yes, but we'll know they didn't, and that's what matters. Did you call Rick and Shellie?"

"Yes. Rick was pretty excited. I had trouble getting a word in. They're climbing the cliff face; he said he could see *Vengeance* over his left shoulder. I'm supposed to look for them with the binoculars."

"The cave's up there?" Dani asked, staring at the exposed rock face on Petit Piton's northwest side.

"He said it wasn't all that high up," Liz said. "They're working their way across a series of ledges, maybe 75 to 100 feet up. Mostly it's going sideways, he said." She scanned the cliff face with the binoculars. "I see them. They're almost to that crevice I was telling you about. Here." She passed Dani the binoculars.

"I see them," Dani said. "Gerald just disappeared into the crevice."

"I'll bet that's the entrance to the cave," Liz said. "I meant to tell you earlier, but I forgot in all the excitement."

"Tell me what?"

"Rick had printed out that sketch map, remember?"

"Yes. What about it?"

"It hit me when I was sketching. That crevice is shown on the sketch map, running down the side of the mountain that would be Petit Piton. And there's a line that could be that ledge they were traversing. It intersects with the crevice, and there's a crude circle around the intersection."

"You're serious?"

"I am."

"We all missed that, then," Dani said.

"It would have probably come to us eventually. But I'll bet anything they're going to find the cave in there."

"Thanks to that crazy Gerald," Dani said.

"Well, there's nothing wrong with a little good luck, is there?"

"I don't know," Dani said, "but I'm glad I'm here on *Vengeance* instead of with them in some cave. Got any snacks? All that exercise they're getting is giving me an appetite."

28

"Hey, Bert," Ed said.

"Yeah?"

"Let's head into town and see what's going on with Leila and Ashley."

"I thought you just called them."

"I did. They're set up in a restaurant. They watched the Everetts scale a cliff with some Rastaman. Said they disappeared into a crevice; it might be the cave. I think we should join them. See what we can see. It's getting late; the Everetts will probably be coming back down soon. Maybe we can see if they're carrying anything."

"What about keeping an eye on their boat?" Bert asked. "Shouldn't we do that, in case they come back a different way?"

"They can see *Vengeance* from the restaurant, too."

"All right. You gonna call a water taxi?"

"Already did. He said he'd be here in no time — here he is, now."

"Hello, *Aquila*," the water taxi operator said, as he came alongside.

"Give me just a minute to lock up," Ed said, as Bert climbed down into the water taxi.

"No problem, mon," the operator said.

Ed, a backpack slung over his shoulder, joined Bert, and the water taxi sped away, rounding Petit Piton. In a few minutes, they were at the town dock in Soufrière. As the water taxi bumped against the dock, the operator said, "Whoee! Mon, somebody gon' have a bad day. That dinghy be sunk, if it not tied to the dock."

Ed looked at the shriveled rigid inflatable dinghy. The tubes were nearly flat, and the outboard engine was submerged, its weight pulling the back of the dinghy underwater.

"Shit!" he said. "That's ours. Now what the hell are we going to do?"

The water taxi operator tied his boat to the dock and rummaged in a small locker, coming up with a bellows pump. "Mebbe we jus' pump up. You unlock it an' pull it over here, okay?"

Ed did as the man suggested. When the dinghy was secured next to the water taxi, the operator reached down into the flooded dinghy and connected the hose from the pump to one of the valves.

"We pump up the back firs'," he said. "Get the engine out of the water."

"I don't understand," Ed said. "The back?"

"The dinghy have t'ree air chambers. One across the bow, one on each side. You can use it wit' the bow one flat, but you mus' have air in the sides." He set the pump on the seat of the water taxi and stood, one foot working the bellows pump. With every stroke, a cloud of bubbles rose from under the inflatable tube. He shook his head. "Got a big hole; not gon' hold air, mon. Somebody mus' take the dinghy out of the water an' patch him."

"Is there anybody around here that can do that?" Ed asked.

"Mebbe. We see how bad this one, firs'." The man had shifted the hose to the other aft inflation valve. He pumped a couple of strokes and shook his head as air bubbled to the surface again. He reached down into the water, running a hand along one of the inflatable tubes. He shook his head and sat up. "Hole mebbe foot long. Somebody cut this dinghy, mon. Mebbe not fix. Not easy, like the mon here can do. I t'ink mo betta you call the charter people. Mebbe they get you 'nother dinghy. You charter in Rodney Bay?"

"Grenada," Ed said.

"Mebbe they got a base in St. Lucia. Rodney Bay got some charter companies. Big dealer for inflatables, too. They might could fix. Marigot got some other ones. You call me any time you need to go somewhere. I give you my bes' special rate. I am Rupert." He offered Ed a business card.

"I already have one. You gave it to my friend earlier. But why would anybody do that to a dinghy?"

"Don' know, mon. Bad people. Mebbe upset wit' you 'bout something. Mebbe jus' plain evil." He shook his head. "You call when you ready. I be waitin', no problem, mon."

After Ed paid the water taxi, he and Bert climbed onto the dock. Ed watched as Rupert cast off and let his boat drift out into the harbor.

"What are we gonna do now?" Bert asked.

"Find Leila and Ashley," Ed said.

"What about calling the charter company?"

"Ashley's the one who signed the contract," Ed said. "She'll need to make the first call, anyway. We'll go from there. Come on. Leila said to follow the road along the waterfront toward Petit Piton. We'll see the sign when we get to the end of the road."

DANI PUT down her Kindle when her cellphone rang. Liz looked up from her sketch pad.

"Hello?" Dani said, answering the phone.

"Dani?"

"Rick?"

"Yes. Can you pick us up now?"

"Sure. Same place?"

"No. Shellie's twisted her ankle. She can't really walk; I'm half-carrying her. If you follow the road south from town along the water toward Petit Piton, it ends at the parking lot for a restaurant. Gerald says you can use their dock on the beach. We'll be there in a few minutes — on the dock."

"All right. I know that spot. I'll grab the first aid kit and — "

"No, that's okay. We've got it wrapped up well enough for right now. We just need to get her back to the boat."

"Okay. I'm on my way." She turned to Liz. "I'm — "

"I heard. Go ahead. I'll get an ice pack put together."

Dani nodded and got in the dinghy. She headed for the spot where the shoreline merged with the base of Petit Piton, and soon spotted Rick and Shellie. He had one arm around her waist and was waving with the other one as they hobbled out onto the rickety little pier. When Dani arrived, they were waiting at the end of the dock. She stopped the dinghy at their feet.

"Just hold it steady, Dani," Rick said. "I'll ease her down into it, okay?"

"Yes. Shellie, use me for support," Dani said. She was standing in the dinghy, bending over with her hands on the dock. "Pretend I'm a handrail."

"I'm okay now," Shellie said, after she got both feet in the dinghy, her hands gripping Dani's shirt.

"Sit down on that tube and I'll climb across to the other side," Rick said.

When he was settled, Dani asked, "Ready?"

"Ready," Shellie said.

Rick nodded, and Dani pushed the dinghy away from the dock.

"Hold on," she said, opening the throttle and heading across the harbor to *Vengeance*.

"What a klutz!" Shellie said, over the whine of the outboard. "I made the whole climb up and back and then tripped right at the end of the trail. Practically fell into the parking lot."

"How's the ankle?" Rick asked.

"Throbbing, but I don't think it's too serious."

"Liz has an ice pack ready for you," Dani said. "And we've got a pretty good medicine chest aboard if you need something for pain."

"I don't like heavy duty painkillers. Ibuprofen will do it for me."

"We have plenty of that, too," Dani said, throttling back and standing up to grab *Vengeance's* toe rail. "Think you can make it up the boarding ladder? If not, we can hoist you aboard — it's no big deal. Put you in the bosun's chair and up you go."

"It's only two steps," Shellie said. "Rick, you go up first, and I'll use my good leg on the ladder to heave myself up. You can catch me, so I don't have to put my weight on the bum ankle."

Dani held the dinghy and Rick went up, turning around to grab Shellie's hands as she mounted the ladder. Rick and Liz helped her back into the cockpit while Dani secured the dinghy. By the time Dani joined them in the cockpit, Shellie had removed her shoe and wrapped the ice bag around her ankle.

"How is it?" Dani asked.

"Better already, but I'm probably stuck on the boat for a few days, darn it."

"Keep it elevated and iced," Liz said. "We can get you back to Castries if you think you need x-rays."

"Oh, I'm sure it's just sprained," Shellie said. "I'm bummed. I wanted to go back with you guys tomorrow and see what's in that box."

"Box?" Liz asked. "So you found something?"

"Something, yes," Rick said.

"You don't sound as excited as when we spoke on the phone this morning," Liz said.

"Well, yes and no. It seems a little too easy," Rick said. "You can see the crevice in the cliff face." He turned and looked. "Maybe not, in this light. Anyway, there's a crevice — "

"We could see you going into it with the binoculars," Dani said.

"Oh, okay. Once you work your way in there, there's a small cavern that opens up to the left. It's maybe twenty feet across, and high enough to stand up in, barely. In the far back corner, there's a tunnel that you can squeeze through. It opens into a big chimney, I guess you'd call it. I'm not a spelunker. Anyway, it's a vertical shaft, maybe 10 feet in diameter, and it goes down to water, maybe 50 or 60 feet. We could lean over and see down all the way with our flashlights. At the bottom, there's a little shelf, like a rocky beach, maybe halfway across. But it was hard to tell. It looked like we might be seeing part of another cavern, like a room that extended off into the water. And there was a stash of stuff stacked on the rocky shelf."

"What kind of stuff?" Dani asked. "You mentioned a box, Shellie."

"There was a box, of some kind, and a jumble of odds and ends piled around it," Shellie said.

"A jumble?" Dani asked.

"Oh, it looked like maybe stuff had been stored in bags at one time, and the bags had rotted away. I don't know for sure. It was a little tough to make out," Rick said.

"Gerald climbed down there," Shellie said, "but Rick didn't want him to touch anything."

"So you didn't go down yourselves?" Dani asked.

"No way," Rick said. "That guy, Gerald, I swear he's part spider. I could never get down that chimney. The walls are vertical, and sheer rock. Too far apart to wedge yourself between them, too."

"You were afraid he'd mess something up?" Liz asked. "Contaminate it or something?"

"Exactly," Rick said. "And then we found out he'd already been poking around down there, but there's nothing to be done about that."

"So he'd found this before?" Dani asked. "He knew it was there?"

"Yes, but I couldn't figure out how long he's known. It's tough to communicate with him, especially about abstract things like how much time has passed. He seems to speak some kind of patois, mostly."

"Every so often, there's a French word," Shellie said. "But they don't always fit the context. He's not too articulate in English."

"That patois would be *Kwéyol*," Dani said. "Or *Creole*, in the French islands."

"Could somebody translate for us?" Rick asked.

"Maybe, but it's tough," Dani said. "There are so many variations from island to island, and even place to place on a given island. You could probably get the gist of what he's saying, though, if we had a *Kwéyol* speaker with good English."

"I'm not so sure about him," Shellie said. "I think he might be on drugs, or hallucinating, or something."

Dani and Liz traded looks. "That crossed my mind the other night," Dani said. "It's hard to know, when there's a language barrier."

"Anyhow, I don't think he'd picked through the stuff," Rick said. "At least not much. The box looked intact from up where we were. When he came back up, he had these." Rick reached into his pocket and took out a short, circular string of beads. He handed them to Dani, who studied them for a few seconds and passed them to Liz.

"They look like ivory," Liz said.

"Old, and stained from handling," Dani added. "And with

some kind of medallion that looks like it has Arabic script carved on it. Ivory, too, I think."

"They're prayer beads," Shellie said. "Thirty-three beads. Typical *Misbaha*. Sometimes, they're strung with three groups of 33, for 99 beads total. A Muslim would use them to count prayers, in a sequence of three. The first prayer was repeated 33 times, then the second, and then the third."

"Are these old enough to have belonged to your mullah?" Liz asked.

"From the appearance, the style, especially of the medallion, I'd say they could be," Shellie said. "It would take a lab analysis to be sure of the age, though."

"Did Gerald pick them up from the stash?" Dani asked.

"I think so," Rick said. "He was kind of vague about it, though. I didn't see him pick them up today. He was just shining the flashlight around, so we could see from up at the top of that vertical shaft."

"What's your next step?" Dani asked.

"I want to go down and have a look at the stash myself," Rick said. "Grid it off with some mason's cord and make a detailed survey, with photographs. Get it thoroughly documented before it's disturbed."

"How's Gerald feel about that?" Liz asked.

Rick shrugged. "He seems okay. I don't know how well I explained it to him, but he's willing to take us back in tomorrow."

"How are you going to get down the chimney?" Dani asked.

"Gerald said something about a chair of some kind. You would use it to go up the mast, from what I got from him."

"A bosun's chair?" Dani asked.

"That's it," Rick said. "I couldn't tell what he was calling it, except the chair part. He thought you might have one."

"We do have one," Dani said. "But we both prefer to use a rock climber's harness for going aloft. It's more secure when conditions are wild, which they often are when you need to go up the mast at sea. I'd recommend it over the bosun's chair."

"How does it work?" Rick asked.

"I'll show you." Dani rummaged in one of the cockpit lockers and took out a drawstring bag about a foot long and a few inches in diameter.

After untying the drawstrings, she extracted a handful of webbing with metal fittings. She shook it out and held it up. There was a heavy length of webbing about three and a half feet long with two smaller loops of webbing suspended from it. She stepped through the smaller webbing loops, one with each leg, working them up high around her thighs and adjusting them for a snug fit. She wrapped the heavier piece of webbing around her waist and buckled it, cinching everything up tight.

"That's it," she said. "These metal loops are for tools, or whatever you want to hang on them. You take the line that's going to hoist you and pass it through these two big D-rings and tie it off, and you're ready to go. It's safer than a bosun's chair because there's no way you can fall out of it. I went up the mainmast in a storm to clear a fouled halyard so we could drop the sail once, and the boat rolled through about 90 degrees. I was thrown off the mast and ended up hanging upside down for a while, until I got sorted out."

"Wow," Rick said. "Could we use that?"

"Sure," Dani said.

"What would we use to lower it? And raise it back up?"

"Liz and I use a four-part block and tackle. That lets you raise and lower yourself without taking too much strength. We've got one that's good for a lift of around 80 feet. All you'd need is something to anchor it at the top."

"How about tying a loop of rope around that boulder in the middle of the cavern, Rick?" Shellie asked. "You could run it through the tunnel."

"Seems to me that would do it."

"You want to watch out for sharp edges that might chafe through your line," Dani said.

"What are the chances of you coming along to help us?" Rick asked. "Just for advice, like that."

"I ... uh, how skinny is this cave?"

"Skinny?" Rick asked.

"Any tight spots? Do I have to slither on my belly or anything?"

"Oh," Shellie said. "No. Nothing like that. A couple of places are kind of like doorways, where you have to turn sideways to squeeze through. And there's one place like a tunnel, going into the cavern with the chimney. You have to crawl on all fours for a few feet."

"How few?" Dani asked. "Two? Twenty?"

"Ten, maybe," Shellie said.

"Okay, then, I'll give it a shot," Dani said.

"Who's ready for a sundowner while I get dinner started?" Liz asked.

"I thought you'd never offer," Shellie said. "Any chance of something a little stronger than wine?"

"She mixes a mean rum punch," Dani said. "And I'll have one, too, Liz. Make mine a double."

29

"I finally got through to the charter people in Grenada," Ashley said, rejoining the group at the table on the restaurant's patio. "For all the good it did."

"What did they say?" Ed asked.

"They started by telling me to get the pump out of the cockpit locker and try to re-inflate it. After some discussion, I got them to understand that it had been vandalized, that somebody had slashed it. Then they wanted us to bring it back to them; they'd swap it for another one."

"Back?" Leila asked. "Back to Grenada?"

"That's what I asked. And their answer was 'Yes, back to Grenada.' Our other option is to find somebody up here to fix it, get an estimate, get them to okay it, and pay for it. They'll reimburse us."

"Shit," Ed said. "That's no good. They don't have a base here?"

"Nowhere but Grenada," Ashley said.

"Rupert didn't think anybody around here could fix it," Ed said.

"Rupert?"

"Our favorite water taxi driver."

"We need a dinghy," Leila said. "We're handicapped without one. Let's just buy one; we've got the cash. There must be a dealer in St. Lucia."

"In Rodney Bay," Ed said. "Rupert told us there was a big dealer there who might be able to fix it."

"Can you check it out online, Ash?" Leila asked. "I'll tell Ed and Bert what's going on with Everett."

"Sure." Ashley took her smartphone and went back inside.

"WiFi's better in there," Leila said, seeing the frown on Ed's face.

He nodded. "So you saw them go into a cave up on the cliff?"

"We saw them disappear into a crevice. Given how long they were in there, we think it must lead to the cave they're looking for. Did you bring the stuff?"

"Yeah. A handful of .380 rounds, a couple of light bulbs from the 12-volt fixtures, and that plastic bag of stuff you bought in the hardware store in Fort-de-France."

"Those two throwaway prepaid phones?" she asked.

"Yes. And a quart of engine oil. Does this mean what I think it means?"

Leila smiled. "Maybe. We need to go up and see if the cave's really there, and if it's the right one."

"Are they still up there?" Bert asked.

"No. They came down a little while before I called you. Everett's wife's limping, like she hurt her leg or something. Ed, did you bring the empty backpack?"

"Yeah, it's inside this one." He nudged the one he'd been carrying with the toe of his shoe.

"I'm ready to go, then. You coming? Bert can stay here with Ash and keep a lookout, in case they come back. I could use your help getting the stuff up there."

"Yeah. One thing, though," Ed said.

"What?"

"We don't have any fertilizer."

She grinned. "You don't, but I do. That's what the extra backpack's for."

"Where is it?" Ed asked, looking around.

"I stashed it in the woods, off the side of the trail. I didn't want to bring a 25-pound bag of fertilizer in here."

"Where'd you get it? Somebody will remember a tourist buying fertilizer. Especially when the cops start asking around after the explosion."

She shook her head. "That's why I didn't buy it."

"You stole it? That must have been a challenge."

"Not really. There's a kind of truck farm off the side of the road back to town. I found it in a shed."

"You're not worried about somebody seeing us on the cliff?"

"It'll be dusk by the time we get out on the exposed rock. Let's go."

"We got an email from Phillip. He wants us to give him a call," Dani said, as Liz finished cleaning up the galley after dinner.

"Shall we take a phone up on the foredeck?" Liz asked. "I don't want to disturb Rick and Shellie. They seemed exhausted."

"Yes, they did. You ready?"

"Sure. Let's go."

Thirty seconds later, they were sitting on the foredeck, the phone between them with the volume turned low.

"Hey, Dani," Phillip said. "Liz with you?"

"Yes, I'm here."

"Hi, Liz. How about your guests?"

"They had a big day," Dani said, "scaling the cliff at Petit Piton. They turned in early. What's new?"

"Scaling a cliff? I thought he was looking for a cave."

"They found it. Or found something. He's not quite sure what's in there yet. We're going back tomorrow."

"We?" Phillip asked.

"Rick and I. His wife sprained her ankle, so she and Liz are staying on *Vengeance*."

"You're going in a cave?" Phillip asked, the pitch of his voice rising. "I didn't think you'd ever — "

"They said you can practically walk in; it's not like that one in Jamaica, okay?"

"Okay. Did the guy Sharktooth put you in touch with show him this cave?"

"No. He turned out to be a typical tour guide. Didn't know much about caves, other than the one they show all the visitors. But this odd character — a Rasta who lives in the woods around Petit Piton — he saw them and overheard Rick asking about other caves. He came by the boat last night and told Rick about this one. It was a weird conversation."

"And it gets even more weird," Liz said. "But that's not why you wanted us to call. We'll tell you about the weird guy another time. What's new?"

"Not too much, actually, but I heard back from Luke Pantene, and Marie got the feedback from Interpol, so I wanted to let you know."

"Sounds like you didn't find out much," Dani said.

"That's right. As Luke put it, they're so clean they're not even normal."

"Does that mean he's suspicious of them?" Liz said.

"Yes, but only because there's no reason to be suspicious. Not even a parking ticket out of the four of them, let alone any moving violations. That puts them in a tiny minority of the population. Their identities all check out. They're in the credit agency files, but none of them has a fixed address or an automobile. They've got Florida drivers' licenses that match everything else. They each have accounts at the same mail forwarding service that they use as a mailing address. Checking accounts, credit cards. All graduated from college about the same time, in different places, and none of them has had a job since they graduated."

"How do they make a living, then?" Liz asked.

"Good question," Phillip said.

"Can Luke get a look at their bank accounts? Or credit card charges?" Dani asked.

"Not without a warrant, and there's no probable cause."

"How about what we found on their computer?" Liz asked. "That's probable cause, isn't it?"

"That's probable cause for somebody to get a warrant to arrest you two," Phillip said, with a chuckle. "But it's worthless for going after them."

"What did Marie get from Interpol?" Dani asked.

"More of the same. She did get a little more information about their travels, but nothing that's helpful. They seem to live out of their suitcases, and they're generally together."

"That's pretty odd," Dani said. "A foursome, with enough money to travel internationally on a full-time basis."

"They could be independently wealthy," Phillip said. "We don't know."

"They're not related to one another?" Liz asked. "Married?"

"Not married," Phillip said. "As for being related, there's nothing to indicate that, but it's always a possibility."

"This is bullshit," Dani said. "We know they're dirty, and they're up to no good. Those have to be false identities."

"I don't think there's any doubt about that, Dani," Phillip said. "And that's all we need to know. You have to keep watching your back, that's all. Any sign of them in Soufrière?"

"They're here, on a mooring between the Pitons, conveniently out of sight from *Vengeance*," Liz said.

"And they don't have a dinghy anymore," Dani said. "It sunk."

"So they're stuck on their boat, or using water taxis?" Phillip asked.

"That's right," Dani said.

"What happened to their dinghy?"

"Dani," Liz said, with a grin.

"Dani?" Phillip asked. "I don't — "

"Dani happened to their dinghy," Liz said, laughing now.

"I was pretty sure they were going to run over something sharp and puncture the tubes," Dani said. "It's always better if that happens at the dock, don't you think?"

"Safer, anyway," Phillip said. "Kind of you to be looking out for them, but won't they just patch it?"

"There's not enough patching material in all of St. Lucia," Dani said.

"Okay," Phillip said. "I take it you're going to be there for a while, since Rick found the cave?"

"Yes, I think so. Why?" Dani asked.

"Sharktooth and Marie are planning to head down there tomorrow morning. They thought you might need some back-up, given what we know — and don't know — about the bunch on *Aquila*."

"Are they bringing *Lightning Bolt*?" Liz asked.

"Of course. You know Sharktooth doesn't like to fly. Besides, they'll need the boat to get around. They'll be calling you sometime tomorrow, but they'll probably stay out of sight, at least for now."

"Okay," Liz said. I'll be on *Vengeance* all day with Shellie, so they know where to find me."

"I'll pass that along. Stay safe," Phillip said.

"You, too," Dani said. "Thanks for calling. We'll be in touch."

She put her phone in her shirt pocket. "I can't wait to see how Sharktooth stays out of sight on *Lightning Bolt*. It practically glows in the dark, with that new paint job."

"Hiding in plain sight," Liz said. "Maybe he'll be able to communicate with Gerald, though."

"Maybe. If Gerald even shows up tomorrow."

"You don't think he will?" Liz asked. "I assumed he'd be going with you and Rick."

"That's a reasonable assumption about a normal person. But I'm not sure about Gerald." Dani smiled.

"Are you okay with going in the cave?"

"I'm dealing with it."

"I could go, and you could stay with Shellie, you know."

"Thanks, Liz. But this is something I need to do, to face up to."

"Face your fear?"

"Something like that. It's the one thing that sends me into pure panic; I can't just throw up my hands and walk away from it. You know I'm not made that way."

"I know. I just thought I'd offer."

"Thanks. Maybe another time, but I'm going to beat this. Let's go to sleep. It's getting late."

30

"Look," Leila said, sweeping the cavern with the beam of her flashlight. She and Ed had located the entrance to the cave with little difficulty once they had found their way back into the crevice in the cliff face.

"What?" Ed said. "You see these drawings? They look prehistoric."

"Yeah. Those are called petroglyphs; I read about them."

"You read about this cave?"

"No, about petroglyphs in other places in the islands. Do you see the shadow back there where I'm shining the light?"

"Yeah. What about it?"

"Let's work our way back there. I think it's an opening of some kind, maybe to another cavern." She began to pick her way across the rock-strewn, uneven floor.

"Spooky," Ed said. "Shit!" He tripped and caught himself.

"Careful," Leila said. "You okay?"

"Yeah, okay. Cut my damn hand, though."

"Shuffle, kind of, and don't shift your weight until you're sure of your footing. Follow me; I'll let you know if there's anything big in the way."

In thirty seconds, Leila reached the back wall. She dropped to her hands and knees. Peering through an opening that was just big enough for her to crawl into, she thought she saw a deeper shadow on the floor several meters ahead. She couldn't be sure, because the tunnel through the rock curved just enough to obscure the size of the opening at the other end.

"I'm going in," she said, dropping the backpack that she had filled with fertilizer. "Wait here."

"Gladly," Ed said. "That tunnel gives me the creeps. There's no room to turn around once you're in there. What if you get stuck? Or get hurt, or something?"

"Then you'll have to get me out."

"And if I can't?"

"Then I'll die. Shut up, Ed. It's just a hole in the rock. It'll be okay."

Pushing her flashlight ahead of her, she crawled into the tunnel. About six meters in, the tunnel opened up enough so that she could rise to a crouch. As she thought, the floor fell away sharply.

She swung the beam of her light around, taking in her surroundings. She was in another cavern, smaller than the first one they'd been in. Less than a meter in front of her, the floor dropped off into a vertical shaft that was three to four meters in diameter. Looking over the edge, she could see water at the bottom, 15 or 20 meters below. There was a strip of rocky beach against the wall of the shaft that was closest to her.

The beach extended about halfway across the shaft, and she could see a sizable box, well above the water line. There were other, smaller things stacked around the box, but she couldn't make out what they were. The other wall, opposite the beach, was in deep shadow. She played the light over it, but she couldn't quite tell what she was seeing.

It could be another tunnel. She wasn't sure of directions, but she wondered if it led out to the cliff face at sea level. That would explain how somebody got all that stuff into the cave. She couldn't see a way to climb down the shaft. It would make sense that there might be another entrance to the bottom of the shaft, if somebody used it for storage.

She shrugged. It didn't matter. This had to be the place, but she'd know for sure if Everett came back with climbing gear tomorrow. She turned around and entered the tunnel that she had crawled through before. This time, having learned that the floor of the tunnel was smooth enough, she lay on her back and scooted herself along. Examining the rock over her head, she was looking for a good spot to put her explosives.

She found one area where the overhead surface had a number of open crevices. Using her abdominal muscles and resting on her left elbow, she reached up with her right hand, exploring the openings. There was room here to wedge the backpack filled with fertilizer up into the overhead gap.

The seams in the rock would shatter under the force of the explosion, and fragments of rock would seal the tunnel. Anybody who survived the explosion would be trapped, and whatever was down in that vertical shaft would never be seen again.

She would snorkel the base of the cliff in the morning to be sure there wasn't an underwater entrance. Once she blew the tunnel closed, she would keep watch at the outer entrance on the cliff face long enough to be sure no one who might be in the outer cavern survived the blast.

Satisfied, she tried to roll onto her stomach so that she could crawl out to where she'd left Ed, but the tunnel was too narrow. She scooted along on her back until she got to a wider spot, then turned over and crawled out.

"Well, what did you find?" Ed asked.

"This is it. It has to be the place." She gave him a quick summary of her plan.

"So I don't have to crawl into that tunnel?" he asked.

"Only if you want to critique my plan; I'd be glad for your suggestions." She smirked, knowing he couldn't see her face.

"No, it's a great plan. What else do we have to do in here?"

"You mix the ammonium nitrate fertilizer with that quart of motor oil. Right in the backpack will be fine. I need to go back in there with one of the burner phones and see if there's a decent signal. I think we're close enough to the entrance."

"What if there's not?"

"Don't worry; I've got an alternate plan. Get to work."

She took a phone from the backpack Ed had been carrying and powered it on. "So far, so good," she said. "Five bars out of five."

Clamping the phone in her teeth, she crawled back into the tunnel, rolling onto her back and skidding into place. She took the phone from her mouth and held it against the top of the tunnel, touching a button to illuminate the screen. "Four bars," she said, moving the phone up into the lower part of the crevice. "Still four bars. It's meant to be." She worked her way back toward the entrance on her back.

"Well?" Ed asked, his hands in the backpack, kneading the mixture.

"We're good," she said, reaching into the other backpack, the one that held her supplies. Withdrawing a plastic bag, she took out the two improvised blasting caps she had rigged earlier.

After they left the restaurant, but before they began climbing, she'd pulled the bullets from the brass cases of two .380 caliber rounds, careful not to spill the powder. She had soldered pigtails of insulated wire to two 12-volt incandescent bulbs using a butane soldering iron.

Then she'd broken the glass envelopes of the bulbs, taking care not to damage the fragile filaments of tungsten. Sliding the tungsten filament of each bulb into the gunpowder in its own brass cartridge case, she'd fastened the base of the bulbs into the cases with duct tape.

Applying voltage to the pigtails would cause the tungsten filaments to burn in two, sparking and igniting the gunpowder, which would set off the primer in the shell case. The resulting small explosion would detonate the mix of fertilizer and oil.

Earlier, on the sail from Martinique to St. Lucia, she'd performed surgery on the two cheap cell phones and tested them. She had left a pair of thin wires coming out of the case of each phone. The wires were energized by the phone's battery when it rang. Now, she powered on each phone and stuck the ends of the wires to her tongue, making sure there was no voltage present. Satisfied, she connected a blasting cap to each phone.

"Ready with the mix?" she asked.

"Yeah." Ed hefted the backpack.

She put a roll of duct tape around her wrist, took a phone in each hand, and lay on her back again, her head in the tunnel opening.

"Put the backpack on my chest," she said. "Top toward my face, straps down."

"Okay?" Ed asked, as he watched her slide into the tunnel.

"Yeah, sure."

"Be careful," he said.

"Would you rather do it yourself?"

"Uh-uh," Ed said. "I'm not trained for it."

"No?" she asked.

"No."

"Then shut up. All your bullshit's making me nervous, and you don't want my hands shaking while I do this."

THE SAUDI COLONEL studied the report from his agent in St. Lucia, nodding as he saw that their work was bearing fruit. The American professor had found the cave, though that was not surprising.

It was clear to anyone who made an effort to learn about crossing the Atlantic under sail that the most likely landfall would be in the latitudes of St. Lucia or Martinique. Further, the foundation had sent Everett a 'revised translation' that referenced a cave in a cliff that overlooked the bay where Khashkhash had established his shore base.

That, along with the fragmentary sketch of the island's shoreline, had apparently been enough of a clue to send Everett to the cave where the goods were hidden. They'd done everything but put an 'x' on the sketch and label it 'cave.'

The report mentioned that Everett had engaged a local guide who had shown him a cave that was a popular tourist attraction, but it was on the wrong side of the mountain. Today, Everett had met another local who helped him scale the cliff above the anchorage and make his way across a ledge to the correct cave.

He had come away empty handed, but that was to be expected. The stash was in plain view from the main part of the cave, but it was at the bottom of a 15 to 20-meter vertical shaft. Everett would need some climbing equipment to get to the prize.

The cave was perfect, the agent wrote, as there had once been a passage from a small beach which afforded sea level access to the storage cavern. The passage was under water now, and closed, too, as the roof had collapsed at some point, probably centuries ago. While no longer useable, the ruined passage would be evident once Everett explored the cavern. That would explain how Khashkhash and his men would have come to use the cave.

The agent expected that Everett would return in a day or two with equipment that would enable him to descend into the storage cavern. Meanwhile, there might be a problem. There was a second group of Americans on another yacht, and they appeared to be shadowing the Everett party.

The agent was asking for instructions. He wanted to know if the colonel was aware of the party. He provided details of their yacht, descriptions of the men and women in the party, and even their names, which he had obtained from a contact in the customs office.

The colonel was alarmed. He needed time to ponder this. He would make a discreet inquiry through his back-channel contact in the Directorate of Intelligence. Maybe they would have some record of these four people. Or perhaps they were part of some rival operation. He needed to know as much about them as he could learn before he briefed the Prince tomorrow.

"DID YOU FIND WHAT YOU EXPECTED?" Ashley asked, as Leila and Ed pulled out chairs at the table. The remains of the dinner Ashley and Bert had shared were still on the table.

"Yes, I think so," Leila said. "We left a surprise behind, as well."

"Ah!" Ashley said. "That's good, then. You can still order dinner, if you're hungry. Bert and I split a salt-fish curry."

"I'm okay," Leila said. "I'd like to get to bed early tonight; I've got an early project in the morning. You hungry, Ed?"

"I guess I'll just make a sandwich back at the boat. Should I call Rupert to pick us up?"

"There's no need," Ashley said, smiling. "I solved that little problem."

"You got a new dinghy?" Ed asked, eyebrows rising.

"Close. The owner of this place overheard my phone calls about the dinghy. His brother-in-law has a business taking people on kayak tours of the Bat Cave, and he's in the midst of upgrading his kayaks. He had some he wanted to sell. I bought two of them. He threw in the paddles, so we're all set."

"But there are four of us," Ed said.

"They're two-seaters," Ashley said.

"Where do we have to go to get them?" Leila asked.

"He delivered them. They're tied to the dock down on the beach, ready to go."

"Good job, Ash," Leila said. "That'll make things a little more manageable."

"Yeah," Ed said. "I've even recovered my appetite. Think this place can do a quick burger?"

"I'm sure they can," Ashley said, waving at the waitress who was hanging back in the shadows.

The woman ambled over to the table and took Ed's order. "We got the bes' burgers in St. Lucia," she said.

"Should I order two?"

"Not 'less you powerful hungry; they half-poun' burgers. Beer?"

"Sure. And some French fries."

"I be right back wit' the beer. The burger an' fries be a minute or two. Anybody else need anyt'ing?"

Everyone shook their heads, and the waitress went back to the kitchen.

"You and Ash can go ahead back to *Aquila*, if you like," Ed said, looking at Leila. "Since we've got two kayaks."

"We need to talk about tomorrow," Leila said. "You think it's okay to talk here, Ash?"

Ashley waited until the waitress put a beer in front of Ed. When the woman left, she said, "Sure. They had a couple of other customers while you were gone, but there's nobody here but us, now."

"Wonder why they're still open?" Ed asked.

"They do some late evening business, they told us," Bert said.

"So, what about tomorrow?" Ashley asked.

"Okay," Leila said. "I'm going out early to snorkel along the base of the cliff. There's a chance that the cave opens to the sea somewhere around that reef we noticed. If it does, we'll need to make sure nobody gets out that way. And if there's access, we'll want to make sure whatever's in there is destroyed. If there's no access, the stuff will be hidden forever, because the cave's going to be sealed off."

"That sounds easy enough," Ashley said. "I could do that, if you want."

"I'd rather do it; I've got a better sense of where the opening might be," Leila said. "Once I've done that, Ed and I will get in position to watch the entrance to the cave from the cliff. I'll want you and Bert to keep an eye on whoever's left aboard *Vengeance*. That's probably going to be Everett's wife, at least, because she's hurt."

"We can handle that," Ashley said, "but I don't think this place will make a good base for us tomorrow."

"I agree," Leila said. "It's going to be early, before they open up here, for one thing."

"Right," Ed said. "And hanging out here two days in a row might attract attention."

"Yeah," Leila said. "You and I can wait along the road with the camera, pretend we're taking pictures of birds or something. Once we see them traversing the cliff face, we can move onto the wooded part of the trail."

"Bert and I can get some coffee and hang out on one of those benches along the waterfront in town," Ashley said. "That'll give us a good view of *Vengeance*." She paused as the waitress returned with Ed's order.

"That was fast," he said.

"The cook, she quick; she gettin' t'ings ready for the people soon come. We get people from the resort up the hill, mos' nights. But they come late. Jus' wave if you need anyt'ing else."

"So, what's the rest of your plan, Leila?" Ashley asked.

"We need to stay flexible. All those people need to die, and their boat needs to vanish without a trace."

"And whatever's in that cave," Bert said. "We're supposed to destroy that."

"The blast will take care of that," Leila said. "And it'll probably take care of anybody in the cave, but I'll want to go up there and check afterward to be sure we've sealed it off, and clean up any survivors."

"What about *Vengeance*, then," Ashley asked. "Whoever's aboard is going to hear the blast, maybe see smoke or something. They'll be raising an alert."

"You need to be ready to jump in that kayak," Leila said. "I'll give you a heads-up a few minutes before the blast, so you can get in position. Then you board *Vengeance* and subdue whoever's aboard."

"You want them alive?" Bert asked.

"Yes, until we've got a handle on the situation."

"How about their boat?" Ashley asked.

"Stay on their mooring until I tell you to leave. We may need it, or the people, if something unforeseen happens. There'll be plenty of time to get it out of the harbor in the confusion after the blast."

"What about *Aquila*?" Ed asked.

"It depends on how things play out," Leila said. "But most likely, you and I will take her and meet up with Ash and Bert."

"Where?" Bert asked.

"Due west until we're out of sight of land. Then we can sort everything out, sink *Vengeance*, and head back to Grenada. Just make sure your phones are charged. Like I said, we need to stay flexible. There are a lot of moving parts here, and we only control some of them."

"How's the burger, Ed?" Bert asked. "Maybe I should get one."

Leila looked at Ashley and rolled her eyes. "I'm going back to the boat and get some rest. You guys do what you want." Leila stood up

"I'm with you," Ashley said, getting to her feet.

"Let's go, then. See you in the morning, Ed, Bert," Leila said over her shoulder as she and Ashley left.

31

"Let's move to the trail," Leila said. She and Ed had been waiting on the road, watching the cliff face through the camera's telephoto lens while they pretended to photograph birds. "Something changed?" Ed asked.

"Yes. That Rasta that was with them yesterday just came out of the undergrowth. He's maybe three or four minutes behind them, crabbing his way across that ledge toward the crevice."

"Okay," Ed said, as they began to walk along the deserted stretch of road. "I wonder what the story is on that cave."

"You could have gone through the tunnel last night," Leila said.

"No, that's not what I meant. You told me about that."

"What, then?" she asked, as they trudged along.

"Well, you said there used to be an opening to the beach. I was trying to imagine what it would have been like when Khashkhash and those people were here."

"You've bought into that story, then?" Leila said.

"Why not? You said there was that stash of stuff down there, and no way to get to it."

"That's not quite what I said, Ed. I don't buy all that bullshit about the Moors."

"Then why are you doing this?"

"I have my reasons. I don't owe you an explanation."

"Okay, but do you think somebody put that stuff in the cave before that sea-level entrance caved in?"

"I have no idea. What difference does that make to us? We've got our mission; there's nothing unclear about it."

"But Leila, don't you wonder? Where's your sense of history, of romance?"

"You sound like a teenage girl, Ed. Now I get it. I finally understand."

"Get what?"

"Those pictures of you and that other ... never mind."

"I told you, those were from a fraternity skit, Leila."

"Uh-huh."

"You can be a real bitch, sometimes. You know that?"

"It's what I was trained for. Now shut up. Everett and that woman from *Vengeance* just went into the crevice. The guy with the dreadlocks is catching up to them. Save your breath and let's hustle."

"If you can see the cave entrance from here, we could stop now," Ed said. "It might be better if we didn't get too close. There's no telling what that much explosive is going to do to the cliff face."

"It's only the equivalent of around 10 or 12 pounds of TNT," Leila said.

Ed squinted at her and shook his head. "It's not out in the open, though."

She stopped for a few seconds, thinking about that. "Yeah, okay. You're right. It is pretty well tamped by all that rock. We can wait here until I set it off. Who knows?"

"You have a cell signal?" he asked.

She took out her phone and touched the screen. "Yeah, it's a solid five bars, just like up in the cave."

"That skinny Rasta just went into the crevice," Ed said. "How long are we going to wait?"

"Let's give it a few minutes," she said. "It would be best for us if all of them were through that tunnel before I set it off. Say another five minutes?"

"Yeah, okay," Ed said. "You going to call Ash?"

"Yes." Leila poked at the screen of her smartphone and held it to her ear. "Ashley?" She was silent for a couple of seconds. "Yes. Can you be aboard *Vengeance* in — say five minutes?" She listened again. "Good. Go for it." She listened again. "No. Just call me if you run into trouble. I'll blow it in about five minutes from the time we hang up. You get aboard and sit tight. Ed and I will need about 15 minutes after the blast. We're going to scale the cliff and make sure nobody got lucky. I'll call you when it's all clear. Remember what we talked about last night, in case something goes wrong." She disconnected and made note of the time.

"Everett's wife and the one with the reddish blond hair must be on the boat," Ed said.

Leila nodded. "So?"

"We're going to just waste them?"

"You got a problem with that?"

"It's pretty cold, Leila."

"Damn right. That's the best way. Cold. Then we know for sure."

"But ... " he shook his head.

"Hey, Ed?

"What?"

"Blowing up the cave with three people in it's not cold?"

"It's ... but we'll be right there with them, the Everett woman and what's her name."

"Liz," Leila said. "Liz Chirac."

Ed didn't say anything. Leila checked the time and looked at him. She saw the sweat beading on his forehead.

"Ed?"

"Yeah?"

"You don't have a problem killing people as long as you don't have to watch them die. That it?"

"Yeah, maybe it is."

"You know what that makes you?"

"What?"

"A coward. You have no respect for human life. If you're going to kill someone, you should at least show them the courtesy of looking them in the eye when you do it."

"What about the people in the cave?"

"That's one of the reasons we're going up there afterward — to pay our respects."

"You're fucking insane, Leila."

"And you're a chickenshit, Ed."

"Watch it. I'm your superior."

"In a pig's ass, you're my superior. Want to try proving it?" She glanced at her watch. "We've got a little over four minutes to go. That's plenty of time for you to die." She locked eyes with him for several seconds, until he looked away. "That's what I thought," she said. She raised her phone and scrolled through her directory, stopping at the number for one of the burner cellphones she had modified.

"Four minutes to show time. If you want to change your mind, just say the word," she said, staring at him.

"Is that the tunnel Shellie mentioned?" Dani asked. She was crouching, looking up over her shoulder every few seconds, eyeing the roof of the cavern. She'd bumped her head several times already.

"Yes," Rick said.

"Should we go back outside and wait for Gerald?" Dani asked.

"I don't see any point," Rick said. "It's all straight forward, from here. Traversing the cliff face is the tricky part, but we did okay with that. You were like a mountain goat on that ledge. I'm glad you were leading the way; I've got a thing about heights. Clearly, you don't."

"No, heights don't bother me. You don't think Gerald's coming?"

"Maybe he had something else to do. He's pretty flaky, you know? And if he shows up, he knows where to find us."

"Okay, I guess. If you're sure we don't need to wait for him."

"Nah," Rick said. "Nothing to it from here. Should we tie this rope to the boulder before we go through the tunnel?" Rick shined his flashlight on the three-foot rock embedded in the floor behind Dani.

"How far is it to the lip of the chimney from here, about?" she asked.

"You mean from the boulder?"

"Yes."

"You're worried about whether this rope's long enough?" Rick had the coiled line draped diagonally across his chest.

"Yes."

"I don't know. Maybe 40, 50 feet at the outside." He lifted the coil over his head, dropping it on the floor. "How long's this rope, anyway?"

"A hundred-fifty feet."

"Do we just tie the end around the rock and pull the rest of it behind us?" Rick asked.

"No, I think it would be better to leave the extra length out here, where it won't be in our way. Maybe you can tie the end to your belt and crawl through, and I'll feed the line out behind you, so it doesn't get tangled. Once you've got enough to dangle a few feet of it over the lip of the chimney, give me a yell and I'll tie it off to the rock."

"Good idea," Rick said. "But let's tie it around my ankle so it's out of the way of my knees and thighs. There's one pretty tight spot in there."

Dani worked her tongue around in her mouth, which had gone suddenly dry. "How t-tight?"

"You have to kind of slump down in one spot, and slither along on your belly, sort of like ducking under an archway. But it's only a foot or two, and then you're through." Rick had looped the line around his left ankle while he was talking. "Did you see me tie that bowline?" He grinned. "I was a Boy Scout."

Dani licked her lips and nodded. "Ready?"

"Sure," Rick said. "Here goes."

Dani watched as he positioned his flashlight on the floor of the tunnel, pushing it in as far as he could reach. He ducked his head and crawled into the opening, blocking the brief glimpse she'd had of what lay ahead. She worked up a mouthful of saliva and struggled to swallow.

"Hey!" Rick called, his voice muffled.

"What's ... " Dani choked, her voice breaking. She swallowed again. "What's wrong?"

"Give me some slack, will you?"

"Oh! Sorry," Dani said, unclenching the fist that held the line. "Tangled. Should be okay, now."

She focused on paying out the line as he began moving again. She tried to ignore the sound of his clothes and shoes scraping along the rough rock of the tunnel. The images conjured by the sounds set her pulse racing.

"Dani?"

She realized Rick had shouted. "Yes," she yelled. "Can you hear me?"

"Yeah. Did you hear me? I said you could tie off the rope now and come on through."

"Okay. Sound must not carry well in here. Give me a minute, and I'll be right with you." She looped the line around the rock a couple of times and made it fast to itself, leaving the excess coiled at the base of the rock.

She turned back to the tunnel entrance and dropped to all fours, pushing her flashlight into the tunnel as Rick had done. Noticing the dank, musty odor in the tunnel, she began to breathe through her mouth. She could make out what she thought must be the other end.

In her mind, it looked to be a hundred meters away, the walls of the tunnel tapering to a small spot of light in the distance. That must be from Rick's flashlight. She knew from paying out the line behind him that it was only a few meters through the tunnel, but it looked much farther to her.

Shaking her head, she took a deep breath. "I can do this," she whispered. She moved forward, only to be stopped by resistance in her shoulders. Fighting her rising panic, she realized she still wore her backpack. The climber's harness was in it, along with a couple of bottles of water, and the block and tackle. The pack had snagged on the edge of the opening to the tunnel.

She backed up and took off the backpack, sliding it into the tunnel with her flashlight. Ducking her head, she took a deep breath, noticing how much of the tunnel was blocked by her backpack. She closed her eyes and began to crawl, pushing the flashlight and the backpack ahead.

After a few feet, she felt her shoulder blades strike the roof of the tunnel. She remembered what Rick had said about having to slouch to get under a low spot. Maybe the tunnel would be more open after that. She gave the backpack and the flashlight a shove and bent her elbows, putting her face close to the floor. Inching forward, she could feel the rock scraping along the muscles in her back. She fought the urge to scream and pushed on.

Just as she thought she might squeeze through the tight spot, a phone rang in the tunnel behind her. She jumped, startled, and felt a sharp pain in her head, accompanied by a blinding flash of light. Then she embraced the darkness that enveloped her.

32

"What!" Dani barked, slapping Rick's hand away from her face as she squinted into the flashlight he pointed at her eyes. She shook her head and sat up. "What happened?"

"You hit your head in the tunnel and — "

"There was a phone ringing," she said.

"I am mos' sorry, Miss Dani."

"Gerald?" She turned her head, looking in the direction of his voice.

"Yes. I go in the hole behind you, mebbe not so far. The phone ring, and you jump. Hit the head."

"How did I get out here? This is the main cavern, right?"

"Gerald pulled your legs," Rick said, "and I guided your shoulders and protected your head. How are you feeling?"

"Okay. How long was I out?"

"Not long," Rick said. "Minute, maybe a minute and a half, tops. You started coming around before we got you out. We rolled you on your back, and I was about to check your pupils when you slapped at my hands and sat up."

"Where were you, Gerald?" Dani asked. "I didn't know you had come into the cave with us."

"Late. Sleep long. Watch people las' night. Tired."

"Watch people?"

"Yes. People come in cave las' night. I watch. They don' stay long, but they leave bag. And phones."

"Somebody left a bag in the cave?" Rick asked.

"An' phones," Gerald said, nodding.

"Where was it?" Dani asked.

Gerald pointed at the tunnel. "In the hole. Up in top."

"Did you move it?"

"I look in bag, take phones. Put bag back." He reached into the cloth pouch tied at his waist and took out a cellphone, extending it toward Dani.

She took it and glanced at it. She scowled, her eyes going wide. "What about these?" She tugged on two thin, insulated wires.

"I break," Gerald said. "Sorry."

He reached into his pouch again and handed her a one-inch-long cylinder covered in black duct tape. Two wires protruded from one end.

She studied it for a moment. "You said, 'phones.' More than one?"

He nodded and held up two fingers. Reaching into his bag again, he brought out the other phone, this one with a similar cylinder still attached by two wires.

Dani took the phone in one hand and jerked on the cylinder with the other, breaking the wires.

"What're you doing, Dani? What are those things?" Rick asked.

"Improvised detonators. Blasting caps. I'd say somebody just tried to blow up the cave, with us in it. Can you get that bag they left, please, Gerald?"

Gerald nodded and scooted into the tunnel on his back, head first. He was back in thirty seconds, a backpack balanced on his chest. He set it on the floor and wiped his hands on his ragged shorts. "Nasty," he said.

"There was only the one bag?" Dani asked.

"One," Gerald said. "Full wit' mess. Nasty," he said, again.

Dani unzipped the bag and Rick shined his flashlight into it. All three of them peered at the grainy, glistening mixture inside.

Dani touched a finger to the surface and brought it to her nose.

"What is that?" Rick asked.

"Ammonium nitrate fertilizer and some kind of oil," Dani said. "Enough to blow that tunnel shut, at the least. Probably fill both caverns with rubble, in the bargain."

"Fertilizer?" Rick asked.

"It's a common explosive," Dani said. "Used for everything from blowing stumps on farms to terrorist attacks."

"Is it powerful?"

"About 40 percent as powerful as TNT, pound for pound." She picked up one of the improvised detonators. "Was this inside the bag? Down in the 'mess?'"

"Yes," Gerald said. "Both in mess."

"We're lucky you found it, Gerald," she said. "We'd be dead otherwise."

Gerald's bleary eyes held her gaze, but he didn't say anything.

"Whoever set this is wondering why it hasn't blown up," Dani said. "I'm surprised — "

The second phone began ringing. They stared at it until it stopped.

"Why'd they call again?" Rick asked.

"Because there was no blast. The second phone was for backup."

"What should we do?" Rick asked. "Call the cops?"

"That would be a waste," Dani said. "By the time we got through explaining, it would be too late for them to help us."

"I don't understand," Rick said.

"Whoever did this is out there watching. I'm not sure why

they waited as long as they did before they called the backup phone, but now they're going to come after us."

"Come after us? Why?"

"To finish the job. They obviously want us dead."

"Why?" Rick asked. "Who are they?"

"I don't know why," Dani said, "but it's almost sure to be the people on *Aquila*." She glanced at her watch. "If they're watching from the base of the cliff, I'd say they'll show up in 15 or 20 minutes. Maybe sooner, if they're already on the ledge."

"Shouldn't we get out of here?" Rick asked.

"No. There's only one way out. There's nowhere for us to go. I don't want to be exposed on the cliff face so they can pick us off at their leisure. Do you?"

"No, but what can we do?"

"We'll arrange a couple of little surprises for them. While they're distracted, we'll jump them."

"I don't understand," Rick said.

"That's okay. You and Gerald retrieve that line that we ran through the tunnel. See if you can find a way to tie it across the entrance, maybe six inches above the floor, where they'll trip over it. I've got work to do."

She took her multi-tool out of the pouch at her belt and began to strip the broken wires coming from the phones and the blasting caps. Before she reconnected them, she checked the phones and set them to vibrate instead of ringing. Then she entered their numbers into her own smartphone.

She took one of the rewired phones and crawled to the entrance of the cavern. Staying low, she reached out and ran her hand over the surface of the ledge they used for access. She found a gap in the rock at the juncture of the ledge and the cliff face and slipped one of the phones with its attached detonator into it. Lying on her stomach, she was able to crane her neck enough to see that the phone was hidden from view, at least for someone standing on the ledge.

She wedged the other phone into a crack between the wall and the floor of the cavern, a few feet to the right of the entrance from the ledge.

As she finished, Rick and Gerald began stringing the rope.

"Not many good places to tie it off," Rick said.

"Just do the best you can. Any distraction will help, even if they just get tangled in it. We've only got a few minutes before they get here, so listen up."

"Okay," Rick said.

"Once you're done with the rope, you and Gerald hide in the tunnel. Take my phone, and when I yell, 'One,' you hit the speed dial button labeled 'one' on the screen." She held the phone so that he could see where she was pointing on the screen. "Same thing when I yell 'two,' Okay?"

"Yeah, but what are you going to be doing?" He took the phone from her.

"Taking out my frustration on whoever comes through the entrance."

"Don't you want help?"

"No, it'll be better if I'm alone."

"Why? That's crazy."

"You ever been in a knife fight in the dark?" Dani asked.

"No, but you'll be outnumbered."

"Exactly. That gives me the advantage."

"How can that be?"

"Because I can cut anyone I touch without worrying about hurting somebody who's on my side. They'll have to be careful not to hurt one another. Now, get in the tunnel, both of you. There may be shooting, so get in there and stay until I tell you it's over. I think I hear them coming." Dani nodded and snapped open her rigging knife as she backed up against the wall on the side of the entrance opposite where she'd hidden the second phone.

"NICE," Liz said, looking over at the sketch that Shellie was finishing. They had both been sketching the town of Soufrière since Dani and Rick had left an hour earlier. "I like the way you captured the change in the light since that last one you did."

"Thanks. I still don't have quite what I wanted, but I don't want to overwork this one. Better to try again with a fresh start."

"I understand how frustrating that can be, but go easy on yourself, Shellie. That one's great. Nobody but you will ever know it's not what you intended."

"Hey, *Vengeance*." A woman's voice seemed to come from the water behind where they were sitting.

Liz put an elbow on the cockpit coaming and rose a few inches, twisting to see where the woman was. She found herself staring down the barrel of a pistol. Glancing up, she recognized one of the women from *Aquila*. She was kneeling on a yellow plastic kayak, the kind that was available for rent to tourists everywhere in the islands. There was a man sitting in the front, holding on to *Vengeance* with both hands, steadying the kayak.

"Hi, Liz," the woman said. "Stay quiet and calm, and I won't have to shoot you or Shellie."

Shellie turned at that, her face going pale when she saw the gun swing toward her.

"Behave, Shellie. Nobody has to get hurt."

"What do you want?" Liz asked. "Who are you?"

"We'll get to that in due time," the woman said. "We're coming aboard to enjoy your company. I'm Ashley, and my friend is Bert. Now, when I tell you, and not before, I want you to move over and sit on the other cockpit seat, facing me. One at a time, Liz first. Keep your hands where I can see them. No sudden movements, okay?"

Liz and Shellie both nodded.

"Okay, Liz, move now."

When Liz was seated again, Ashley said, "Your turn, Shellie. Careful of your ankle."

"How did you know I — "

"Uh-uh," Ashley said, chuckling. "Not now. I told you, all in due time. Bert, when I tell you, I want you to go aboard and step toward the bow a couple of feet, out of my line of fire. Make sure you have a clear shot at both of them. I want you to cover them while I come aboard. If either of them moves, shoot to wound, not to kill. But shoot them both, okay?"

"Yeah, I got it," Bert said.

"Go," Ashley said.

When Bert was in position, Ashley tucked her pistol in the waistband of her shorts and climbed aboard. She bent and tied the kayak to a cleat on the starboard quarter. Turning around, she stepped into the cockpit and drew her pistol. She sat, facing her two captives, the pistol held low, out of sight of anyone passing in another boat.

"Okay, Bert. Put your weapon away and join us, please."

Bert came into the cockpit and sat next to Ashley.

"Now, as I said, I'm Ashley, and my friend here is Bert. We're going to keep you company while the other members of our team meet up with Dani and Rick. Once everybody's properly introduced, we'll probably go for a nice little sail. How's that sound?"

"Just delightful," Liz said. "How is it that you know our names, Ashley?"

Ashley smiled. "Oh, we know quite a lot about you. We know all the details of Rick's little archaeological project with the Saudis, too."

"Are you from a rival organization?" Liz asked.

"You might say that, yes," Ashley said. "We're here to make sure that what Rick has found will never be seen. Life will be better for everyone if those things in the cave disappear forever."

"Whatever you say," Liz said.

"Good for you, Liz," Ashley said. "Bert, I could use a cup of coffee while we wait. How does that sound?"

"Great," Bert said.

Liz said. "I'll go — "

"No, I don't think so, Liz. It was my idea; you needn't go to any trouble. Bert?"

"Yeah?"

"Would you go below and check the boat for weapons? While you're down there, make some coffee for us. Liz can tell you where everything is, I'm sure."

"Most of what you'll need is still on the galley counter from breakfast," Liz said. "But just ask if you don't see what you want."

Bert got up and went below.

"Don't forget to check for weapons," Ashley said. "We don't need any surprises."

DANI HEARD SCRAPING sounds from outside the cave. She tilted her head away from the wall far enough to see a person silhouetted in the entrance. Pressing herself back against the wall, she watched from the corner of her eye as the shadowy figure came into the dark cavern, right hand extended as if holding a pistol. She heard more scraping from outside.

Yelling, "One," Dani dove and rolled across the floor. The figure in the entrance fired a shot at where Dani had been standing moments before. The bullet ricocheted twice, and then there was a sound like another gunshot from just outside the entrance.

Dani grinned at the yelp of pain that followed the blast of the detonator she'd placed on the ledge. There was a shuffling of feet and a muttered curse from the shooter, who tumbled to the floor, feet tangled in the rope.

Dani waited, lying still, holding her breath, watching. She saw the shooter stand, methodically scanning the inside of the cavern. Picking a moment when the person's head was turned away, Dani yelled "Two," and rolled again as a shot rang out, the bullet ricocheting off the floor inches from where she had been.

Then there was a buzzing sound, followed a second later by the explosion of the detonator inside the cavern. The shooter turned, firing three rounds in the direction of the sound, and Dani lunged, her weight driving the shooter to the floor. Worried, she wasted no time on finesse, grabbing the person's hair and smashing their head into the floor repeatedly, looking over her shoulder toward the entrance.

The person underneath her — a woman, Dani realized — went limp. Dani snatched the pistol from her hand and rolled away just as the second figure limped into the entrance. Dani stuck the pistol in the waistband of her shorts. Her rigging knife hung from her right wrist by a short lanyard. Deftly, she flipped her wrist and gripped the big knife.

She rushed the figure in the entrance — a man, this time, she registered, with a gun in his right hand. She grabbed his pistol with her left hand. Driving the point of her knife into the outside of his forearm just above his wrist, she leaned into it, putting her weight behind the knife and slicing his forearm open from wrist to elbow.

He screamed, releasing the pistol, and she stepped in and drove the butt of the knife's handle into the left side of his head with all her strength. He was unconscious before he hit the floor. She took a deep breath and stepped back, glancing at the pistol in her hand. She recognized it as a MAC-11, a machine pistol. She had just noticed that it was set for automatic fire when the woman she had thought was unconscious hit her from behind, knocking her down.

Dani rolled as she fell, avoiding most of the force behind the follow-up kick that the woman aimed at her ribcage. She scrambled to her feet as the woman struck again with another powerful kick aimed at Dani's torso. Dani shifted to the side, trapping the woman's lower calf with her left arm. She locked the woman's knee with her left hand and fell forward, her right forearm across the front of her opponent's thigh.

They crashed to the floor, and Dani heard the satisfying pop as the woman's knee bent the wrong way. To her surprise, the woman didn't scream. With a soft grunt of pain, she cupped Dani's chin in her right hand and grabbed Dani's hair with her left, beginning the twisting motion that Dani knew would break her neck. Dani stiffened her neck and drove the rigging knife into the woman's right hip, twisting and slashing.

Still, the woman was silent, but her surprise distracted her long enough for Dani to jerk her chin free. She trapped the woman's left hand, still gripping Dani's hair, with her own left hand. She got her right hand on the woman's left elbow, locked her arm, and rose to a crouch. Dani's continued pressure on the woman's extended left arm drove her to the floor, and Dani lunged to her feet, breaking the arm.

She released it and stepped back, delivering a vicious kick to the side of the woman's head for good measure. She swung her own head from side to side, working the kinks out of her neck and keeping an eye on her attackers for a few seconds.

Satisfied they were out of action for a while, she called, "Rick? Gerald?"

"Yeah," Rick answered.

"It's over. You guys come on out and help me tie these two up."

33

Bert reached through the companionway and set two cups of coffee on the bridge deck. After climbing into the cockpit, he handed one to Ashley. She took a sip and wrinkled her nose.

"Yuck," she said. "Instant?"

"I was in a hurry," he said. "No weapons below; I looked while the water was heating."

"This is terrible, Bert. It's not even good instant. Don't you guys have real coffee?" She looked at Liz.

"Yes," Liz said. "Should I make a pot?"

"No, that's okay. Just chalk up another screw-up for Bert." She smirked.

"Make your own damn coffee, then," Bert said.

Ashley took another sip and looked at her watch. She shifted her gaze to the cliff face, and then said, "Okay, Bert. Sorry for picking on you. Enough foolishness. Cover these two again. I need to make a call."

Bert drew his pistol and held it low, pointed at Liz and Shellie. Ashley stood, tucked her pistol in her waistband, and took a smartphone from her pocket. She went up on the foredeck and made a call, speaking briefly in a hushed tone. She was frowning when she came back to the cockpit.

"What's up?" Bert asked.

Ashley shook her head. "Not now. Let's secure these two. Then we can talk."

"That's what I thought," Bert said. "Want me to take them below?" He gave Liz a hungry look.

Ashley reached in her pocket and brought out a handful of cable ties. "I'll cover them; you cuff them — wrists behind their backs, and ankles together— okay?"

"Okay, but — "

"Hang on," she said, leveling her pistol at Liz. "Okay, Bert. Put your pistol away." She watched as he put it in his waistband at the small of his back. She handed him the cable ties. "We're going to do this one at a time, now, ladies. Bert, you go below and wait for Shellie."

Bert climbed down the companionway ladder. "Okay, come on, Shellie," he said.

As Shellie stood, Ashley said, "Go down the ladder and lie down on the floor, face down. If you don't cooperate, I'll shoot Liz in her knee, okay?"

Shellie nodded and went below, favoring her ankle, but doing as Ashley had instructed.

"Good girl," Ashley said, watching as Bert cinched cable ties around Shellie's wrists and ankles. She waited until he dragged Shellie back into a corner, then said, "Liz, it's your turn. Same drill."

Liz went below, and Bert secured her wrists and ankles. He shoved her back on top of Shellie, taking his time, letting his hands wander. Liz moaned softly as he fondled her.

"You like that?" He grinned.

She smiled and licked her lips. Holding his gaze, she blew him a kiss. "Come back when you're not busy?" she asked.

He gave her an evil smile. "Count on it," he said, climbing back into the cockpit.

In a low voice, he asked Ashley, "Did you get Ed or Leila?"

"No," she said, whispering. "Both phones went straight to voicemail — no ringing — like they were turned off."

"We should have been able to hear the blast," Bert said.

"Yeah. Something's wrong."

"Should I go look for them?" Bert asked.

Ashley chewed her lip for a few seconds. "No, I don't think so. Leila said if things went haywire, we should get under way and head due west until we're out of sight of land, then just wait. She and Ed will bring our boat and use the tracker to find us. No matter what happens in the cave, we can't leave these two alive. And this boat has to be sunk."

"So we just head out and wait for them? What if they don't show up?"

"One step at a time. They'll show up. The improvised detonators can be flaky, she said. She was half expecting that she and Ed would have to go into the cave and kill Everett and whoever was with him."

"What about destroying whatever's in there?"

"Not our problem. She and Ed will deal with it, I'm sure. Maybe set off the explosives manually, somehow. Let's get moving." She bent to the instrument panel and started the engine. "Go on up to the bow and drop the mooring pennant."

DANI WAS PLAYING the beam of her flashlight over the two unconscious people when Rick crawled out of the tunnel, Gerald right behind him. Rick switched on his flashlight, and he and Gerald spent a few seconds looking at the two people.

"They're in bad shape, Dani," Rick said, dropping to one knee and feeling for a pulse in the woman's neck.

"Is she still alive?" Dani asked.

"Yes," Rick said, "but she's lost a lot of — "

"What about him?" she asked, swinging the beam of her flashlight.

Rick shifted his position and rolled the inert man onto his back. "Jesus!" he said, seeing the man's right arm, the white bone exposed in the light. "What happened? He's bleeding out, too."

"They made a mistake," Dani said. "Take that rope and — "

"We need to stop the bleeding," Rick said, "or they'll both die."

"If they wake up, they may not live long enough to bleed to death," Dani said.

Rick had begun to tear the man's shirt. He looked over his shoulder and saw the pistol in Dani's hand. "What do you mean?"

"Tie them before you bandage them," Dani said. "Especially her. If they recover consciousness and decide to fight, I'll have to blow them both away."

"Did you cut his arm like that?" Rick asked.

Ignoring the question, Dani stuck the pistol in her belt, picked up the rope, and used her bloody rigging knife to cut off four lengths, each about three-feet long. She knelt beside Rick, shouldering him aside, and pulled the unconscious man's wrists together. Using a length of the line she'd cut, she tied them in a matter of seconds.

Tugging the final knot tight, she said, "Go ahead and bandage his arm if it makes you feel better." She moved to the man's feet and lashed his ankles securely together.

She crawled to the woman, who moaned as Dani rolled her onto her stomach. Dani crossed the woman's wrists at the small of her back and secured them. She turned and tied the woman's ankles together.

As she finished, the woman groaned again. Dani squatted back on her heels and took the pistol from her belt, looking over her shoulder to check on Rick.

She realized that Gerald was nowhere to be seen. "Gerald!"

"Yes?" His voice came from the cave entrance.

She crouched and turned in that direction. "Where'd you go?"

"Out. Make sure nobody come. They got two frien's, mebbe come look for them. I watch. Nobody come now."

"Okay. Good for you."

Dani turned back to see that Rick had bound a pad made from the rest of the man's shirt over the wounds she had inflicted on the woman's hip. He had tied it in place with the rope. He looked up at her.

"Can you cut this off?" he asked. "The excess?"

Her rigging knife still hung from her right wrist. She slipped the lanyard over her hand and handed it to him, noticing that the woman was conscious, her eyes following the knife.

"Thanks," he said. "You weren't kidding about a knife fight in the dark, were you?"

"No, I wasn't. And trust me, they're still dangerous."

"You got that right, bitch," the woman said. "You're going to be sorry you ever saw me before this is over."

"I already am," Dani said, turning her flashlight on the woman.

"You should have killed me while you had the chance, *Dani*," the woman snarled, putting emphasis on the name.

"It's not too late, *Leila*. You looked much more attractive in your passport picture."

"So you stole them, then, not some petty thief. I thought so."

"It seemed only fair," Dani said. "I'm attached to my handheld radio, and you stole it. But I'd say we're about even, now."

"I'm enjoying getting to know you, shit-head, but you're wasting time you don't have."

"What am I missing here?" Dani asked.

"Ashley and Bert. They have your girlfriend and Everett's wife."

"Maybe," Dani said. "Maybe not. Liz is sweet, until you piss her off."

"Why don't you call her and check on her? Cell service is pretty good in here."

"I don't know about that. The phones you rigged didn't do a very good job. Or maybe you were as bad at that as you are at hand-to-hand combat."

"Keep talking, Dani. You'll find out the hard way that I'm not bluffing about Liz and Michelle Everett."

Dani shrugged and took her phone from her pocket. She touched the screen and listened as the call went to Liz's voicemail. She disconnected and put the phone back in her pocket.

"Well," Leila said. "What do you think?"

"The voicemail said she was busy kicking Ashley's ass. Bert's feeding the fish right now."

"Uh-huh, smart-ass. You'd better cut my hands loose and let me make a call, or you'll never see either of them again."

"You have a phone?" Dani asked.

"In my left front pocket. Cut my hands loose, Rick."

"Give me my knife, Rick," Dani said.

Rick looked down at his hand and saw that he still held the bloody knife. "Dani, I think we should do what she says."

"Give me the knife, Rick." She locked eyes with him until he looked away.

"I'll cut her loose. You can hold the pistol on her," Rick said.

"Don't make me ask again, Rick. If you make me take the knife from you, you'll get hurt."

Not looking at her, he extended the knife, handle first.

"Thanks," she said, taking it.

She put a foot on Leila's bandaged hip and rolled her onto her right side. Leila grunted in pain, but didn't say anything. Dani knelt in front of her and made a quick motion with the knife, slicing her pocket open. The phone tumbled to the floor of the cave, and Dani picked it up, powering it on.

"What's the unlock code?"

Leila laughed. "Funny. Now cut my hands loose, and I'll make the call. Liz may still be alive. I think Bert had the hots for Shellie, so she's probably okay, too. He can be a little bit of a sicko, sometimes, though. Better hurry."

Dani knelt and put the point of the knife in Leila's nostril. "The unlock code?"

"Fuck you. Cut me all you want. I'm not telling you anything."

"That's the only thing you've said that I believe." Dani reversed her grip on the knife and smashed the butt of the handle into the side of Leila's head, watching as her eyes rolled back. Leila slumped, unconscious again.

"Why'd you do that, Dani?" Rick asked. "She —"

"I could tell she was in pain, Rick. I didn't want her to suffer needlessly while we were gone."

"Gone?"

"Yes. Let's get out of here. We're going to see about Liz and Shellie."

"But ... " Rick said, shaking his head.

"Rick, we don't even know if she was telling the truth about them. If she was, I'll guarantee that she wasn't going to set them free. And we don't know for sure where her two friends are; they may be coming after us, for all we know. Now, come on. Let's get moving. Shellie and Liz may need our help."

"What about them?" Rick asked, looking at Ed and Leila.

"They're not going anywhere. Go. I'm right behind you."

34

Rick was on the ledge, having just left the cave's mouth. He was about to come out of the crevice and go around the corner onto the cliff face when he saw an oversized, brown, scaly hand snake around into the crevice. He hoped it was Gerald, but he decided not to take a chance on it. Sidestepping back to the cave, he was looking back over his shoulder when he reached the entrance and bumped into Dani.

She was backing out onto the ledge. Startled, she whirled, in a crouch, ready to attack. Rick lost his balance, flailing his arms. She grabbed two fistfuls of his shirt and pulled him toward her, into the cave.

"Somebody's coming in," he said, ducking his head and pushing past her into the cave entrance.

"Probably Gerald," she said, taking a pistol from her belt and stepping back into the shadows.

"Hallo, Miss Dani? Mr. Rick?" Gerald peered into the darkness, silhouetted in the opening.

"What's up, Gerald?" Dani asked, putting the pistol away again.

"*Vengeance* goes," he said.

"Goes?" Dani asked. "She's leaving?"

"Yes. Goes jus' now, few minutes past. I t'ink I bes' come tell you."

"Good. Thank you. Rick and I were just coming out; we're going to the dinghy."

"Then I stay here wit' the bad people, make sure they don' get loose, yeah?"

"Okay," Dani said.

He opened the pouch at his waist and took out one of the two cellphones he had found. "How I call you, Miss Dani?"

Dani reached for the scratched, blackened phone, surprised to see that the display was still working. "You found this on the ledge?"

"Yes, tha's right."

"Let's see if it survived the blast," she said, fiddling with it, finding the incoming call log. She saw her number in the received calls and copied it to the first speed-call button.

"Let's try it," she said, handing the phone back to Gerald, her finger pointing to the '1' key. "Press this button, and it should call my phone."

He took the phone and studied it for a moment.

"Go ahead. Try it," she said.

He touched the button and held the phone to his ear, grinning and nodding when he heard the ringtone from the phone's speaker. A split second later, Dani's phone rang in her pocket.

Taking it out, she accepted the call and said, "Hello, Gerald."

He cackled with pleasure. "He work!"

"Let's disconnect," she said, taking his hand in hers and showing him the 'end' button. "Say goodbye, and press that button."

"Goodbye." He pressed the button, a grin on his face.

As he started to put the phone away, Dani said, "Wait. I'll call you, now." She touched the screen of her phone, and the one in Gerald's hand began to ring.

He looked at it, frowning.

"Press the green button," she said.

He did, and raised the phone to his ear. "Hallo, Miss Dani."

"Hello, Gerald. Can you remember all that, or do you want to do it again?"

He shook his head. "Goodbye," he said, and disconnected. "No problem, thank you."

"You're welcome. Rick and I are going to get the dinghy and see if we can catch *Vengeance*, okay?"

"No problem. I stay wit' these bad people. We talk on phone if trouble come." He raised the hand that held the phone.

Dani nodded. "Ready, Rick?"

"Yes." Rick backed out of the entrance and began sidestepping toward the corner where the crevice met the cliff face, his arms spread as he leaned into the rock, his head turned to the left to see where he was going.

Dani waited until he turned the corner and then followed him.

"ALMOS' there," Sharktooth said, his voice raised.

"Should I call Dani?" Marie asked, also speaking up because of the roar from the three big V8 engines. *Lightning Bolt* was leaping across the waves' crests, making about 80 knots in the two-meter seas a couple of miles off the western shore of St. Lucia.

"Le's wait 'til we there. They on a mooring in Soufrière. Won't be hard to find."

"Is that a sailboat?" Marie asked, rising from her seat and holding on to the top of the windshield with both hands, peering a little to the right of their course.

"No sails," Sharktooth said.

"But I thought I saw sunlight reflecting from a mast a few seconds ago."

Sharktooth opened a small locker in the console in front of his seat. He took out a padded, camouflaged case and snapped it open, extracting a bulky pair of binoculars. He handed them to Marie. She sat down again and looked at the binoculars.

"On the right side," Sharktooth said.

"Thanks," Marie said, flipping the switch she'd found at his direction. "These are different."

"New model," he said. "Jus' tryin' them out."

She held them in one hand as she stood back up. This time, she wedged a knee against the dash to leave her hands free. Raising the glasses to her eyes, she said, "These are better than the ones I've used before. The stabilization is quite good."

"The button on top turns on focus tracking, once you got your target in the reticle," Sharktooth said.

"Okay. It is a sailboat, with no sails up. Two people on deck. Do these have zoom?"

"Little lever on top of the left side."

"Got it ... okay. A man at the helm, and a woman in the cockpit with him. They look uncomfortable. Why would they not put up some sail? At least enough to stop the rolling?"

"I don' know," Sharktooth said. "Mebbe somet'ing broke? Sails ripped?"

"It's a ketch rig," Marie said. "They could at least put up the ... Sharktooth?"

"Yes?"

"It looks a lot like *Vengeance*. But the woman's not Dani or Liz."

"Mebbe their guests?" Sharktooth asked.

"Maybe, but why wouldn't Dani and Liz have sails up?"

"Don' know. An' why they goin' way out wes'? Nothin' out that way 'til Central America. Le's swing by an' take a closer look. Mebbe not *Vengeance*. Bes' sit down; I open her up."

Marie dropped back into her seat and Sharktooth grasped a

knob on the dashboard. He pulled it toward himself and opened the exhaust cutouts as he shoved the throttles forward. *Lightning Bolt* surged forward, the acceleration pressing both of them back into their seats.

In a little more than a minute, they were within a few hundred meters of the sailboat. Sharktooth throttled back and closed the exhaust cutouts. Marie looked over at him, raising her eyebrows. He nodded, and she got to her feet again, wedging herself in and lifting the binoculars.

"It's *Vengeance*," Marie said, after a few seconds, "and they're both staring at us."

"You recognize them?" Sharktooth asked. "Rick an' Shellie?"

"I don't think so." She handed him the binoculars.

Steering to cross their bow at a distance of around a hundred meters, he raised the binoculars for a quick look. Shaking his head, he handed the binoculars back to Marie.

"Well?"

"Couldn't see the woman's face," he said, "but her hair is wrong, and man is not Rick."

By now, *Vengeance* was a quarter of a mile astern of *Lightning Bolt.*

"What do you think?" Marie asked. "Should we pull alongside?"

"Call firs'," Sharktooth said. "Rude to drop in unannounced."

Marie took out her phone and scrolled through her directory. She raised the phone to her right ear, covering her left ear. She shook her head. "No answer on their sat phone. I'll try Dani's cellphone."

"YOU SHOULD HAVE LET her make that call, Dani," Rick said. They were a few feet apart on the ledge, working their way across the cliff face.

"It wouldn't have helped, Rick. She could have passed them a coded message and let them know that she and the other asshole were in trouble."

"But they've got Shellie and Liz."

"And *Vengeance*," Dani said. "They've signed their death warrants. They're not getting out of this alive."

"Shellie?" There was a tremor in Rick's voice. "And Liz? You think ... not really?"

"I wasn't talking about Shellie and Liz. I meant those two scumbags that stole my boat. I'm going to kill them both. And Leila and that numb-nuts with her, too."

"But Dani, they've — "

Dani's phone rang, interrupting Rick. She paused and reached into her pocket, balancing precariously as she extracted the phone.

"Hello?" she said, pausing for a few seconds. "Marie? Hang on for a second." She brought the phone around in front of her face and switched it to speaker mode, then slipped it into the breast pocket of her shirt. With her hand free, she extended her arm, putting her palm against the cliff face again, restoring her balance.

"Marie? Can you hear me okay?"

"Yes. We are about a mile south of your position. Who are those people on deck?"

"You're where?"

"We just passed across your bow. Sharktooth and I don't recognize the people in the cockpit. Are you okay?"

"You've seen *Vengeance*?"

"Yes. We just passed you. What's — "

"Ask her about Shellie," Rick interrupted.

"What? I didn't understand that," Marie said.

"Hold on, Marie. Rick, let me talk, please."

"But I — "

"Rick!" Dani snapped. "Sorry, Marie. Rick and I aren't aboard

Vengeance. You were saying you've spotted her?"

"Yes. There's a woman at the helm, and a man with her. We don't recognize either of them. Where are you?"

"Rick and I are traversing the cliff face at Petit Piton. Where are you and Sharktooth?"

"About three miles west of Soufrière. Who are those people?"

"They have to be Herbert and Ashley. The other two are tied up in the cave."

"Cave?" Marie asked.

"I'll tell you later. There's a beach bar with a dock at the south end of the bay at Soufrière. Rick and I will meet you at the dock as soon as we can get there — maybe five or ten minutes, okay?"

"Okay, but what about *Vengeance*? And where are Liz and Shellie?"

"They're aboard *Vengeance*. My guess is they're tied up below deck, unless these people are even dumber than I think they are."

"You don't want us to check on them?"

"Yes, but I want to be there. Pick us up, and we'll double back to *Vengeance*. They can't get far in a few minutes, and the odds will be better with three of us to deal with them. Somebody's got to run *Lightning Bolt* while we board. They're dangerous people."

"Your call. We'll be waiting when you get to the dock."

"Okay. While you're waiting, can you get somebody to pick up the two injured prisoners from the cave?"

"Yes. I'll send for one of the sightseeing helicopters. Clarence has one on standby for us, with a few men. Are the prisoners mobile?"

"No. They'll need basket stretchers. And there's a Rastaman keeping an eye on them. He's a good guy. I'll call and tell him what's going to happen, but if one of your men speaks *Kwéyol*, see what you can find out from him. He's mentioned some men who were in and out of the cave a month or two before we got here, but we've had a language problem. See what he knows about that, please."

"We can handle that," Marie said, "but where is this cave you are talking about?"

"There's a crevice in the rock face on the west side of Petit Piton. About 50 meters above sea level, there's a ledge that cuts across the face and intersects the crevice. Just inside the crevice from the intersection on the north wall, there's a cave. That's the place."

"Got it. That would be maybe 150 meters to your right, facing the cliff?"

"Yes. You know the crevice?" Dani asked.

"No, but I see the two of you."

Dani craned her neck around, squinting into the glare. "I can barely make out a speck on the horizon to my northwest. Is that you?"

"Yes. Get busy with your climbing. We'll be at the dock in a couple of minutes."

"Can you scoot forward a little bit?" Liz asked. "I need room; I don't want to elbow you."

"Okay," Shellie said. "I'll try. What are you going to do?"

Bert had wedged the two of them into the narrow space between the companionway ladder and the nav station in front of the entrance to the aft stateroom. He had lifted Liz and tossed her across Shellie's extended legs, leaving Liz leaning back against Shellie, who had her back to the door into the stateroom.

"First," Liz said, "I need to try to get my arms out in front."

She rolled onto her side and spun herself around until her feet were against the bulkhead. Shellie watched, frowning, as Liz drew her knees up to her chest and scooted closer to the bulkhead, pressing the soles of her feet against it.

"That guy's creepy," Shellie said, as she watched Liz scrunch her spine into an arc, forcing her wrists down toward her buttocks. "His hands were all over me. You don't think she'll let him, uh ... "

"I hope so," Liz said, as she wriggled, working her arms under her hips. She kept shifting her weight as the boat rolled, using the movement to work her left arm between her body and the cabin sole. "I did my best to encourage him. Didn't you hear me making kissy sounds at him?"

"Is that what I was hearing? I thought he was making those disgusting noises."

Liz chuckled. "He was too busy licking his lips and drooling while he groped me."

"Why were you encouraging him?"

"Because she's not my type. Besides, she's the brains of the pair."

"I don't understand why you were teasing him," Shellie said. "I just hope he doesn't decide he wants to ... what are you doing, Liz?"

Liz had rolled onto her back, her feet still against the bulkhead. She had managed to get her arms past her hips, and her wrists were now behind her knees. She curled into a tight crunch and slipped her bound wrists past her feet.

"All right. Now I need to get to a sitting position."

She scooted herself around until her back was against the side of the seat at the chart table. Twisting to one side, she used an elbow to lever herself up until she sat on the edge of the cushion, facing into the aisle. She wriggled her arms, twisting them until she had her palms together.

Extending her arms to the front, she balled both hands into fists and jerked her arms back with all her strength, her elbows bending. The momentum pulled her fists in tight to her stomach, and her forearms were forced apart by her ribcage. She repeated the movement, and the second time, the cable ties came loose. Liz pulled her right hand free and slipped the loose ties over her left hand.

"How did you know to do that?" Shellie asked.

"Dani taught me," Liz said, massaging her wrists.

"Where did she learn something like that?"

"She had some strange experiences in her teens," Liz said, extracting her rigging knife from its pouch on her belt. "She picked up all kinds of odd skills." She opened the knife and cut the ties at her ankles. "Let's get you free, and then I'll see if Bert was serious, or if he's just a tease."

"What are you going to do?" Shellie said. "They've got guns."

"I noticed. It's not fair that they have two and we have none. I'm hoping maybe I can get Bert to share; he seems like that kind of guy."

"They'll kill you, Liz."

"I'm sure they think so. I could use a little privacy, if you don't mind."

"What?" Shellie frowned.

"I'd rather you didn't watch what I'm about to do, okay? Why don't you close yourself in your stateroom? I'll let you know when I finish with Bert."

"I don't ... "

"Trust me, Shellie. This is not going to be pretty, and you might be in the way. You could get hurt. Now, go."

Once Shellie closed the door, Liz sat back down on the cabin sole, wedged back where Bert had left the two of them a few minutes earlier. She put her ankles together, laying a cut cable tie across them in case Bert noticed.

She pulled first one lip and then the other into her mouth, chewing and sucking on them until they were swollen. Tucking her hands behind her back, she called, "Bert," raising her voice to carry over the sound of the engine. She did her best to sound seductive. "Oh, Bert?" She parted her lips and ran her tongue over them, looking up toward the companionway entrance.

In a few seconds, Bert's head and shoulders appeared. "What?"

"I like to do it when I'm tied up," she said. "I've been thinking about it ever since you touched me. You made me really hot, Bert. Help a girl out?" She made big eyes at him and ran her tongue over her lips. "You won't even need to untie me, or anything. Just come down here and stand in front of me. I'll do the rest; you won't be sorry, I promise. I'm really good at it. Please?"

He looked back over his shoulder and said something to Ashley, but Liz couldn't hear their conversation. Then she saw him coming down the ladder and braced herself, grinning.

"HOW LONG WILL it take to reach *Vengeance*?" Dani asked, as she climbed aboard *Lightning Bolt*. Rick was already in one of the seats.

"Five minutes, at mos'," Sharktooth said. "How you want to do this?"

Dani looked at Marie as Sharktooth pulled away from the dock. "You said they were in the cockpit?"

"Yes," Marie said. "And we didn't see Liz and Shellie."

"They're below, then," Dani said. "That's good; they'll be out of the way."

"We will need to move fast," Marie said, "to get aboard before they can make hostages of Liz and Shellie."

"Or take them out before they know what's happening," Dani said. "Is your .50 caliber Barrett aboard, Sharktooth?"

"Mm-hmm." Sharktooth grinned. "No prisoners?"

"That's what I'm thinking. If we try to take them alive, they might damage *Vengeance* or hurt somebody."

"You aren't planning to shoot them down in cold blood?" Rick asked.

"Me?" Dani asked. "Of course not. I'm angry as hell. There's nothing cold-blooded about it. I'm going to blow them away in the heat of the moment, and feel badly about it later. For about a nanosecond."

"You can't just ... " Rick shook his head. "But ... "

"Rick, if we can make a clean kill before they know what's happening, it's less likely that they'll hurt Shellie and Liz. Don't you see that?"

"But we don't even know why they're doing this," he said.

"Good point," Dani said. "Marie, can your people interrogate the two in the cave before they dispose of them?"

"Yes, certainly. You wish to know who sent them, and why. Is that correct?"

"Yes. Can you think of anything else we should ask them, Rick?"

"That's not what I meant, Dani. You can't just kill people like that."

"Why not? They tried to kill us; they were going to blow the cave up with you and me in it. Surely you don't think they hijacked *Vengeance* with the idea that they were going to let Liz and Shellie go free at some point."

"That is *Vengeance*, I think," Marie interrupted. She was pointing at a white speck on the horizon to the west.

Sharktooth throttled back and *Lightning Bolt* settled in the water. "Sea state's not too bad," he said. "I get the Barrett." He ducked into the companionway that led to the cabin under the long foredeck of the ocean racer's hull.

"How close did you get to them earlier?" Dani asked.

"One hundred meters at the closest," Marie said. "Why?"

"Think they'll recognize *Lightning Bolt*?"

"Oh, I don't think so. We were going too fast. I was using stabilized binoculars."

"Eighty-five knots," Sharktooth said, rejoining them. "Jus' a cloud of spray. Tha's all they saw. Mebbe thought it was a waterspout." He grinned and handed Dani the .50 caliber sniper's rifle. "Hundred yards?" he asked.

"I think so, with this sea state," Dani said. "I'll go for center of mass. Shouldn't be a problem. I'll take up a prone position aft, on the sunbathing pad."

Sharktooth nodded. "Aim low. It's sighted-in for 500 meters."

Dani crawled out onto the padded sundeck, the rifle in her right hand.

"Dani?" Rick asked.

She looked at him. "What?"

"Will you at least shoot to wound them? Please?"

"Of course. I'll do that. No problem. Wound them. That's what I'll do."

"She's coming toward us," Marie said, braced against the windshield, binoculars pressed to her eyes as Sharktooth began closing the distance.

"What?" Dani asked.

"And under sail," Marie said. "I can't make out who's on deck yet, but still only two people. Range is under a thousand meters and closing fast."

Sharktooth slowed the boat down and said, "I pass to the north and put us beam to the sea when we at 100 meters, Dani. Jus' enough speed for bes' stability, okay?"

"Good. So you'll be stern to the target, then?"

"Mm-hmm."

"Perfect," Dani said.

"Hold it," Marie said. "They've spotted us. Somebody's coming forward on the windward side deck — she's on the bowsprit, waving — it's Liz!"

Dani scrambled back into the cockpit, holding the rifle at the ready. Sharktooth swung *Lightning Bolt* in an arc, turning onto a parallel course a hundred meters behind *Vengeance*. He pulled up even with her stern on the downwind side as Liz returned to the cockpit. Sharktooth matched their speed, and they saw that Shellie was at the helm.

Liz cupped her hands around her mouth and yelled, "Heaving to!"

Sharktooth made a thumbs-up sign and opened the distance between them a bit. *Vengeance* turned smartly to port, sails flogging violently as she swung through the eye of the wind.

Then the headsails were back-winded, working against the main and the mizzen. *Vengeance* was fore-reaching at less than a knot, rising and falling gently with the swell. Sharktooth brought *Lightning Bolt* close alongside, and Rick yelled, "Are you okay?"

"We're fine," Shellie said.

"We thought Ashley and Bert had you," Dani said.

"We dropped them off a few minutes ago," Liz said. "They were bleeding all over the place, making a mess."

"Should we pick them up?" Dani asked.

"No need. They took a little chain with them," Liz said.

"What happened? Chain?" Rick asked.

"They died, Rick. We buried them at sea," Shellie said.

"What happened?" Rick asked again, frowning.

"They tied us up below deck. They were going to kill us and sink *Vengeance*," Shellie said. "Bert told us right before he died."

"How did you get free?"

"Liz broke the cable ties on her wrists and cut us free. Then she tricked Bert into coming below deck. She stabbed him and took his gun. Then she shot Ashley."

"And you just threw them overboard?" Rick asked.

"Well, threw isn't the right word," Liz said. "We hoisted them with the main halyard and lowered them gently. They were too heavy for us to lift, what with the chain around their ankles."

"But what about ... shouldn't we call the police, or something?" Rick asked.

"We were in international waters," Liz said. "No police around when you need them. Let's get underway, Shellie. We'll finish this conversation on the mooring, in, say about an hour?"

"See you there," Dani said, as Sharktooth pulled away.

35

"Where's Marie?" Liz asked, as Sharktooth snugged *Lightning Bolt* up against the fenders she and Shellie had hung along *Vengeance's* port side.

"We dropped her off at the beach bar. Gerald's going to take her up to the cave. She needs to talk with her troops," Dani said, scrambling over the lifelines.

"They're still in the cave?" Liz asked.

"Yes. Things didn't quite work the way Marie thought they would. Her guys couldn't swing using the chopper to access the crevice. They climbed the cliff instead."

"I wondered how that was going to work," Liz said.

"And it's too exposed to view from that restaurant, too. They're going to wait until after closing time. Then they'll drop lines from the cave entrance out and down the cliff face and bring a big RIB up to that reef at the base of the cliff. The RIB's *en route*. Once Marie debriefs her people, she'll come by and fill us in."

"Hey, Dani?" Sharktooth asked.

"Yes?" She paused, halfway down the companionway ladder.

"I'm gon' borrow your dinghy for a little while, okay?"

"Sure," Dani said. When they dropped Marie at the beach bar, they had taken the dinghy in tow. It was bobbing behind *Lightning Bolt* as they spoke. "Where are you going?"

"The bakery in Soufrière got some of the bes' fried chicken in the islan's. Need a little snack. I bring back a bucket full. Anybody want anyt'ing else?"

They all shook their heads, and Sharktooth climbed in the dinghy and motored away toward town.

"It doesn't look bloody down here," Dani called, from the base of the ladder.

"I cleaned it up while Shellie sailed us back in. It wasn't too bad; I stuck him in the kidney. Most of his bleeding was internal. The varnish could probably stand to be refreshed, though. I had to use scouring powder," Liz said.

"What about the woman?" Dani asked.

"She was coming out from behind the helm when I shot her. She made a mess, but we were able to hose it down with seawater before it soaked into the deck."

"Not a nice clean head shot, huh?" Dani asked.

"No. Bert had a MAC-11, and I didn't have much time. She must have heard me scuffling with him. I snatched his weapon, whirled, and she was almost at the top of the ladder. I pulled the trigger. That's when I discovered it was set for full auto. Not only that, but it was loaded with hollow points. Her upper torso looked like hamburger."

Rick was scowling, looking off into the distance. He shook his head. "I'm having trouble with this," he said.

Shellie sat down next to him. "Rick, it was them or us, honey. Thank goodness for Liz, or we wouldn't be here."

"But they're dead, Shellie."

"They put us in the position we were in. Our only other choice was to die in their place, Rick," Liz said.

"How can you be so clinical about this, Liz? You and Dani both. You just ... "

"I chose to live, Rick," Liz said. "I'm not thrilled about the price

I paid, but as Shellie said, I didn't put myself in that position. I'm sorry you're upset by it, but what would you have me do? Or say?"

"And what about those two we left in the cave?" he asked. "Shouldn't we get them to a hospital? Dani? How will you feel if they die?"

"Alive, Rick. I'll feel alive. They tried to blow us up. You heard what Leila said. You think she'd feel bad if she'd succeeded? What is it that you don't understand about that?"

"I've just never ... I'm ... "

"You'll just have to deal with it, Rick," Liz said. "It'll take some time. I'm not over the shock, but I'm not going to lose any sleep over this, and you shouldn't either. Sometimes bad things happen. You just have to put it behind you."

"I'm working on it."

"Here comes Marie, I'll bet," Dani said, as a gray, 10-meter-long RIB with three big outboards approached.

The RIB coasted to a stop, its bow almost touching *Vengeance*. Marie stepped on the bow tube and vaulted over *Vengeance's* lifelines, landing like a cat on the side deck. She waved at the man behind the helm of the RIB, and it backed away, headed out to sea.

"They didn't make it, those two people in the cave," she said. "Our medic did his best, but they were too far gone. The man never recovered consciousness. The woman, though, she was lucid until the end."

"Did you learn anything from her?" Dani asked.

"They were Iranian agents," Marie said. "Part of Iran's special forces. Their mission was to kill the four of you and destroy whatever's in the cave."

"Why would Iran care about any of this?" Liz asked.

"She thought it was because the Saudis are behind this whole expedition. There are supposed to be documents in the cave. She said they would prove the Sunnis are right."

"The Sunnis?" Dani asked.

"That's all we got before she was gone," Marie said. "The Shiites are running Iran. The Saudis are Sunni Muslims. I'm not sure anybody can really understand that conflict. Anyway, that's what we know."

"I'm surprised she talked, the way she acted with Dani," Rick said.

"She was heavily medicated," Marie said. "She didn't know what was happening."

"Do you believe what she said?" he asked.

"I'm in no position to judge whether she was right, but from experience, I think she told us what she believed to be true."

"Has anybody been down to look at the things in that vertical shaft?" Rick asked.

"Not since my people arrived," Marie said. "But, Dani, you asked us to question Gerald."

"Yes. Did he have anything interesting to say?"

"I will let you all decide. This is what he told us: about two, maybe three months ago, some men came on a large motor yacht. They stayed on one of the moorings on the other side of Petit Piton for a week, perhaps. They went into the cave several times, and they left all of those things down in the bottom of that shaft. Always, they came and went in the darkness, he said."

"They left those things?" Rick said. "You mean they planted them?"

"Gerald said that none of the things were there before. He has known this cave since his childhood. There was never anything in that shaft before the men came."

"I see," Rick said. "that's something of a disappointment."

Marie shrugged.

"Will you want to go back into the cave, Rick?" Dani asked.

"Yes, I suppose I should," Rick said. "Tomorrow?"

"We will be finished tonight," Marie said. "We will leave it as it was before the Iranian agents disturbed you. We found a rock-climbing harness and a block and tackle. Are those yours?"

"Yes," Dani said, "and one hundred-fifty feet of line."

"As I thought," Marie said. "We will leave those as we found them. So, tomorrow, it is all yours."

"I think rum punch is in order," Liz said. "I see Sharktooth coming with his bucket of chicken. Let me get to work."

"I must get to work, as well, Liz," Marie said. "Thank you, but I will pass on the refreshments. I may not see you before I leave, so good luck to everyone."

"Thanks, Marie," Dani said. "Liz and I will see you in Martinique soon, I'm sure."

"Yes, I hope so. Keep well, all of you." Marie spoke into a small radio transceiver and the RIB appeared, rounding the point to their north. She stood on the side deck, and within a minute, she was in the RIB, headed back toward the beach bar's dock.

"ARE you going to the cave with Rick in the morning?" Liz asked. She and Dani were in their berths, but neither was sleepy. Liz had served a light supper and everyone had retired early, exhausted from the stress of the day.

"I can't, Liz. I almost died in there this morning."

"You mean from the bomb?"

"That too," Dani said. "But that's not it."

"No?"

"No. I was having a panic attack when that phone rang."

"Phone? You and Rick never told us what happened, exactly."

"They'd set an explosive charge in the roof of that tunnel and rigged it to a cellphone," Dani said.

"And the phone rang, but it didn't blow?"

"That's right. Gerald watched them go in the cave last night, and after they left, he went in and found it."

"It? The explosive charge?"

"Right. He didn't know what it was, but he took the cellphones out of the fertilizer mix. They'd used two, one for backup. With improvised detonators wired to the phones. I guess he wanted the cellphones, maybe. I don't know."

"So he pulled them out and left the explosives?"

"Yes. He broke the detonator wires to one of the phones, but the other one was still connected. He had them both in that cloth pouch he wears, and he was behind me in the tunnel. Rick had already gone through, and we'd rigged a line to anchor the block and tackle."

"Rick went first, then you, and then Gerald? In the tunnel?"

"We didn't know Gerald was even there. He didn't show up when we were on our way up the trail. He sneaked into the cave after we were already in the tunnel."

"Okay. Then one of the phones rang?"

"The one he'd pulled the detonator loose from."

"And you say you were having a panic attack then?"

"Liz, I tried to make myself do that, get through that tight spot, but I ... " Dani gulped and shook her head.

"This is where Shellie said it was like ducking under an arch, or something? This tight spot?"

"It's no arch. The ceiling of that tunnel comes down so close to the floor that you have to turn your head sideways and put one cheek on the floor and then scooch your way along on your belly for a couple of feet. I could feel the roof of the tunnel pressing down on my back, across my shoulder blades, Liz."

There was a tremor in Dani's voice. She took several deep breaths. Liz waited, saying nothing.

"It ... it was narrow, too. My arms were straight out in front of me; I was pushing my backpack, and I couldn't breathe. Then the phone rang in the tunnel. Behind me. I didn't even know Gerald was back there." Dani paused again, panting.

After almost a minute, Liz said, "What happened then?"

"I don't know. The next thing I remember, I was out in the entrance cavern and Rick was shining a light in my eyes. They said I hit my head when the phone startled me, but I don't think so. I think I just blacked out, scared out of my wits. Liz, I'm so disgusted with myself. All evening, I've been having this raging argument in my head. I need to go back in there, to beat that stupid irrational fear. But I can't, Liz. I can't do it." Dani groaned through her clenched teeth, pounding her fist on her thigh.

Liz got up and moved across the narrow space between their berths. Sitting on the edge of Dani's mattress, she put a hand on her friend's shoulder, patting her, massaging the knots of tense muscle.

"Easy, Dani," she said. "It's okay. You don't have to go back in there. Rick and Gerald can handle it. Don't be so hard on yourself."

"I'm a coward, Liz," Dani said.

"Leila and Ed might disagree."

"What?"

"You're not a coward, Dani. And that's not an irrational fear. It's a normal reaction to a confined space. You always manage to do the things that you have to do. Squeezing through a crack in the rock underground isn't one of them, not then, and for sure not right now."

"But Rick went through there. So did Shellie. Why can't I?"

"Everybody's different. For whatever reason, they're not wired the same way you are. Leila would have killed you and Rick if you hadn't stopped her. Rick owes you his life. You're no coward. Now ease up on yourself."

"But I can't deal with a close space like that."

"You don't have to, Dani. Stop it, now."

"But what if I did have to? Like it was the only way out?"

"Then you'd do it. Your determination to survive would overcome your fear; you're the bravest person I know."

"You think I could? If I had to?"

"You and I both know that you *would*, if you had to. Don't test yourself unnecessarily. That's pointless."

"What do I tell them?"

"Tell who? Rick and Shellie?"

"Yes. How do I explain that I'm too scared to go back in that tunnel?"

"Just tell them you need to take it easy for a day or two. They'll be okay with that."

"You think?"

"I do." Liz patted her shoulder again, feeling Dani's muscles relax. "Are you going to be able to sleep now?"

"Mm-hmm. Thanks, Liz." Soon, her breathing fell into a deep, smooth rhythm.

Liz went back to her own berth, but she couldn't sleep at first. She was too tense from the terror that Dani's description of her ordeal had evoked. When she heard Dani start snoring softly, she dropped off to sleep herself, hypnotized by the sound.

"YOU WERE AWFULLY QUIET THIS EVENING," Shellie said, her head on Rick's shoulder. They had turned off the light several minutes earlier, but she knew he was too worked up to sleep. "Still upset?"

"Upset?"

"About the four people who died," she said.

"Oh. No ... well, yes, I guess so. But I'm coping with that. I know all of you are right; there wasn't any other option. I'm still struggling with the idea of just dumping the bodies at sea, but I'll get over that. I can't fault the logic or the ethics, but on some emotional level, it just seems wrong."

"I understand that," she said. "Something else bothering you?"

"Yes. What's really bugging me is that they played me for a fool."

"They?"

"The Saudis, it seems," he said.

"You mean because that stuff was put there for you to find?"

"Exactly. I've been going over the whole thing in my mind ever since Marie told us what Gerald said."

"And?"

"And I think the Saudis were using me. The foundation's got to be a front of some kind. That's why I never heard of it before they called me."

"What do you suppose they intended?"

"I'm not sure. There's the obvious propaganda angle, if they managed to make a case that the Moors beat Columbus. But there's that whole Sunni versus Shiite thing, too."

"What are you going to do?"

"I want to see what's in that cave, before I decide. At least get a look at what's in the box — and grid the whole stash off and make some good photographs. Then I'll go from there."

"That makes sense. I'd like to go with you, but I don't think my ankle can stand it."

"That's okay. Dani and Gerald can help me. Let's try to go to sleep. I'm exhausted."

"Me, too," she said, as he gave her shoulder a squeeze.

36

"Anybody need anything else?" Liz asked, as she brought a thermal carafe of fresh coffee up into the cockpit.

"Everyt'ing good," Sharktooth said. "Sit down an' eat, Liz, befo' the eggs get cold."

"I need some of that coffee," Marie said, reaching for the carafe. "I didn't sleep much last night."

"I'm surprised to see you this morning," Shellie said. "I thought you were leaving last night."

"That was what I thought, as well. But we had to wait until the restaurant closed to lower the bodies, and then it was very late. I'll go back with Sharktooth, the way I came. You were a big help last night, Sharktooth. Thank you again."

"My pleasure." Sharktooth grinned and took a bite of his salt-fish patty.

"Did you go into the cave?" Dani asked.

"Uh-uh. Not me. No way," Sharktooth said. "Big mon like me, I don' do so good in little places. Make me too nervous. Gotta have plenty room to breathe."

"I know what you mean," Dani said, trading glances with Liz, who smiled and gave her a wink.

"I wondered where you went after we all went to bed, Sharktooth. I heard the dinghy in the middle of the night," Liz said.

"I decided to help Marie and her folks get that boat, *Aquila,* ready."

"What about that?" Shellie asked. "I wondered what was going to happen to it. Is somebody going to return it to the charter company?"

"You do not hear, last night?" Marie asked.

"Hear what?" Rick asked.

"*Aquila,*" Sharktooth said. "She 'splode las' night. Wit' the dead people on her."

"She exploded?" Shellie asked.

"Cookin' gas, mos' likely. Cookin' gas leak into bilge sometime. Ver' dangerous."

"I guess Petit Piton is a pretty good acoustic barrier," Liz said. "I didn't hear anything."

"Neither did I," Dani said. She took a sip of coffee. "The explosion was a good idea. I was worried about how four people could just disappear. Now there's an explanation."

"But only two bodies," Rick said. "Won't the authorities notice?"

"Hard to know how many bodies in a 'splosion like that. Not much lef'," Sharktooth said. "Pass the salt-fish, please."

"Are you still going back into the cave today, Rick?" Liz asked.

"Oh," Marie said, before Rick answered. "I am glad you reminded me, Liz. Gerald asked me to say he will wait for you on the path this morning, Rick."

"Okay. Thanks," Rick said. "I'm going to take a quick look, and document what's there, but then I think I'm going to back out of this deal with the foundation. I'm afraid this was a hoax of some kind, after what Gerald told your people, Marie."

"Yes, I think that is so," Marie said.

"What will you do, then?" Dani asked. "What about the stuff down at the bottom of the vertical shaft?"

"That depends on what I find in there. Are you coming this time?"

"Um, if it's okay, I'd like to freshen up that patch of varnish where Liz used the scouring powder," Dani said.

"That's fine. Gerald can help me. You do what you need to; you've done more than enough, you and Liz both. I just want to finish this off. Guess I'd better get going. Can one of you run me ashore?"

"Let's go," Liz said.

"I WONDER HOW RICK'S DOING," Dani said, as Liz served coffee in the shade of their cockpit awning.

Since Liz had taken Rick ashore earlier, she and Shellie had passed the time sketching the town of Soufrière. Dani had been stretched out in a hammock on the foredeck, reading.

"I'm sure we'll hear all about it soon enough," Shellie said. "He must be about done; there really wasn't that much stuff down in that shaft."

"I wish we could — " Dani was interrupted by the ringing of Liz's cellphone.

"Hi, Rick," Liz answered. She listened for a few seconds. "Sure. I'll be there in a couple of minutes." She disconnected and put the phone in her pocket. "He's almost to the dock at the restaurant," she said.

She stepped to the side deck and climbed down into the dinghy. Once she'd started the engine, she untied it and raced away toward the beach bar's rickety little dock.

"There he is," Dani said, watching as Liz slowed the dinghy and coasted in to the dock. "Perfect timing."

In two minutes, they were back. Rick climbed out of the dinghy, his cellphone held against his ear. He gave Shellie and Dani a grin, holding his left thumb and forefinger an inch apart as he squeezed past them and went down the companionway. Liz secured the dinghy and took her seat.

"He's talking with your lawyer," she said. "He was already on the phone when I picked him up; he interrupted the call long enough to let me know they want to deal with some things before the close of business on the East Coast."

Shellie nodded. "That's my guy. He's always in a hurry to get things done. No word on what he found, I guess?"

"Not really. He said there was nothing exciting, that he'd tell us everything once he wrapped up the loose ends."

Two hours later, Liz had served rum punch and was passing a tray of cold appetizers when Rick poked his head through the companionway and said, "Pour me some of that, please. I'll be up as soon as I wash my hands.

"Okay, give it up," Shellie said, as he joined them a few minutes later. "We're dying to hear what you found."

Rick grinned and shook his head. "There were a lot of intact ceramic vessels from the Ostionoid Period. They're what was stacked around the box we saw. They're consistent — "

"Sorry, but what's the Ostionoid Period?" Liz asked.

"The chronology of the people of the islands is divided into cultural periods," Rick said. "There were a number of periods in the settlement of the islands before people began to make pottery, but around 500 B.C. the people we refer to as the Saladoid culture appeared. The Saladoid Period lasted until around 600 A.D. They left behind some decorated pottery, some of it in the shape of animals, incense burners, that kind of thing. As they became more settled and agricultural, their culture evolved into what we call the Ostionoid culture. The Ostionoid Period stretched from around 600 A.D. until 1500 A.D. The pottery from that era is more utilitarian.

"The ceramic vessels in the cave are what you'd expect from Caribs of that era — the Ostionoid Period. It's rare to find so many pieces that are intact, though. Remember, these were like every-day dishes, as opposed to Grandma's Sunday china.

"I suspect whoever put them here must have pilfered them from somewhere, maybe several different places. They went to some lengths to assemble such a collection. Somebody wanted to make it look like the Moors had taken them in trade, maybe, or were using the pottery themselves."

"What about the box?" Shellie asked.

"That's ivory," Rick said, smiling. "Intricately carved. A beautiful piece of work. It's probably worth a fortune, all by itself. It's typical of the period when Khashkhash lived, and typical of Moorish Spain. Elaborately decorated cases like that were often used to hold a Koran, or important manuscripts. Still are, sometimes. That box once held a collection of documents of some sort."

"Once?" Dani asked. "Leila told Marie's people that there were supposed to be records of some kind in there that would prove the Sunnis were right, or something like that."

"What's in there now is the biggest nest of termites I've ever seen," Rick said. "They're just a writhing mass, in that brown, damp mess they make — the whole box, full. There may have been documents in it when it was put there, but there aren't any now. That's a shame, too, if they were really ancient manuscripts. An utter waste, all for some kind of scam."

"What are you going to do about that?" Shellie asked. "I mean, with the artifacts, knowing they were planted."

"I talked to the curator at the museum in Martinique. He put me in touch with somebody at the University of the West Indies, here in St. Lucia. They'll send someone out to survey it and take care of it tomorrow. That seemed like the right thing to do, given that we know somebody put it here recently. At least everything will be preserved and studied. And that's the end of that story, at least as far as I'm concerned."

"What do you want to do, from here on?" Liz asked.

"Well, I'm stuck here until the woman from the University gets here tomorrow. Shellie and I can talk it over tonight, but I think it would be fun to just enjoy the islands for a while. I'd like to pursue the question of the Caribs and whaling, too."

"What about the foundation?" Dani asked.

"Okay. About the foundation," Rick said, grinning. "I was on the phone with my lawyer for most of that time I was below. Here's the deal. Ready?"

"Yes, please," Shellie said. "Tell us."

"In exchange for our agreement not to sue them or expose their plot, the foundation is releasing us from the contract, Shellie. Not only that, but they've agreed that we can continue the three-month charter, at our discretion. There's a 30-day notice required to terminate, they said. If we do opt to terminate, we get to keep whatever's left of the fees as liquidated damages after we square things with Dani and Liz. That's on top of what they advanced us already for our time and anticipated expenses."

Dani and Liz looked at one another. Dani raised her eyebrows, and Liz nodded. "We won't hold you to that 30 days," Dani said.

"That's nice of you, but if Shellie's willing, I'd like to finish out the charter with you, if you agree."

"I'm in!" Shellie said.

"I thought you'd say that." Rick said.

Shellie nodded. "Are you okay with that?" she asked, looking from Dani to Liz.

"That would be great for us," Dani said.

"We're thrilled to have you aboard for as long as you'd like," Liz said, pouring a fresh round of rum punch. She raised her glass. "A toast to new friends and fine shipmates."

The others touched their glasses to hers, and they all took sips of the punch.

"I'm so excited," Shellie said. "Oh! Look at that sunset!"

They watched in silence until the show ended, and then Liz said, "Hey, Dani?"

"Yes?"

"Come below and give me a hand peeling the shrimp for dinner."

"WHAT DO YOU THINK ABOUT THIS?" Liz whispered, once they were below.

"What do you mean? The charter?"

"Yes."

"It's going to be fun," Dani said.

"Even though they're boring academics?"

"I like them, Liz. They're not boring. Pass the shrimp."

Liz handed her the bowl of fresh shrimp. She began peeling as Liz started the sauce.

As she picked up the second shrimp, Dani said, "There is one thing, though."

"What's that?" Liz asked, looking over at her.

"I know I can't have everything, but I do wish I'd gotten to help Sharktooth and Marie blow up *Aquila*."

THE END

A NOTE TO THE READER

Thank you for reading *Bluewater Quest,* the fourteenth book in the **Bluewater Thriller** series. I hope you enjoyed it. If so, please leave a brief review on Amazon. Reviews are of great benefit to independent authors like me; they help me more than you can imagine. They are a primary means to help new readers find my work. A few sentences can help others find the pleasure that I hope you found in this book, as well as keeping my spirits up as I work on the next one. If you would like to be notified by email when I release a new book or have a sale or giveaway, please join my mailing list at http://eepurl.com/bKujyv. I promise not to use the list for anything else; I dislike spam as much as you do.

If you haven't read the other **Bluewater Thrillers**, please take a look at them. If you enjoyed this book, you'll enjoy them as well. I write another series of sailing thrillers — the **Connie Barrera Thrillers**. Connie had a key role in ***Deception in Savannah***, my first book. I enjoyed writing about her so much that I wrote her into the **Bluewater Thrillers**. She plays prominent parts in both *Bluewater Ice* and *Bluewater Betrayal.* The **Connie Barrera Thrillers** are a spin-off from the **Bluewater Thrillers**, and feature some of the same characters. Dani and Liz taught Connie to sail, and they introduced her to Paul Russo, her first mate and soon-to-be husband.

In December of 2017, I released ***Bluewater Quest***, the fourteenth novel in that series. Now I've turned my attention back to Connie and Paul for their ninth adventure. You'll find progress reports and more information on my web page at www.clrdougherty.com. Be sure to click on the link to my blog posts; it's in the column on the right side of the web page. Dani has begun to blog about what's on her mind, and Liz and Connie are demanding equal time, so you can see what they're up to while I'm writing.

A list of my other books is on the last page; just click on a title or go to my website for more information. If you'd like to know when my next book is released, visit my Amazon Author's Page at http://www.amazon.com/author/clrdougherty and click the "Follow" link near the upper left-hand corner. I welcome email correspondence about books, boats and sailing. My address is clrd@clrdougherty.com. If you'd like personal updates, drop me a line at that address and let me know. Thanks again for your support.

JOIN MY MAILING LIST

Join my mailing list at http://eepurl.com/bKujyv for notice of new releases and special sales or giveaways. I'll email a link to you for a free download of my short story, ***The Lost Tourist Franchise***, when you sign up. I promise not to use the list for anything else; I dislike spam as much as you do.

ABOUT C.L.R. DOUGHERTY

WELCOME ABOARD!

Charles Dougherty is a lifelong sailor; he's lived what he writes. He and his wife have spent over 30 years sailing together. For 15 years, they lived aboard their boat full-time, cruising the East Coast and the islands. They spent most of that time exploring the Eastern Caribbean. Dougherty is well acquainted with the islands and their people. The characters and locations in his novels reflect his experience.

A storyteller before all else, Dougherty lets his characters speak for themselves. Pick up one of his thrillers and listen to the sound of adventure as you smell the salt air. Enjoy the views of distant horizons and meet some people you won't forget.

Dougherty has written over 25 books. His **Bluewater Thrillers** are set in the yachting world of the Caribbean and chronicle the adventures of two young women running a luxury charter yacht in a rough-and-tumble environment. The **Connie Barrera Thrillers** are also set in the Caribbean and feature some of the same characters from a slightly more romantic perspective. Besides the **Bluewater Thrillers** and the **Connie Barrera Thrillers**, he wrote ***The Redemption of Becky Jones***, a psycho-thriller, and ***The Lost Tourist Franchise***, a short story about one of the characters from ***Deception in Savannah***.

He has also written two non-fiction books. ***Life's a Ditch*** is the story of how he and his wife moved aboard their sailboat, *Play Actor*, and their adventures along the east coast of the U.S. ***Dungda de Islan'*** relates their experiences while cruising the Caribbean.

Join my mailing list for news of upcoming releases and special offers.

www.clrdougherty.com
clrd@clrdougherty.com

OTHER BOOKS BY C.L.R. DOUGHERTY

Bluewater Thrillers

Bluewater Killer

Bluewater Vengeance

Bluewater Voodoo

Bluewater Ice

Bluewater Betrayal

Bluewater Stalker

Bluewater Bullion

Bluewater Rendezvous

Bluewater Ganja

Bluewater Jailbird

Bluewater Drone

Bluewater Revolution

Bluewater Enigma

Bluewater Quest

Bluewater Thrillers Boxed Set: Books 1-3

Connie Barrera Thrillers

From Deception to Betrayal - An Introduction to Connie Barrera

Love for Sail - A Connie Barrera Thriller

Sailor's Delight - A Connie Barrera Thriller

A Blast to Sail - A Connie Barrera Thriller

Storm Sail - A Connie Barrera Thriller

Running Under Sail - A Connie Barrera Thriller

Sails Job - A Connie Barrera Thriller

Under Full Sail - A Connie Barrera Thriller

An Easy Sail - A Connie Barrera Thriller

Other Fiction

Deception in Savannah

The Redemption of Becky Jones

The Lost Tourist Franchise

Books for Sailors and Dreamers

Life's a Ditch

Dungda de Islan'

For more information please visit www.clrdougherty.com

Or visit www.amazon.com/author/clrdougherty

Made in the USA
Coppell, TX
07 June 2022

78574000R00175